KILL DEVIL FALLS

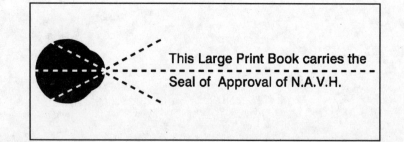

This Large Print Book carries the
Seal of Approval of N.A.V.H.

KILL DEVIL FALLS

BRIAN KLINGBORG

THORNDIKE PRESS
A part of Gale, Cengage Learning

GALE
CENGAGE Learning·

Farmington Hills, Mich • San Francisco • New York • Waterville, Maine
Meriden, Conn • Mason, Ohio • Chicago

LIBRARY OF CONGRESS CATALOGING-IN-PUBLICATION DATA

Names: Klingborg, Brian, 1967- author.
Title: Kill devil falls / by Brian Klingborg.
Description: Large print edition. | Waterville, Maine : Thorndike Press, a part of Gale, Cengage Learning, 2017. | Series: Thorndike Press large print peer picks
Identifiers: LCCN 2017007854 | ISBN 9781410499141 (hardcover) | ISBN 1410499146 (hardcover)
Subjects: LCSH: United States marshals—Fiction. | Bank robberies—United States—Fiction. | Sierra Nevada Region (Calif. and Nev.)—Fiction. | Large type books. | BISAC: FICTION / Mystery & Detective / General. | GSAFD: Suspense fiction.
Classification: LCC PS3611.L5629 K55 2017b | DDC 813/.6—dc23
LC record available at https://lccn.loc.gov/2017007854

Published in 2017 by arrangement with Midnight Ink, an imprint of Llewellyn Publications, Woodbury, MN 55125-2989 USA

Printed in the United States of America
1 2 3 4 5 6 7 21 20 19 18 17

ACKNOWLEDGMENTS

A big shout-out to the following: Lindsay Friedman for telling Bob Diforio he should represent me, and Bob for listening to her; Terri Bischoff, Amy Glaser, Katie Mickschl, Sandy Sullivan, and the gang at Midnight Ink; Chris Alexander, Nicholas Sigman, and Jon Klingborg for notes and suggestions; mom and dad for the obvious; and Lanchi, Sophie, and Sylvie for everything else.

1

Before she walked through the door, Lee Larimer had never once laid eyes on Helen Morrissey. Didn't know her from Adam. Could be she was a real sweetheart. Active in the local church. Volunteered at an old folks' home, emptying bed pans, spooning baby food into toothless mouths. Rescued stray kittens. Lee could give a good goddamn.

Within two minutes of her arrival, he'd pegged her for a cop. And decided, odds were she was going to die.

Rosa's Café (*Home of the Chili Cheese Fries Burger!*) sat on the outskirts of a slowly decaying town in the Sierra Nevada foothills, just off Highway 80. It was a ramshackle structure, approximately the size of a shoebox, reeking of old bacon grease, frequented by three kinds of clientele: long-haul truckers, geriatric gamblers heading to Reno for the nickel slots, and unwashed backpackers.

When Helen entered, the only other customers, aside from Lee, were two truck drivers in nearly identical flannel shirts, down vests, and fly-specked ball caps. The one sitting closest to the door was thickset, with Popeye forearms, aviator sunglasses, and a mustache. The other was rail-thin apart from an almost perfectly rounded gut, like a python who'd just swallowed a kid goat.

Helen was dressed in dark pants, a blue shirt, a medium-weight coat, and black tactical boots. Her hair was drawn into a tight ponytail. She wore a trace of lipstick and sensibly modest gold studs in her earlobes. Lee guessed she was thirty or so. Her features were a tad sharp to be considered beautiful, yet she was striking in a tightly wound sort of way.

Lee's impression: given the surroundings, the lady stuck out like a diamond in a mangy dog's asshole.

Helen paused in the doorway, her eyes sweeping the cafe, noting the patched vinyl booths on the left (the one farthest from the entrance occupied by Lee), a bathroom door in the corner, a peeling Formica counter on the right where the two truckers slouched, the swinging door leading to the kitchen behind it.

As her gaze fell on Lee, he lowered his head and shoveled a wet forkful of eggs, dripping yolk and Tabasco sauce, into his mouth.

He was wearing one of his many thrift-store disguises. Enough to not look himself, but not so much he garnered unwanted attention. His normally longish, jet-black hair was cut short and speckled with gray, aging him a good ten years. His customary week-old scruff was shaved clean. He wore glasses with black plastic frames. A touch of bronzer darkened his complexion.

The *piece de resistance* was his Operation Enduring Freedom camouflage fatigues. Military personnel were a common enough sight in small-town America these days. Nobody batted an eye or gave a soldier a hard time. Quite the contrary. Most folks bent over backward for a man in uniform. Accorded him an extra measure of respect. Didn't ask too many questions, just thanked him shyly for his service on behalf of the country.

Already, the waitress had refilled his drink twice without being asked.

Lee certainly didn't resemble his mug shots or the grainy surveillance photos released to the media. Still, it was always better to be safe than sorry. He switched the fork to his left hand, slipped his right beneath his coat.

One. Two. Three. Four. Five. He glanced up from his plate.

Helen was frowning at the Formica counter. The seat closest to the front door was free, but frigid air leaked through the poorly sealed window facing the parking lot. She hesitated a moment, then walked over and slid onto the open stool sandwiched between the two truckers.

Lee let out a breath. If she had any clue who he was, no way she'd take a seat with her back to him. Maybe she was just a real estate agent checking out summer rentals. Or a bank employee in town to foreclose on some unemployed single mother's house.

Whatever. As long as she wasn't there for him.

But as Helen shifted into a more comfortable position on the stool, her coat bunched up and Lee spotted the squared tip of a black leather holster dangling down her hip. Judging from its size, he guessed she was carrying something standard issue, like a Glock 17. A dependable, rugged little gun. A favorite of cops and feds alike.

Lee fondled the smooth, cold surface of the enormous revolver resting on his lap; it was a Smith & Wesson X-Frame, with an 8 and 3/8ths-inch barrel. The X-Frame possessed the highest muzzle velocity of any mass-produced revolver on the market. It fired .200 grain, .460 caliber rounds at two thousand three hundred feet per second. If Lee were to line up everyone in the diner single file, including the waitress, line cook, and even the Mexican dishwasher, a single bullet from the X-Frame would punch right through all of them. And still have enough zip to knock the black off a crow on the other side.

He leaned sideways to peer through the ice-streaked front window. Down in the valley, spring was slowly prying at winter's blue-tipped fingers, but at six thousand feet, daytime temperatures remained in the thirties and patches of black snow clung stubbornly to sidewalks and gutters.

Only two cars occupied Rosa's tiny parking lot. His, a shit-brown Honda Accord (stolen, plates switched with an unsuspecting soccer mom's Highlander in a Safeway parking lot); and hers, a slightly battered white Dodge Charger.

Lee was envious of the Charger. A V6 engine, zero to sixty in 6.6 seconds, more than enough horsepower for climbing mountain roads. He'd be lucky to squeeze a top speed of forty mph from the Honda on a steep upgrade.

He didn't see any police cruisers. No Crown Vics or vehicles with suspicious antenna clusters. Just two eighteen-wheelers parked on the street, no doubt property of the truckers sitting at the counter.

Turning his attention back to the Charger, however, he spied a metal screen extending across the width of the cab behind the front seats. A cage. The kind you put criminals in when hauling them to jail.

Lee wiped his mouth with a napkin, tossed it on his plate. He was no longer hungry.

Helen rested her forearms on the counter. Her goal was a quick bite, and then back on the road. She desperately wanted to make it up the mountain and down again before dark.

Her left hand landed in a patch of something moist and sticky. She lifted her palm — grape jelly. She tugged a few napkins from a metal dispenser.

The trucker to her right chuckled. "Got a little jam on ya?"

He was in his late fifties, with a purplish nose that looked to have been broken more than once. An ancient scar ran diagonally across the sun-roughened skin of his chin.

Physically, he reminded her a bit of her father. Probably the toughest kid on his block growing up, now getting older but refusing to do so gracefully, beating back time with desperate hooks and savage uppercuts.

Of course, her father wasn't nearly as solicitous as the trucker. Didn't matter if it was jam, blood, or tears, he would've just told her to stop being such a whiner, wipe it off, and get on with her day.

"Yeah." She wiped her palm with the napkins.

"You want to save the napkin, I could lick it off for ya."

Helen stopped wiping. "Excuse me?"

A waitress pushed through the kitchen door. "Hi, hon." She smiled broadly, revealing a wad of gum squeezed between her premolars.

Still processing the trucker's offer, it took Helen a moment to answer. "Hi."

The waitress slipped a laminated menu on the counter. "Something to drink?"

"Coffee."

"Cream and sugar?"

"Just black, thanks."

"You bet."

Helen finished cleaning her hand, crumpled the napkin, dropped it on the counter.

She decided to ignore the trucker.

The waitress set down a chipped brown mug, filled it with coffee. She was around forty, a bleached-blonde, her hair parted down the middle and feathered. Probably the same haircut since seventh grade.

"Know what you want, hon?"

Helen scanned the menu. "How's the Greek omelet?"

The waitress scrunched her nose. "Butch, the cook? Closest he's been to Greece is the gyro place on the other side of town. Try something else."

"I'll go with two eggs, over hard, wheat toast, side of bacon, crispy."

"Okay. Even Butch can't fudge that up."

Helen's coat pocket buzzed. She pulled out her cell phone. The caller ID read *Chowder.*

She slipped off the stool and answered the phone as she headed for the front door. "Morrissey."

Supervisory Deputy Marshal Rick Choder, whom Helen called Chowder but not to his face, wheezed into the mouthpiece.

"Where you at, Morrissey?"

She pushed through the front door of the diner and stepped into the parking lot. An icy breeze snatched at her coat. She

14

squeezed the cell phone between her shoulder and ear and zipped up.

"I stopped for a quick bite. I think I'm about an hour and change from Donnersville."

"Well, you're not going to Donnersville anymore."

She felt a flush of hope. "You mean I can turn around?"

Choder's laugh betrayed a hint of spite. "You wish. The sheriff wasn't able to run Crawford to the county jail, so you'll have to pick her up where she was apprehended."

Helen took the phone from her shoulder with her left hand, slipped the right into her coat pocket. "What happened to the sheriff?"

"He got an emergency call and had to take it."

"Why can't one of the deputies transport her to Donnersville?"

"I don't know. I'm not your social secretary. Just do your job and go get her, okay, Deputy?"

Helen clenched her fist, nails digging painfully into her palm. She pictured Choder, stupid cowboy boots he affected propped on a corner of his desk, wet grin on his punch-worthy face.

"Where am I going now?"

"Some Podunk town, north of Donnersville."

"Suck it," she muttered.

"What did you just say?"

Helen was nominally a Catholic and still suffered a twinge of guilt each time she swore, which, since her recent assignment to the US Marshal's Sacramento office with its high school locker-room ambience, had become excessive. For the past few weeks, she'd been making an effort to curb her potty mouth, substituting favorite curse words with more benign expressions.

Hence, *suck it,* instead of *go fuck yourself, Chowder.*

"Nothing, sir. You have directions?"

"I'll email them."

"Can you do it now? Cell coverage seems pretty intermittent up here."

"Roger that."

Chowder. She suspected he'd designated her for this crap duty out of pure vindictiveness. Because she refused to sleep with him. Or date him, or have a drink with him, or interact with him in any way at all outside the bounds of their professional relationship.

"What's the name of the town?"

Again, that malicious little laugh.

"Get this. It's called Kill Devil Falls."

■ ■ ■

Lee watched Helen's body language through the window as she spoke on the phone. He saw her shoulders hunch, her angry pacing. She didn't care for what the person on the other end of the line was telling her. And she didn't even glance in his direction when she came back inside. The lady was either a hell of an actress, or she truly had no clue a wanted man was sitting five feet away.

Lee removed a roll of cash from his pocket, peeled off a twenty, and laid it on the table. He thought about it, took back the twenty, and replaced it with a ten and a five.

Here's what bothered him: if she was a cop, but wasn't after him, it was a hell of a coincidence they'd both ended up in the same crappy diner in a jerkwater town halfway up the Sierra Nevadas. One *hell* of a coincidence.

Like the saying goes, it's a small world. But not that small. She must be bound for the same place he was.

And now Lee had to make sure she never got there.

Helen's plate of eggs arrived just as she

resumed her seat at the counter. She picked up her fork and took a bite. The trucker on her left leafed through the *Chronicle*'s sports pages. The waitress busied herself wiping menus with a wet dishcloth. The trucker on her right leaned over and murmured into her ear.

"What?"

"Like a man," he said. "Your coffee. You drink it like a man."

Helen lowered her fork. "Really? How do you mean? Through a hole in my dick?"

The waitress looked up from her menus, made a little "O" with her mouth.

"Black. You drink it black. That's what I meant."

"Oh. Gotcha. Thanks for clarifying."

The trucker chewed a corner of his mustache, watched her take a bite of bacon. "Why? You got one?"

Helen sighed. "What?"

"A dick. 'Cause if you don't, I'll be happy to lend you mine for a spell."

"Hey, now," the waitress said.

"That's okay," Helen said, holding a hand up to the waitress. She finished chewing her bacon, swallowed, turned to the trucker.

"Sir, consider this a warning. You have just surpassed your allowable limit for douche-baggery. Any further unwanted sexual advances will incur severe penalties, including, but not limited to, a slap across the face, a kick in the ass, and a hot cup of coffee dumped directly onto your ball sack. Please acknowledge this message by saying, 'I understand.' "

The trucker flushed. Helen heard the newspaper rattle sharply behind her.

"Say it. 'I understand.' "

The trucker outweighed Helen by a hundred pounds, at minimum. He was thirty years older, but built like a Sherman tank. And if those forearms were any indication, he pumped heaps of iron.

Helen was trained in hand-to-hand combat. Not just the basics she'd learned during her stint in the Navy and at the Marshals Academy. She could box, throw a kick, execute a decent hip throw; rolled Brazilian jiu-jitsu a couple times a week. And she'd been in a brawl or two, but never one-on-one versus a guy who looked like a finalist in the Mr. Senior Olympia powerlifting championships.

Yet, if there was one thing she'd learned as a petite and reasonably attractive female in a work environment positively seething with alpha males, it was to never let an aggressor get the upper hand or assume a position of psychological dominance. Au-

thority must be established right away. Doing so required taking a risk — and sometimes bluffing like a cardsharp down to his
last wooden nickel.

She slid off her stool.

"Say it," she growled.

The trucker gave it a few seconds, looked
away.

"I ain't saying a goddamn thing," he
mumbled. But that was it. He was done.

"Fine. You stick to that."

She climbed back onto the stool, picked
up her fork, cut into her eggs.

"Stuck-up bitch," the trucker muttered.

He laid money on the counter, got to his
feet. The waitress gave him the hairy eye as
he walked out the door.

"I'm real sorry about that, hon," the
waitress said when he was gone. "Food's on
the house."

"Oh, don't worry about it. I can handle
myself."

"Well, I guess you can."

The waitress refilled Helen's coffee mug.
The remaining trucker whistled and went
back to his sports page.

After finishing her meal, Helen checked her
phone and located Choder's directions in
her email inbox. It looked like a circuitous

but straightforward route: Highway 80 to Route 89 to Route 49, and finally onto a smaller, unnamed access road. She punched "Kill Devil Falls" into Google. It showed her Kill Devil Hills in North Carolina, but no California town by that name. Not a good sign. She located Route 49 and traced it on the display until it linked to the access road. After that, the access road quickly dead-ended into a splotch of green empty space. What the hell? Even Google didn't think the place was worth the effort of mapping.

The estimated drive time from her present location to the access road was one hour and ten minutes. It was unlikely she'd reach Kill Devil Falls, collect Crawford, and get back down to the valley before nightfall. She was anxious at the prospect of navigating steep, treacherous, and unfamiliar mountain roads in the dark.

Helen paid her bill over the protests of the waitress, used the restroom, and stepped out into the chilly parking lot. She glanced at her cell phone. Already past three. And dusk fell early this time of year.

Her Dodge and a brown Honda occupied neighboring spots in the parking lot. As she was reaching for the Charger's door handle, a blur of movement flashed kitty-corner though the rear window.

She walked around to the back of the car. A man squatted between the Charger and the Honda. She recognized him from the diner. Tall, lanky, combat fatigues. She glanced at the insignia on his jacket, saw that he was a sergeant.

"Hi," Helen said.

"Hi," Lee said.

She waited. Lee was holding a small tool with a black plastic handle and long sharp metal shaft. His hands were black with oily dirt. He looked down at the tool, back up at her.

"This looks kinda weird, don't it?"

"Kinda. What are you doing?"

"I got a hole in my tire. I'm plugging it. Till I can get to a garage."

"Ah. You need a hand?"

"No, ma'am. I got it under control." Lee held up a small brown tube which resembled a Slim Jim. "I just gotta jam this sucker in the hole and I'm good to go."

"Okay."

Helen took a step forward, leaned down to look at the tire.

"Ingenious," she said.

"What?"

"The plug thing. Very clever."

"Yeah."

She wasn't really interested in his tire. She just wanted to examine her own without being obvious. She gave it a quick once-over as she straightened up and backed away. It seemed fine. But what did she know?

"Can't be too careful on these mountain roads," Lee said. "A blowout can send you right over the side of a cliff."

"No kidding."

"You headed up or down?" he asked.

"What's that?"

"You headed up or down the mountain?"

"Up," Helen said. "You?"

"Same. On leave. Visiting family in Reno."

"You have a long drive."

"Sure do. That's why I got to get this tire sorted out. Where you headed?"

"Up," Helen repeated. "You have a good day."

She walked back to the front of the Charger, climbed inside, started the engine. She checked her side-view mirror. The guy stood up, flattened himself against the side panel of the Honda, waved her on. Helen backed slowly out of the parking lot. As she passed by, he flashed a thumbs-up sign.

2

Helen navigated the serpentine curves of Route 89, ascending steadily, the Charger chugging along like the Little Engine that Could. She switched on the CD player. A forceful female voice flowed crisply from the car speakers:

"Let's face it, ladies. It's still a man's-man's-man's world."

Helen was an avid, but exceedingly secretive, consumer of self-help titles. *Nice Girls Don't Get the Corner Office*, *The Seven Habits of Highly Effective People*, *The Secret*, *The Road Less Traveled*, *Awaken the Giant Within* — she'd read them all. This one was called *The Superior Sex.*

"Let's review a few statistics," the narrator continued. "By the time a college-educated woman turns fifty-nine, she will have earned eight hundred thousand dollars less than her male counterparts due to the gender wage gap. Women make up almost half the workforce, but only account for 4 percent of Fortune 500 CEOs. As recently as 2013, Congress proposed seven hundred bills designed to regulate women's health and reproductive rights. In fact, it's now easier for your average woman to get her hands on a gun than it is for her to obtain an abortion."

Helen estimated another twenty or thirty minutes to Route 49, and perhaps fifteen or twenty more to reach the access road. Beyond that, she had no idea how long till Kill Devil Falls. Could be ten minutes on the access road, could be half an hour.

"The fact remains, we live in a patriarchal society," the narrator declared. "Power is still concentrated in the hands of men, whether they be senators, bosses, fathers, or husbands."

"Eh." Helen shrugged, not entirely convinced. She decelerated into a curve, eyes flickering to the edge of the road where a flimsy metal barrier was all that separated her from a deadly plunge straight down a cliffside. The mountain scenery was truly breathtaking — snow-frosted peaks, a thick carpet of fir trees, sheer granite rock faces, and deeply cut valleys — but a second's carelessness and the Charger would become a twisted, buckled, deformed metal coffin.

On the far side of the curve, the road inclined sharply. The Charger's V6 whined in protest as Helen pressed on the gas pedal.

"In the corporate world, when a woman does not conform to the male beauty standards, she is less likely to receive promotions and leadership roles. If she does conform to these standards, she is assumed to be pretty, but stupid. If she dresses conservatively, she is called a frump. If she dresses in a manner that plays up her sexuality, she is considered a slut. An aggressive male CEO is tough, while an aggressive female CEO is a bitch."

Helen nodded to herself, thinking of how Choder enjoyed tossing out the occasional comment on her appearance, suggesting she dress in a more feminine manner or let her hair down. "Just because you carry a gun doesn't mean you have to wear men's pants," he'd say.

"So what is a woman to do? The simple answer is this: A woman has to work twice as hard, and be twice as good, as her male colleagues. When the deck is stacked against you, you have to bring your own aces to the table. You have to prove you are the superior sex."

Helen eased up on the gas and navigated a tight turn, skirting very close to the safety barrier. The road started to level out. The Charger's engine settled into a comfortable purr.

Although she didn't label herself a hard-core feminist, Helen was no stranger to the challenges of being female in a predominantly male environment. For one thing, she'd been raised by a single father, an ex-Navy officer with little patience for emotional outbursts and menstrual cycles. For another, she'd chosen a profession dominated by men with a high tolerance for personal risk and violence, where sexual innuendo and crude jokes were the norm. For the most part, she ignored the wisecracks and pick-up lines or just laughed them off. After all, there weren't enough hours in the day to call her coworkers on all their bullshit, and besides, she didn't want to earn a reputation for being hard to work with.

But she had her limit, and when a colleague crossed it, she let him know. Just like with the trucker in the diner. She found a dose of humor usually helped the pill go down, but if that didn't do the trick, she was willing to draw a line in the sand and then throw a punch when some meathead stepped over it.

"I developed the following questionnaire

to help you evaluate your strengths and vulnerabilities, so you can determine how to reach your full potential as the superior sex," the narrator said. "Check the statements below which apply to you."

"Go for it," Helen said.

"I have a good relationship with my father."

"A beeline straight to Freud, huh?" Helen said.

"I have a good relationship with my mother."

Helen tapped her fingers on the steering wheel, frowned at the CD Player console. Her mother had died when she was ten. Car accident.

"I go the extra mile to please my partner."

Helen laughed. "What partner?"

"I like to call the shots in bed."

"Oh, for God's sake."

"I'd rather shoot pool with the boys than go shoe shopping."

"That's an affirmative."

The next question was cut short by the sound of an explosion. The steering wheel leaped from Helen's grasp. The Charger swerved left, straight for the rocky mountainside, then shot right, toward the safety barrier overlooking the cliff.

Helen clamped her hands on the wheel

and slammed on the brakes. The Charger's right fender scraped along the safety barrier, spewing sparks like a black market Roman candle. Helen maintained a grip on the wheel with her left hand, reached down and yanked on the emergency brake with her right. The car fishtailed. The view through the windshield careened wildly, like a ship tossed on the ocean by gale-force winds.

Helen lifted her foot from the brake, gave the car some leeway. When the Charger's direction stabilized, she went back to the brakes, adjusted the wheel. Slowly, grudgingly, the Charger responded. Another fifty feet, and she brought it to a sliding halt on a narrow dirt shoulder.

She put the car in park and shut off the engine. Her heart was hammering so violently against her sternum, it threatened to crack a rib. She inhaled deeply, started mentally counting backward from one hundred, gradually brought her pulse rate under control.

"Fuck your fucking FUCK!" she screamed at the windshield. The struggle to curtail her habitual cursing continued, but in some situations, *frick, eff,* and *dang* weren't sufficiently cathartic.

Helen waited out a bout of the shakes.

Then she opened the car door and walked around to the rear of the Charger. The smell of hot rubber and burning motor oil hung in the air.

The right rear tire was flat. Not just flat. Deflated, shredded, a hollow skin of tattered black sludge.

She shuffled a few feet over to the side of the road, peered down into the valley below. Just beyond the safety barrier was a nearly vertical drop of at least one hundred feet. Nothing clung to the cliffside apart from a scatter of scree and a few stunted trees, which grew at awkward angles in a desperate bid for sunlight.

Helen attempted to open the trunk with her key, but her hand trembled too much to fit it into the slot. She returned to the driver's side door and popped the trunk using the release under the dashboard.

She removed a jack, lug wrench, and spare tire, dumped them on the graveled shoulder. She fit the wrench over the first of the wheel's lug nuts, twisted. It was stuck fast. She leaned all of her weight on the wrench, grunted with effort, felt it give. By the time she had three of the nuts removed, her arms were as limp as boiled macaroni.

As she was jacking up the car, she heard the putter of an engine approaching. Seconds later, a dirty white sedan whipped around the corner, recklessly fast. Helen froze, hand on the jack lever, certain the sedan would sideswipe the Charger, propelling it and her over the side of the cliff.

The sedan missed by a narrow margin, raced past, engine mewling piteously, and disappeared around the curve up ahead.

"Asshole!" she shouted.

She wiped sweat from her hairline. Could this day *get* any shittier?

Helen wrestled the shredded tire off the axle, dropped it onto the ground. As she rolled the spare over, she flashed back to the guy in the diner parking lot.

He'd been squatting right there, at the back of the Charger. Wielding a sharp tool. Could he have tampered with her tire, rigged it to hold twenty or thirty miles and then basically disintegrate?

Possible. But what reason would a random stranger have for sabotaging her ride?

Helen propped the spare tire against the exposed axle, pulled out her cell phone. Reception was weak but serviceable. She googled "California's Most Wanted," waited several minutes for the mug shots to load. She couldn't remember the name of Crawford's partner off the top of her head, so she scrolled down, searched the photos.

Here he was: Lee Larimer.

Long dark hair, unshaven, pale as a vampire. Handsome in a grungy, struggling-musician-with-a-drug-habit kind of way. Not her type, but she knew lots of women who'd take him in, give him a hot bath, make him a grilled cheese sandwich, and then moon over him for six months after he absconded with all their cash, credit cards, and jewelry.

Larimer didn't look anything like Sgt. Fix-it. Still, it didn't sit right, the blow-out right on the heels of the parking lot incident.

Helen put her phone back in her pocket. She lifted the spare onto the axle, threaded the lug nuts, lowered the jack, tightened the nuts with the wrench. She tossed the wrench and jack into the trunk. She picked up the shredded tire and tossed that into the trunk, as well. When she got back to Sac, she'd ask the boys in motor pool to examine it. See if she was just being paranoid or if maybe, possibly, some punk-ass associate of Crawford's had attempted to send her over a cliff.

The antique chair groaned in protest as Teddy Scroggins leaned his considerable bulk to one side and spat a stream of tobacco juice into an empty coffee can sitting on the floor. He wiped a stray dribble off his beard with the heel of his hand.

He'd found the coffee can in the guard room, on a shelf displaying a dozen or so artifacts dating to the late 1800s — an ivory-handled straight razor and a shaving brush, a tortoise-shell comb, a pocket watch, a deck of cards, a collection of yellowed Penny Dreadfuls, rusted food tins, a dented sheriff's badge.

He wasn't supposed to be using it, certainly not as a tobacco juice receptacle, but they weren't supposed to be using the Old Log Jail to hold a fugitive, either. Of the two, Teddy figured borrowing an old coffee can was the lesser offense.

The Old Log Jail was, as its name indicated, an A-frame structure built of pine logs. Attached to the front of the building was a wooden porch, leading to a thick door reinforced with iron bands. To the right of the door was a window, likewise secured with metal bars.

Inside was a sizable room. On the left, facing out from the wall, sat a massive mahogany desk. This is where the sheriff had conducted his business back when the jail was in active use, and where Teddy sat now. Recessed into the rear wall were two jail cells with doors constructed of crisscrossed flat metal strips. To the right side of the jail cells was a short hallway leading to a separate guard room at the back of the building. The guard room was furnished with a wooden bed frame and mattress, the aforementioned display shelf of artifacts, a round table with two pewter place settings, a pair of chairs, and an old cast-iron wood-burning stove.

The jail dated back to 1876, when it served as the county lock-up. In its heyday, it hosted a rogue's gallery of petty thieves, claim jumpers, drunks, gamblers, debtors, and even a murderer or two. Originally located in Marleesville, it was decommissioned in the 1930s and sat empty and neglected until the 1960s, when it was dismantled and reassembled on the outskirts of town to serve as a Gold Rush-era museum.

In retrospect, no one could remember who had made the decision to move the jail to Kill Devil Falls, and it proved a strange one, as the only tourists who ever visited the museum were those hopelessly off course on their way to a camping or hiking destination.

The county's current jail was located in Donnersville, in the same building as the courthouse and sheriff's department. That was thirty miles as the crow flies, but a good fifty minutes to an hour by car across a twisted, undulating landscape. And in the wake of a biker-rally-turned-violent-street-brawl, it was presently filled to capacity.

Even so, when Big Ed and Teddy rode up from Donnersville, the intention was to take Rita Crawford into custody, bring her back down, and then sit on her until the US Marshals arrived. But shortly after they'd reached Kill Devil Falls, a call came over the radio regarding a shooting in Sardine Valley. It was decided that Big Ed would take the patrol vehicle, a white Ford Explorer with *County Sheriff* printed on the side, and Teddy would wait with Rita.

At the moment, Rita was locked up in the leftmost five-by-six-foot cell and Teddy was chewing tobacco and biding his time.

"Edward," Rita said. Her fingers poked through the slats of the cell door, her nails ragged, dark with dirt.

Teddy pretended not to hear. He folded his hands across his wide belly and closed his eyes.

"Deputy," Rita growled, annoyed.

"Deputy Sheriff," Teddy said.

"Jesus Christ. Deputy Sheriff. May I please have a cigarette? They're in my jacket." Rita pointed at a leather motorcycle jacket resting atop the desk.

"No, you may not," Teddy said. "This is a public building. No smoking allowed."

"Come on. I could really use one. Please?"

"Shouldn'ta let yourself get hooked on such a nasty habit."

"I see. And you're fucking perfect, aren't you?"

Teddy abruptly stood up and strode over to the cell, drawing a baton from his gun belt as he did so. Rita withdrew her fingers from the cell door.

"I don't take lip from criminals," Teddy said. He rapped the baton on the door. "Mind your manners."

"If anyone should be locked up, it's you, *Deputy.*" She spat the word out like a mouthful of maggoty cheese.

Teddy's face flushed a deep shade of crimson. He clenched the baton hard enough to turn his knuckles white. He reached toward the wall behind the desk, where a rusty metal ring holding a large key hung on a hook.

"I didn't mean that. I'm sorry," Rita said hastily. "I don't . . . I'm sorry."

Teddy glowered for a moment, then slid the baton back into his gun belt.

"Your ride should be here any time," he said. "Why don't you do us both a favor and keep your mouth shut till then?"

"Sure thing. After I get that cigarette."

"Don't know when to quit, do you?"

A low rumble vibrated through the wooden floor of the jailhouse. Teddy clomped to the window in heavy boots, peeked out.

"Speak of the devil," he said.

Inside the cell, Rita sank onto a narrow cot placed against the wall. She let out a breath, muttered "Thank God."

Lee Larimer cursed as a branch snapped across his face for the twentieth time.

"Motherfucking . . . cocksucking . . . ball-busting trees!"

Lee wasn't exactly a city boy, having been born and raised in Fresno, but he'd never been the outdoorsy type, into pitching a tent, fishing for supper, taking a shit in the bushes. He preferred the comforts of civilization. Paved roads, drive-through fast food, strip clubs, cable television.

He zipped up his jacket, blew on his hands. He'd known it would be cold up here, but not this cold. His fingertips were numb.

Fucking Rita. Two-faced little bitch. She'd ditched him in the middle of the night, while he was sleeping off a bender. Taken the money he'd risked his life for. Money he'd stolen not for himself, but for *them*. She'd robbed him, stabbed him in the back, and dumped him all in one fell swoop.

And now, because of her, he was going to get frostbite. Or tick fever.

Theirs had not been a stereotypical storybook romance. Less Princess Bride than Bonnie and Clyde. Yet, for Lee, it was something genuine. The closest thing to happiness he'd felt since his family broke up when he was a boy.

They'd met in a halfway house on Fresno's West Side. She was there to kick an Oxycontin addiction. He was a resident by invitation of the court, following multiple drug busts. They bonded on the rickety back porch, amid a backdrop of splintered wood and peeling paint, over cigarettes and tales of rough childhoods. Lee wouldn't say it was love at first sight, exactly, but he and Rita shared a similar "fuck-you" worldview and a fondness for Bud Light, illicit narcotics, and Slayer's musical oeuvre. Plus, she had great legs and a passable pair of tits.

Following their release from the program, Rita and Lee had rented an apartment together on Saginaw Way. Within a week, Lee was back to slinging and using dope. Soon after, Rita resumed her Oxy habit. Lee used more than he sold, and eventually fell deep into a hole with his main supplier, a minor player in the local faction of the Fresno Bulldog street gang named Felix "El Psicopata" Rodriguez. When Felix threatened to drape Rita's intestines over his personal shrine to Santa Muerte, Lee traded his last bags of heroin for a Smith and Wesson X-Frame revolver in the Fashion Fair Mall parking lot. Then he drove over to Felix's house, forced "El Psicopata" into his bathtub, and shot him in the face. It was the first time Lee had killed someone, the first time, in fact, he'd even drawn a gun on another human being. He left with a couple thousand dollars in crumpled bills, a big bag of weed, an eight-ball of coke, an assortment of pills, and a sense of Godlike omnipotence.

That night, Lee and Rita had packed up his '86 Mustang and hit the road. There was no specific plan or destination, just an urgency to leave Fresno before Felix's vatos fingered Lee for the murder and came looking for payback.

Their first joint venture had involved an AM/PM market outside of Chowchilla a week later. Lee wore sunglasses and a hat and used the X-Frame to scare the crap out of a seventeen-year-old kid behind the cash register. Rita was the getaway driver. They didn't net much money, but it was easy. It was a gas.

Lee and Rita then zigzagged up and down California, as far south as LA, as far north as San Jose, hitting convenience stores, gas stations, twenty-four-hour markets. They cobbled together various disguises from magic shops and thrift stores. Lee proved adept at meticulously planning each job, first casing the target, noting specifics such as video cameras and exit routes. A stolen, hotwired car was used as transport, and later ditched. He and Rita wore gloves to avoid leaving fingerprints. She drove, and he did the heavy lifting.

It took four or five months for law enforcement to connect the dots and realize they had a serial robbery team on their hands. The Attorney General held a press conference asking citizens to come forth with any information or leads that might help catch the thieves. A grainy video capture was issued, showing Lee in a hoodie and jeans, with a ball cap and sunglasses. And another of Rita, sitting behind the wheel of a stolen Chevy Impala, wearing a blond wig and big movie-star shades. The media dubbed them Robin and the Hood.

When he saw their photos splashed across the TV news and in the papers, Lee knew it was only a matter of time before the cops got lucky. He decided to go for broke, amass as much cash as possible in a short time, and then — poof! Disappear. So they began hitting country credit unions and suburban bank branches. Between robberies, they laid low at various motels, never staying more than two nights in one place, always paying in cash. They kept the partying and drugs to a minimum. For the first time since about the age of fourteen, Lee was spending more time sober than drunk or high. He was a man with a plan — to build a nest egg, enough for him and Rita to start over somewhere abroad, out of reach of American authorities, maybe Belize or Costa Rica.

But the inevitable eventually occurred. Somehow — maybe a minuscule piece of physical evidence, or someone recognized Lee and Rita from a surveillance video capture — the cops managed to ID them. Game over. Lee suggested they drive down to San Diego, where they would hire a fishing boat to take them into Mexico. It was easy enough to do. American boats took tourists fishing south of the border almost every day.

The night before their planned departure, he and Rita had a little makeover party. Rita cut and dyed his hair. Lee trimmed Rita's bangs, helped her add red highlights and a loose perm. He smoked a shitload of weed and drank eleven or twelve beers. He didn't notice Rita was limiting herself to a couple of bong hits and a few drinks.

When he woke up the next morning, Rita was gone. So was the Mustang. And apart from a few thousand dollars, so was the money.

She'd left him a note, sitting under the short stack of bills:

Lee, I'm sorry. We never would have made it to Mexico. I have to look out for myself, I hope you understand. Don't try to find me.

He was stupid enough to think she might have second thoughts. Get fifty miles down the road, burst into tears, make a U-turn. Realize maybe she loved him. Recognize she couldn't do him like that. He waited. She didn't come back.

He sat on the sagging motel bed, smoking Marlboro after Marlboro, drinking the last of the Bud Light Lime. Where the fuck would she go? Mexico? She wouldn't know how. Canada? She'd never get across the border. Maybe she'd jump a container ship in San Pedro? Or just head up to Portland or Yakima and lay low?

What would he do, if he were Rita? Well . . . if he was a real bitch, he'd stash the money somewhere. A hole where no one would find it. Then he'd turn himself in, throw himself on the mercy of the court, claim that his partner was the mastermind. That he was coerced, or too scared to resist, or Jedi mind-fucked into going along with the crimes. He'd offer to turn state's evidence. Be a rat in exchange for a reduced sentence.

If that was Rita's plan, a good lawyer could probably have her out of jail in three years max. While she was still young. With plenty of time to enjoy the money he'd risked his life to steal, for *them.*

Meanwhile, he'd be doing a twenty-year stretch at least, and perhaps even life if they could pin El Psicopata's murder on him. If that happened, he wouldn't last three weeks into his sentence before some Fresno Bulldog affiliate motherfucker shanked him in the showers.

Yes, it made sense, if you were Rita. It was a logical plan, one that gave her a chance at a future outside of a six-by-eight-foot cage. All she had to do was find a good place to hide the cash. And royally fuck over the man who'd taken care of her, provided for her, sweated his ass off to build a future for her.

As to where she might put the money, it had to be a location that was remote, so no one would just stumble on it by dumb luck. Secure from rot, bugs, animals, fire, floods, natural catastrophes. A place she knew would still be there, relatively unchanged, in three or so years.

He recalled those months on the back porch of the halfway house. The sob stories. How her dad ran off when she was eight. And her mom got remarried to some hard-ass. The abuse. Running away, living on the streets. Now, what was the name of that town? Something weird, messed up. Kill Devil Falls. That was it. Up in the mountains. That's where she would go.

Lee put on his fatigues, the bronzer, and glasses, packed up his meager belongings, wiped down the hotel room, emptied the garbage in a dumpster out back. He took a public bus to a strip mall parking lot and stole a car, the brown Honda. He switched the Honda's plates with an SUV's. He spent ten dollars at a gas station to buy a map of the Sierra Nevadas, traced a route to Kill Devil Falls, and hopped on the highway.

Running into the lady cop in the diner had been a shock. Yet since she didn't seem to be there for him, he was all the more certain he was on the right track. But how did the cop know where Rita was? It didn't make sense for Rita to have hidden the cash and then turned herself in at Kill Devil Falls. She'd have wanted to get as far away from the money as possible before surrendering to the authorities. Maybe she'd been collared. If so, he hoped to Christ she'd buried the money first.

Here's where it got sticky. What if she was handcuffed to some redneck country sheriff's radiator, guarded by dogs and hillbillies with shotguns?

Ultimately, it didn't matter. Lee needed to get up there, determine the lay of the land, and either find the money or make Rita tell him where it was. Short of encountering a SWAT team, he wasn't leaving empty-handed.

As for the lady cop, he'd been lucky enough to find a tire-repair kit in the Honda's glove box. He used the T-reamer and a cigarette filter to doctor her tire. She'd get a flat, or the tire would blow, sending her into a rock wall or over a cliff. Either way, he was going to reach Kill Devil Falls before she did.

As a precaution, he'd ditched the brown Honda and stolen a white Hyundai Sonata parked a few blocks over from the cafe. He would have preferred something with more than just four cylinders, but he was in a hurry and the Hyundai was easy pickings.

After passing the Charger on the mountain (the cop was lucky — or one hell of a driver), he knew she'd be back on the road soon. He stashed the Hyundai off the access road, camouflaged it with broken branches. He picked his way through the forest, tree limbs slapping his face, vines and roots tripping up his feet.

And now, after a twenty minute slog, he reached the edge of town. He saw one road and a smattering of buildings. The closest one was constructed of thick logs and had bars on the window, like a jail in a John Wayne western.

Lee watched from the shelter of the trees for five minutes. Nothing moved. It was a ghost town.

He decided to start searching for Rita, beginning with the log building. But just as he was making his move, he heard the meaty thrum of a car engine. The Charger rolled up, the front door to the log building opened, and a pudgy deputy emerged.

Lee hunkered down. Best to sit tight, see how things played out. And when opportunity reared its head, grab it by the throat and choke the shit out of it.

3

Teddy picked up the coffee can, used a finger to hook the tobacco in his cheek, and spat a masticated wad into the makeshift spittoon. He grabbed his green uniform jacket off the back of the chair and slipped into it as he opened the front door and stepped out onto the porch. Frigid air rushed into the room.

Outside, the mud-splattered Dodge Charger pulled to a stop. Helen switched off the engine, climbed out of the driver's seat. Her back was stiff and she was dying for a cup of thick black coffee.

"Hi! Deputy Marshal Morrissey," she called out. "Are you Sheriff Scroggins?"

"Uh, no ma'am. He ain't here at the moment. Had to run over to Sardine Valley. Probably won't be back for an hour or so. I'm the Deputy Sheriff. Call me Teddy."

Helen mounted the porch steps, shook Teddy's hand.

"Good to meet you," she said. "You have the fugitive inside?"

"Locked up tighter'n a duck's ass." He blushed. "Excuse me."

"No worries."

"Right through there."

He waved Helen inside. She stepped across the threshold, took in the room. No coffee machine, unfortunately.

"What is this place?"

"Old Log Jail. Now a museum. Cells still work fine, though. She's in the one on the left."

Teddy pointed. Helen walked to the cell, peered through the iron slats. All she could see was a shadowy figure sitting on a narrow cot.

"Rita Crawford?"

"Yeah." Rita's voice was low-pitched, scratchy, sullen.

"I'm Deputy Marshal Morrissey, with the US Marshal's Service. I'll be taking you to Sacramento and remanding you to the Department of Corrections."

"Fine. Let's get the fuck out of here."

That was a new one to Helen. Usually people were less enthusiastic about going to prison.

Helen turned to Teddy. "I understand someone from the sheriff's department is

48

going to assist me in escorting Ms. Crawford back to Sacramento?"

"Uh . . ." He fidgeted. Helen sensed a snag coming her way.

"Is there a problem?"

"We had a ruckus in Donnersville. Annual biker rally got a little out of hand. So most of the deputies is busy cleaning up that mess."

"Okay, and? What's the upshot?"

"The sheriff, he said you should take Rita down to Donnersville and see which of the boys is free to ride with you."

"Great," Helen said through clenched teeth. "My supervisor just told me to come all the way up here to collect Ms. Crawford. If you'd transported her to Donnersville, it would have saved me some time."

"Sheriff and I drove up together, Marshal, and he took the vehicle on an emergency call to Sardine Valley, so . . ."

"Okay, I get it. What about you?"

"Me?" Teddy said.

"Maybe you can help me transport her to Sac."

"Oh, well." Teddy looked at his watch. "Actually, Marshal, my shift's over. I'm off duty now."

Helen stared at him.

"Don't worry," Teddy said. "One of the

49

other deputies will help you out."

Helen took a deep breath. "While I have you here, can we at least get this paperwork squared away?" She set a manila envelope down on the desk, started pulling out forms.

"Maybe we should wait for the sheriff?"

"Why?"

Teddy shrugged. "He does the official paperwork, is all."

"Deputy, I'd really like to streamline this process as much as possible."

Teddy got a pained look on his face. He cleared his throat, looked up at the ceiling, fiddled with the keys on his gun belt.

"Just sign the fucking papers," Rita said through the slats of the cell door.

"Quiet!" he barked.

Helen curbed the urge to smile. Rita Crawford was quite the loose cannon.

"You got a pen?" Teddy said.

First they went through Rita's possessions: one leather jacket; one pack of cigarettes, Marlboro Reds; one disposable lighter; one small plastic flashlight; one Samsung pre-paid cell phone; one gold ring; one gold crucifix; one pair sunglasses, generic; one Mickey Mouse watch; seven hundred and thirty-four dollars in cash; one set of car keys.

"Where's her car?" Helen asked.

"She ain't inclined to tell us. But there's a lot of old horse trails around here. Easy enough to hide a car and walk into town."

"Speaking of that, I'm on the lookout for a brown Honda driven by a guy in camouflage fatigues. I don't suppose one passed through here?"

Teddy chuckled. "Passed through on the way to where, Marshal? Main Street dead-ends on the other side of town. Why you on the lookout for this guy?"

Helen shook her head. "Never mind, it's probably nothing. I'll sign here and you sign there."

They painstakingly completed a few additional forms, Teddy adding his signature in a laborious cursive script. When they were done, Helen handed Teddy his copies, stuffed the other papers into the envelope. She put Helen's possessions, apart from the jacket, in a plastic bag and sealed it.

"That should do it," she said.

Teddy took the key from its hook on the wall, unlocked the cell door, pulled it open on creaking hinges.

"Let's go," he said.

Rita appeared in the doorway. She was dressed in jeans with ripped knees and an old, stretched-out cable-knit sweater which hung from her frame like baggy skin on bones. Helen guessed she was maybe thirty-four, thirty-five. Given nicer clothes, a better haircut, and easier life, she might have been pretty. The raw material was there — big dark eyes, prominent cheekbones, a delicately shaped nose. But Rita's hair was a mess of old roots and cheap dye, her skin was weathered and lined, and those dark eyes displayed a hungry, hunted look.

Even so, she stood with her shoulders back, chin up, direct eye contact. No shrinking violet, even in these circumstances. Helen respected her grit.

"Turn around and put your hands on the wall."

Rita waited just long enough to demonstrate silent defiance, then complied. Helen moved closer.

"I'm going to search you now."

"I already did that," Teddy said.

"And he made sure to get his money's worth," Rita said.

"You shut your mouth!" Teddy shook his head at Helen. "She's just trying to get a rise out of me."

"Looks like she's succeeding," Helen said.

Teddy just waved a hand, as if brushing away a cloud of gnats. Helen's gut told her Rita saw a weakness in Teddy — a lack of confidence, a sensitivity to being laughed at

— and enjoyed picking at it like a scab.

She frisked Rita carefully.

"Okay. I'm going to cuff you. Maybe you want to put on that jacket first. It's cold outside."

"Gee, Mom, thanks."

Helen ignored her. She checked the pockets, found them empty, felt the lining to make sure nothing was sewn inside it, held out the jacket. Rita slid her arms into the sleeves.

"Turn around again."

This time, instead of waiting for a response, Helen grasped Rita's elbow and spun her around.

"Police brutality," Rita deadpanned. Helen cuffed Rita's hands behind the small of her back.

"Did the deputy read you your rights?" Helen asked.

"I did," Teddy said.

"Please let her answer, Deputy," Helen said.

"Yeah, he read me my rights," Rita said. "Good thing they're only written at a fourth-grade level."

Teddy started to sputter and Helen quickly cut off his indignant response.

"Did you waive these rights?"

"I asked for a lawyer," Rita said.

"I see. Fair enough." According to law, nothing Rita now said to Helen would be admissible as evidence in a trial. "You got any belongings you want to bring along, aside from what the deputy found on your person?"

"No."

"How about in your car? I'll escort you there and you can claim anything you left inside."

"No."

"Fine."

She put a hand inside Rita's elbow, turned her so that they were face-to-face.

"Let's you and me have an understanding, Rita."

Rita looked Helen in the eye but didn't say anything.

"We've got a two-and-half, three-hour drive back to Sacramento. I'll make a couple of stops on the way to use the bathroom, get some take-out burgers, my treat, maybe even let you smoke a few of those cigarettes. In return, you keep quiet and don't cause any trouble, and most importantly, don't try anything stupid. If you give me a hard time, I'll take you straight to corrections, no food, no cigarettes, no bathroom. You can just piss your pants on the way. Make noise or talk back, and I'll duct tape your mouth shut. Deal?"

Rita thought about it for a moment and said, "Can I have one of those cigarettes now?"

"Sure."

Helen guided Rita out onto the porch. She opened the plastic bag, took out a cigarette, placed it between Rita's lips, lit it with the disposable lighter.

She looked at her watch. Twenty minutes or so and night was going to drop like a lead curtain. She checked her cell phone. No signal.

"I should probably call my office, let them know the situation," she told Teddy.

"You'll have to wait till you get to Donnersville. Sorry about that. If the sheriff was here with the vehicle, you could use the radio. But as you can see, we don't get cell reception, and we ain't got no landline in town."

"No landline?"

"Kill Devil Falls is on condemned land. We got electricity, but the phone company won't run a line up here."

"Condemned? Why?"

"Well, this was a mining town back in the late 1800s, early 1900s," Teddy said. "Gold, mostly. In those days, they used mercury to separate gold from sediment. There wasn't

55

no Environmental Protection Agency or nothing like that — and miners was just looking to get rich. They didn't give a rat's . . . you know . . . behind . . . about the land. All that mercury leached into the soil and made it toxic."

"Is it still toxic?" Helen asked.

"Oh, yeah. I mean, not so bad, but more than is allowed. It ain't like we got kids with two heads stashed in the cellar, but I wouldn't necessarily eat no vegetables grown around here." He laughed. "Besides the mercury, the rock underneath town is riddled with old tunnels, so it's pretty unstable. A medium-sized earthquake or something like that and the whole place might just sink underground."

"I can't believe anyone is even allowed to live here."

Teddy shrugged. "The county ordered us to evacuate years ago, but we fought the case in court and made a deal. The residents that was living here at the time of the agreement are allowed to stay until they decide to leave voluntarily, or . . . pass away. Once the last remaining resident is gone, the county will take back the land and wipe Kill Devil Falls off the map."

"Good riddance," Rita said, cigarette bouncing in her mouth.

Helen didn't mention to Teddy that Kill Devil Falls *already* appeared to be off the map.

"You said *we* fought the case. You live in Kill Devil Falls?"

"Born and raised. Right there." Teddy pointed off the side of the porch at a red farmhouse fifty yards up the road.

Rita muttered under her breath.

"You say something?" Teddy asked.

"Nope. Just smoking my cancer stick, minding my own business."

"Why stay here?" Helen asked. "If the soil is poisoned? And the ground unstable?"

"It's home, Marshal."

Rita spat her cigarette onto the wooden floor of the porch, ground it out with her shoe.

"I'm ready," she said.

The tip of Helen's nose was growing numb in the cold.

"Okay, let's get moving."

She escorted Rita down the porch stairs, opened the back door of the Charger, helped her inside. She pulled the seat belt across Rita's chest, buckled it.

"I gotta ride with my hands cuffed behind my back? It's real uncomfortable."

"Don't start."

Helen shut the back door and climbed

behind the wheel. She dumped the manila envelope and the plastic bag containing Rita's possessions on the passenger's seat.

She glanced up at the sky through the windshield. From her vantage point, the setting sun was a hair's breadth from impaling itself on the jagged tips of pine trees to the west. Which meant a drive down the mountain in the dark, on three and a half tires. She hoped Chowder slipped on a patch of ice heading home tonight and the toe of his cowboy boot got stuck up his ass.

She turned the key in the ignition. The engine clicked, but didn't start.

"What's wrong?" Rita said.

"Hold on."

Helen confirmed the gear was in park and her foot was on the brake. She turned the key again. Same thing. *Click-click-click.*

"What's wrong with the car?"

"Just wait a minute!"

Helen gave it another go. No joy.

"*Suck* it!" she growled.

"You have gas?" Rita said, her voice rising an octave.

"Take it easy, Rita." Helen reached under the dashboard, pulled the hood release. She clambered out of the car, opened the hood, gazed down at a lot of black metal and rubber hosing she knew nothing about.

She fiddled with the battery cables, some random wires. A couple seemed loose, so she connected them more tightly. She scooted back behind the wheel, turned the key. Not even a click this time.

"What the fuck is wrong with your car?" Rita said.

Helen climbed out of the Charger. Teddy smiled at her from the porch, hands in the pockets of his jacket.

"She won't start?"

"No. Can you take a look?'

"Sorry, Marshal. I ain't good with cars."

"Anyone around here who is?"

"Frank and Mike are pretty handy."

"Frank and Mike? Where can I find them?"

Teddy squinted down at his watch.

"It's getting near dinnertime. They might be at the Trading Post."

"What's the Trading Post?"

Teddy laughed. He had one of those snorting laughs that came mainly through the nose and was occasionally accompanied by an expulsion of nasal discharge.

"It's our local market and restaurant. Almost everyone in town eats dinner there every night."

"And where would I find it, Deputy?"

"It's down Main Street a ways."

Helen opened the back door of the Charger, reached for Rita.

"What are you doing?"

"Taking you back inside."

"Why?"

"I would have thought it was obvious. The car isn't working."

"But I want to leave. Now."

"Me too. You know how to fix cars?"

"No."

"Me either. So I'm going to get a mechanic."

"You're putting me back in the cell?"

"Just for a bit, Rita."

"No, no . . . I don't want to go back into the cell."

"Would you prefer the trunk?"

Helen unbuckled the seat belt, tugged at Rita's arm. Rita wriggled and pulled away.

"Hey!" Helen said. "Knock it off!"

"Listen. Listen!" Rita said. Her eyes had that wild, cow-trapped-in-a-barn-fire look. "You can take my car. I'll show you where it is. We'll leave now. No need for a mechanic."

"I can't just use any old car I want, okay? I need to get this car fixed and return it to my motor pool. Now, come out of there."

"This isn't right, Marshal. Don't you understand?"

"Enough." Helen removed a small canister from an attachment on her belt. "You're coming out of the car or I'll mace you. Do *you* understand?"

She put a forefinger on top of the canister, pointed the tiny nozzle at Rita's face.

"Marshal . . . please." Rita's eyes welled with tears.

"I'll give you to a count of one. Then I'm giving you a dose. And you'll ride all the way home with tears and snot running into your mouth because the back seat's going to have pepper spray residue all over it."

There were strict rules against macing prisoners in handcuffs, but Helen figured the threat alone would prompt Rita's compliance.

"Okay, okay," Rita said.

She allowed Helen to pull her from the car, escort her toward the porch steps. But when Helen took her hand from the crook of Rita's elbow to slip the canister of mace back into the attachment on her belt, Rita made a break for it.

"We got a runner!" Teddy yelled.

"Oh, for frick's sake," Helen said.

4

Rita was surprisingly fast, given the handcuffs. Helen was tempted to aim a sweep kick at her heels from behind, but that would dump Rita face first on the pavement. Bringing in a bruised and bloody fugitive, no matter what the excuse, was just asking for trouble.

Helen sprinted, drew abreast of Rita, cut a diagonal, and body-blocked her into the dirt on the side of the road.

She straddled Rita's hips, pressed down on Rita's throat to prevent her from rearing up, took a few seconds to catch her breath.

"Trying to run away . . . falls very much under the category . . . of doing something stupid, Rita. What did I tell you about that?"

Tears cut through the dust on Rita's face. Helen felt a twinge of sympathy. Sometimes, it's not until you're cuffed and in the back of a cop car that the full reality of your situation sinks in. Rita put on a brave front, but now she was going away, possibly for a very, very long time, and the hard veneer was finally cracking.

Helen pulled her to her feet and led her back toward the jail. The fight seemed to have leaked out of Rita like air from an old kiddie bop-bag. She stumbled slightly as they ascended the porch steps. Helen jerked her upright, a bit roughly.

Teddy held the front door open. As they passed, Helen caught him giving Rita a smirk. Rita kept her eyes on the floor.

Helen placed Rita into the cell, closed the door.

"You want to take those cuffs off her?" Teddy asked.

Helen was still pissed about the escape attempt.

"No, leave them on for now."

"If you say so."

He locked the door, hung the key ring back on its hook.

"Nothing like a little excitement, huh?" He snort-laughed.

"I could do without. And I still need to get that car fixed."

"You know, I could use a cup of coffee. How about I take you down to the Trading Post, introduce you to Mike and Frank?"

"I don't think we should leave Rita alone."

"Ah, she'll be fine. Handcuffed, locked in a cell. I'll lock up the front door, too. That thing's two inches of solid oak, reinforced with steel. No way anyone's getting in here without a key."

"I don't know, Deputy."

"Call me Teddy. And I've been sitting in here for a couple of hours. I wouldn't mind stretching my legs. We'll be back in five minutes."

Although she was jonesing for coffee and had a moderately severe need to pee, leaving a prisoner alone was strictly against protocol.

"You go and I'll wait with Rita," she said.

Teddy shuffled his feet. "Well . . . see . . . here's the thing."

Helen readied herself for another irritating snag.

"Frank and Mike," Teddy started. "They're real jokers."

"Really."

"We grew up together, and all. So it might be better coming from you. The request to take a look at the car."

"Do you mean," Helen said, "they won't do it because you tell them to? Even though this is police business and you're a deputy sheriff?"

Teddy scratched his beard and blushed

red. "It's just better . . . it's better if you make it official. You know, in your capacity as a federal officer. Otherwise, they'll take their sweet time. You want to get on the road sooner rather than later, right?"

Helen was at a loss for words. Apparently she was working with the mousiest deputy since Barney Fife.

"All right," she said. "I'll ask them. How do I get to the Trading Post and how will I recognize them?"

"I'll take you."

"We shouldn't leave Ms. Crawford alone."

"We won't be but a moment, Marshal. I need to show you where the Trading Post is, and besides — it ain't safe to walk around town by yourself."

"Why? Are there man-eating bears?"

"It ain't so much the bears that'll get you, Marshal, as the mountain lions. But that's not why. It's the sink holes."

"What?"

"Like I said before, the ground beneath town is riddled with old mining tunnels and there's a bunch of sink holes right on Main Street. One wrong step and you might find yourself at the bottom of a ten-, twenty-foot shaft."

"You gotta be kidding."

Teddy shrugged. "Welcome to Kill Devil Falls."

"Just when I thought things couldn't get any better," Helen said. "We'll have to make it quick. It's against procedure to leave a prisoner unattended."

"I know that," Teddy said. "Five minutes. And she'll be locked up tight. Nothing to worry about."

"Marshal," Rita whispered.

Helen put her ear to the cell door. "What?"

"Don't leave me alone."

"I won't be gone long, Rita."

"What about Big Ed?"

"Who's that?"

"The sheriff."

"What about him?"

"When's he getting back?"

"I don't know."

"Marshal. Please don't leave me in here."

"Sit tight for five minutes. You want me to bring you back some coffee?"

"Marshal!"

Exasperated, Helen turned away.

Out on the front porch, Teddy showed Helen a tarnished skeleton key.

"This locks the front door. It's a reproduction, for the sake of the museum and all, but it looks just like what they used to have in the old days." He slipped it into the keyhole, twisted it, jiggled the door. "Secure as a bank vault."

"Why do you have a key? Are you in charge of the museum?"

"Me? No." He started down the porch steps. Helen followed. "The county is. Only no tourists come up here no more, because the town's condemned. We got some volunteers from the local historical society down in Donnersville who stop by once a month to maintain the place. But that's a long drive, so they gave us a key just in case there's an emergency."

He unsnapped a loop on his gun belt, added the jail key to half a dozen others dangling there, snapped the loop closed. The keys jingle-jangled as he walked.

A two-lane paved road ran through the center of Kill Devil Falls. Its surface was cracked, pitted, and dotted with large round depressions four or five feet in circumference and twelve to eighteen inches deep. Some were roped off with portable safety barriers and orange tape. Others were not.

"Those are the sinkholes you were talking about?" Helen asked.

"Yep. We blocked off the worst ones, but I wouldn't step in the middle of those other ones neither. Just in case."

On either side of the road was a scatter of neglected and, to all appearances, abandoned houses. These dilapidated structures moldered on plots overgrown with weeds. Darkened windows regarded Helen with deep suspicion as she passed. Behind the empty houses, tall pine trees provided a dense backdrop.

"So this here's the main street," Teddy said. "The folks who founded this town didn't have no imagination, so they actually named it Main Street."

"All these places are empty?"

"Most. There's mine."

He nodded at the red farmhouse. Unlike the other homes, this one was in good repair, with a recent paint job and neatly tended yard. A Toyota sat in the driveway.

"That's my 4Runner. Unfortunately, it ain't working right now because the fuel pump is busted."

"You live here alone?"

"No. My dad and me."

"Oh? Is he retired? Or does he work in Donnersville, too?"

Teddy tugged at the beard on his chin. The jangling of his keys alternated with the crunch of his boots on the pavement.

"He works in Donnersville. With me. He's

the sheriff."

"The sheriff?"

"Big Ed Scroggins. That's my dad."

"Oh! I didn't realize."

"Guess you didn't notice his name on the paperwork?"

"To be honest, my supervisor dropped the case on my lap around noon. I was in such a hurry to get up here, I didn't have a chance to review any of it yet."

"But you know about Rita — the robberies and so forth?"

"I know about her because she's on the Most Wanted List," Helen said. "But I haven't been working the case, so beyond that, I'm no more familiar with it than your average crime junkie."

"Watch your step." Teddy guided her around a deep fissure in the pavement.

"This road is a mess," Helen said.

"Yep. And the county won't be sending any crews for repairs anytime soon."

Helen wondered why anyone would want to live in such a ghost town. Miles from anywhere, isolated, with deadly chemicals in the very soil.

"So your dad," Helen said. "The sheriff. He's on a call, where?"

"Sardine Valley."

To Helen, it seemed like the town names

up here had been chosen by a precocious child with a strictly literal grasp of nomen-clature. Sardine Valley. Fiddletown. Poker Flat. Chinese Camp. Kill Devil Falls.

"How did this place get the name Kill Devil Falls?"

"Ah . . . now that's a good little story," Teddy said. "It started with a guy by the name of Franklin Stoppard. Ex-soldier, mountain man, explorer-type. Around 1850, during the Gold Rush, he and his partner were out prospecting when they got lost in the woods. They wandered for days till they came to a spot at the bottom of a ridge where a little waterfall ran into a pool of clear water. Stoppard noticed the pool was all glowing-like. When he got closer, he saw the floor of the pool and the rock behind the waterfall was veined with gold. Natu-rally, before they could take advantage, Stoppard and his partner was attacked by Washoe Indians. Stoppard escaped and made it down to the Yuba River. The partner wasn't never seen again."

The town proper commenced another thirty yards ahead. It consisted of a dozen commercial buildings on either side of Main Street, packed tightly together. There was a mixture of brick, wood, and adobe-style architecture, with balconies fronting a few of the two-story structures.

"Stoppard managed to take a couple of gold nuggets from the pool before running away, and when he got down to the river, he showed them to some prospectors. Of course, their eyes got as big as dinner plates and they agreed to follow him up to the waterfall. That was in the late summer. It wasn't till fall that one of 'em finally came back down to the river, skinny as a reed, crazy as a loon, and with just a stump for a left arm."

"Sounds like a cheap horror flick."

Teddy nodded. "The one-armed guy said Stoppard led them up the mountain but couldn't find the waterfall. They searched for weeks. Stoppard started mumbling to himself and acting more and more nuts. The group of prospectors eventually ran out of patience and took a vote. If Stoppard didn't find the waterfall within one day, they was going to hang him from the nearest tree. Keep in mind, they was in the middle of the forest, so finding a tree wasn't a problem."

Teddy led Helen left, onto a poorly maintained sidewalk. They passed a peak-roofed, wood-paneled building with faded lettering on the front window that read *Auntie's Antiques* in Old West script. Helen took a quick peep through the filthy glass. The inside was empty, apart from yellowed scraps of newspaper on the floor, a three-legged table, and a Queen Anne cabinet with busted glass doors.

"That night, Stoppard knifed most of the men in their sleep," Teddy continued. "He kept a couple alive, including the one who made it off the mountain. He said it was 'cause they appeared to be the juiciest."

"I see where this is going."

"Yeah. He dragged these two around for a couple more days until, lo and behold, he actually stumbled onto the little clearing. Only there wasn't no waterfall there, not really. Just a rock face with a trickle of water and a muddy pool at the bottom. No gold, neither. That's when Stoppard really lost it. He tied the two prospectors to a tree and proceeded to make camp and build a fire. Then he killed the first one, roasted him up, and ate him."

Teddy was enjoying this. Helen pictured him relating the tale to a troop of Boy Scouts around a campfire, scaring the be-jesus out of the little buggers.

"After Stoppard finished with the first guy, he cut off the second one's arm and cooked that. But the one-armed prospector managed to slip his ropes when Stoppard was busy digging in the rock face and make a run for it. When he got back to Yuba, a posse was formed. They went looking for Stoppard but couldn't find the clearing again. So they gave up, went back to working the river. In time, as the gold petered out in the valley, more of them began to search around here. And that's when they started finding wild animals, coyotes and bobcats, with their faces all chewed off. And it wasn't long before a couple more prospectors went missing. The local Indians said Stoppard had turned into a devil. They said once you developed a hunger for the flesh of humans, you just couldn't fight the craving."

"Wendigo. Right? That's what the Native Americans call a cannibal."

"I don't think the Indians in these parts call it that. But same idea, yeah. Here we are."

He stopped in front of a two-story building. Facing the sidewalk, on the first floor, was a door and a rectangular window. A wooden sign dangled from a pole jutting out between two windows on the second floor. It read *The Trading Post.*

"So what happened with Stoppard?"

"The prospectors rounded up another posse. This time, they found the waterfall, and Stoppard, still chipping away at the rock face. All kinds of bones, animal and human, was sticking out of the mud at the bottom of the pool. The posse hog-tied Stoppard, stuck him in the hole he'd dug, and blocked it up with tree limbs and such. As digging for gold was their trade, they happened to have a couple sacks of black powder handy. So they packed 'em in with Stoppard and lit the fuse."

"Charming."

"Frontier justice. That was the end of Stoppard, and the end of whatever excuse for a waterfall we used to have up here. But since that time, this area's been called Kill Devil Falls."

"And where exactly was this muddy pool and sad little waterfall?"

"Not far. You go down to the end of Main Street, where the last few houses are, take a left, head down the hill a ways, cut left again, and it's at the bottom of a ridge. Funny thing, when they blew up that rock face, they actually uncovered a vein of gold. Stoppard's blood wasn't even dry before they got to digging. That was the start of this town. And the Kill Devil Falls mine. Original entrance is still down there."

Helen shuddered. She told herself it was because it was growing chillier as the sun set.

"Let's get that coffee," she said.

Rita waited, seated on the narrow cot, wrists behind her back, cold, sharp edges of the cuffs biting painfully into her skin. Weak light from the front room's lone ceiling fixture leaked through the iron slats of the cell door, casting a distorted checkerboard pattern along the floor.

She held back tears. She'd had years of practice.

Rita felt guilty about leaving Lee. And taking the money. And his precious Mustang. But since the death of her mother, she'd been alone in the world. Long ago, she'd learned there were no knights in shining armor, no Prince Charmings, no happily ever afters. She had no choice but to be selfish. Ruthless, even.

Lee was destined to die of unnatural causes at an early age. Not Rita. She could escape the cycle of addiction, poverty, desperation. All she needed was one lucky break. The kind provided by three hundred and fifty-three thousand dollars in small bills stuffed into a black waterproof Allagash duffel bag.

Turning state's evidence on Lee was supposed to be the hard part. Testifying in front of him at court, seeing the look on his face.

Knowing he wouldn't tell the cops anything about the money in order to protect her, even as she was condemning him to twenty years behind bars. She wasn't proud of herself. But there was no sense in both of them going down.

Unfortunately, Kill Devil Falls didn't believe in lucky breaks and fresh starts. It had caught her in its web and wasn't letting go. Like a fat greedy spider collecting flies just for the pleasure of watching them slowly squirm to death.

Rita had realized early on that she and Lee wouldn't last. He was too mercurial, couldn't hold a conversation that wasn't about drugs, money, booze, death metal, or slasher movies. He didn't have the mental faculties or discipline to do something with his life, apart from drift aimlessly on a haze of pot smoke from one heroin fix to another. She didn't need tea leaves or Tarot cards to foresee his inevitable end: a needle in his arm, probably in a cardboard box under a highway overpass.

But he was so sweet to her at the halfway house, and sometimes, having someone care for you, listening to them snore softly beside you at night, feeling their arm draped over you like a shield, was enough. At least for a time.

After Lee shot El Psicopata, everything moved so quickly, with barely a moment to draw a breath. One minute she was sitting on the couch scrounging enough loose change for a pack of cigarettes, and the next Lee was showing her a garbage bag filled with drugs and money, telling her to pack some clothes because they had to split, like, *right fucking now,* and pushing her into the Mustang.

She was too high on Oxy to object when he proposed, on the spur of the moment, to rob the AM/PM. It probably wouldn't have made a difference either way — Lee was a natural-born desperado, and once he started, he wasn't going to quit, no matter what promises he made. Robbery was in his blood, as much as the heroin he bought with his ill-gotten money. Even before the cops managed to ID them, Rita had resolved to ditch Lee before he got them both killed.

The night their identities were broadcast on the news, Lee proposed hopping a boat to Mexico. She pictured him wandering the San Diego docks, the duffel bag of cash on his shoulder, propositioning random boat captains to smuggle them south of the border. She figured someone would call the cops, and the best-case scenario was prison. Worst case — her brains scattered across the pier, a meal for seagulls. So, when he decided their imminent departure was cause for a blow-out, she saw an opportunity. She kept him plied with beer and weed until he zonked. Then she grabbed the money, car keys, her cigarettes, and snuck out the door.

A few hours later, she'd arrived on the outskirts of Kill Devil Falls and parked the Mustang on a trail off the access road. She'd slung the duffel over her shoulder and navigated through the forest to the edge of town.

In her absence, Kill Devil Falls had barely changed, aside from slipping ever more into entropy. There had been a dozen or so families living in town when she was a kid. Now the only house that showed any signs of upkeep was Big Ed's red farmhouse. Rita kept to the trees, picked her way toward the far end of Main Street, descended to the ridge where the mine entrance was located.

As a teen, with hundreds of acres of open forest to choose from, perhaps it was strange that she'd chosen the mine as her refuge. After all, it was claustrophobic, pitch dark, creepy, dangerous. But it was the one place where *he* wouldn't follow her. She fashioned a sanctuary from one of the rock chambers deep in the hillside and spent hours there, reading books by candlelight, smoking purloined Camels.

Like everyone in town, she heard rumors that old man Yates still worked the mine. She occasionally found evidence of his presence in the tunnels — boot prints, empty beer cans, broken tools. But she never saw him, most likely because he dug exclusively at night. And although he must have known about her private lair, there were no signs that he ever entered it, nosed around. Which made sense. The chamber was a dead end, and Yates didn't give a shit about her teenage drama. He was after gold.

Now, all these years later, Rita found her hideaway pretty much the same as she'd left it. Lots of old candles and melted wax, crude wall drawings, tattered books. She picked up one of the moldering paperbacks — *Flowers in the Attic.* She remembered it well. Child abuse, murder, rape, incest. *Jesus,* she thought. *The story of my life.* She tossed the book into a corner.

After secreting the money, she made her way out of the mine and started the long walk back to the Mustang. She chose a different path uphill, one a bit less steep. But she lost her way and wandered aimlessly for fifteen minutes. Eventually, she pushed through a tangle of underbrush and emerged into an unexpected clearing.

The clearing was rectangular, ringed by pine trees, unnatural in its symmetry, devoid of weeds and other vegetation. Rita saw dozens of tiny depressions in the earth, lined up in neat little rows.

On one side of the clearing sat a plastic shed, the DIY-type from Home Depot. The shed door was closed and padlocked. Beside the shed was a pile of detritus. Plastic tarps, broken gardening tools, brown and shriveled cuttings from some sort of plant.

Rita halted, confused. Who would plant a garden way out here?

A twig snapped. "Hold it," a man said. Rita turned.

Although she hadn't laid eyes on him for more than a decade, she recognized Mike immediately. During her desperately unhappy adolescence in Kill Devil Falls, Mike, his best buddy Frank, and Teddy were the only kids around her age. Back then, Mike and Frank were skinny, runty, gross teenage boys, into guns, video games, comic books, country music, and weed. She was often the target of their crude sexual jokes, but a fear of her stepfather kept them from ever crossing a physical line with her.

Mike was still skinny, runty, and gross. He wore a straw hat and a ridiculous pencil-thin mustache. He held a crossbow, its arrow pointed at her belly.

"Hi, Mike," she said.

"Do I know you?"

"Sure. It's Rita."

"Rita?"

"Rita Crawford, dumbshit."

"Rita . . . holy cow!"

"Can you . . . uh . . ." She waved at the crossbow. He narrowed his eyes.

"What are you doing up here, Rita?"

"I'm just passing through, Mike. Honest. I was just leaving."

"Why you nosing around the woods?"

"I wasn't. I was just trying to find my way back to my car. It's parked outside of town."

"Where you coming from, just now?"

"From . . . down the hill."

"What were you doing down the hill?"

"What's with the twenty questions?"

Mike kept the crossbow pointed at her belly. Rita held up a hand.

"Okay, listen. I'm going away for a while. A few years, probably. I just came back to . . . to see the place one last time. I've done that and I'm ready to go. So, if you don't mind, I'll just —"

"I think you'd better come with me."

"What's the problem, Mike? Why are you hiding in the bushes with a crossbow?"

"We need to go see Frank. This way."

81

He motioned with the crossbow.

It came to her. The clearing, with its symmetrical rows, the dead clippings next to the DIY shed. Way out in the middle of the woods. Mike and Frank were weed farmers. And growing this many plants, on county land to boot, was probably worth a three-to-five-year stretch.

"Ahh . . . I get it. Seriously, Mike. I'm the last person to rat out your little enterprise here to the cops. I mean . . . I'm sure you've heard I'm a wanted woman."

Mike smiled, his teeth chipped and yellow. "A wanted woman."

"How about a little honor among thieves?"

"I ain't no thief."

"No, no, it's just an expression. What I'm saying is . . . armed robbery . . . pot farm . . . You say po-tay-to . . . I say pa-tah-to . . ."

"Let's talk to Frank."

"Mike —"

"Now, goddammit!" He pointed the arrow at her face.

"Okay, Jesus. Chill."

So they trampled through the woods to the double-wide trailer where Frank and Mike lived. Frank walked out the door, totally freaked out.

"Rita fucking Crawford. Holee shit! I saw you on, like, one of those America's Most

Wanted shows. Fucking A, girl!"

"How you doing, Frank? Like I told Mike, I was just on my way out of town. I'm in kind of a hurry."

"Well, now. Maybe we should turn you in. Is there some kinda reward?"

"If you turn me in, I'll tell them about your pot farm, Frank. How'd you like that?"

Frank's grin evaporated.

"Not much."

"Then let's just go our separate ways and each keep our little secrets."

"What's it worth to you?"

"What do you mean?"

"Me letting you go?"

"I suppose it's worth about as much to me as it is to you that I don't tell anyone what you got going in the forest."

"How about a blowjob?"

"What?"

"Is it worth a blowjob? One for me, and one for Mike?"

"Go fuck yourself."

Frank laughed.

"If I had a pretty mouth like yours, I might just do that."

Rita was starting to get butterflies, worse than when she'd sat behind the wheel waiting for Lee to come out of whatever joint he was robbing. No one knew she was up here. Mike and Frank could chain her up in the cellar of one of the abandoned houses and rape her to death over a period of weeks.

"Frank . . . come on." She showed him her winningest smile. "Be cool. I'll tell you what. I have a few hundred in my pocket here. I'll give it to you. Just cut me loose."

"Maybe we should tell Teddy." Frank turned to Mike. "Think we should tell Teddy?"

Mike shrugged. "I mean, Teddy's a sheriff."

Rita was shocked. "That little shit?"

Frank nodded. "Yeah. He's the law around these parts."

"What about . . . Big Ed?"

"Oh . . . he's still the *actual* sheriff. Teddy's just a little old deputy."

She really, really didn't want them telling Teddy and Big Ed she was in Kill Devil Falls.

"Boys . . . please."

Frank motioned at Mike and they walked a short distance away, had a brief huddle, then returned.

"You sit tight," Frank said. "Mike's gonna watch you. I won't be long."

"Where are you going, Frank?"

"I'll be back."

"Goddammit, Frank!"

It was no use. Frank trotted off down Main Street. Mike escorted Rita into their double-wide, told her to sit on the couch. The place was a mess. Empty beer bottles, dirty dishes, comic books, PlayStation game cases scattered around.

"You want a beer or something?"

"No. I want to get the fuck out of here."

Mike took a seat perpendicular from Rita, used a remote to turn on the TV. The reception had issues.

"No matter what we do, just can't get no decent picture," Mike explained.

"That's a real shame," Rita said. She considered making a break for it. As if he could read her mind, Mike shifted the crossbow on his lap so that it lined up with her chest.

Time passed. A lot of time. Frank finally returned to the trailer, told Mike and Rita to wait. Mike complained that he had to piss. Frank took a turn watching Rita with the crossbow.

Rita continued trying to convince Frank to let her leave. He refused. Eventually, Rita heard a vehicle arrive. Frank and Mike took Rita outside.

When she saw the Ford Explorer, *County Sheriff* painted across its side, Big Ed and Teddy in the cab, she almost ran. Instead, her knees gave way and she thumped down onto the ground.

Frank helped her to her feet, whispering in her ear, "Go ahead and tell 'em about the pot farm. They won't do shit."

As they were driving back up Main Street on the way to Donnersville, Rita in the back, Big Ed silent, Teddy scratching and fidgeting, a call came over the radio. Shooting in Sardine Valley. Big Ed and Teddy were the closest law enforcement and a shooting was always a priority. Teddy suggested, timidly, that he watch over Rita while Big Ed drove over to Sardine Valley.

"I can hold her in the Old Log Jail. It's still got working cells."

Big Ed hemmed and hawed, but finally agreed.

"You sit with her until the marshal arrives or I get back, you hear?"

"Yes, sir."

Now, hours later, she was still in the cell. Still waiting to blow town.

Rita's heart leaped as she heard a key jiggle in the front door. She got up, went to the cell door, squinted through the iron slats.

A man stepped through the doorway. He reached over and switched off the overhead light. But not before Rita saw the hunting knife.

She knew then she wasn't leaving Kill Devil Falls. Not ever.

5

The front room of the Trading Post served as a bare-bones mini market. There were a couple of half-empty aisles with haphazardly arranged shelves displaying goods — canned food, bottled water, toiletries, household items, coffee, tea, boxes of crackers, cookie tins, and what looked like a lifetime supply of Hostess Cupcakes and Twinkies.

Along the rightmost wall was a small refrigerator unit with plastic strips dangling down. Inside were a few jugs of milk, egg cartons, packaged meat, cheap beer, and some other perishables.

Straight ahead, in the back right corner, was an open doorway. Helen smelled hot food. Pie crust. Coffee. Her stomach rumbled.

"Restaurant's there," Teddy said. "Restroom's on the other side, if you want to use it." He pointed toward a door in the back left corner.

"Yes, that would be great," Helen said. "I'll wait for you."

Helen passed through the aisles, opened the door to the restroom. The toilet seat was up, its rim splattered with urine. Gross. She wadded up toilet paper, wet it in the sink, thoroughly wiped down the seat. She used the toilet, washed her hands, re-tied her ponytail.

Much better. Now for coffee and hopefully a quick car fix and on the road.

Teddy was waiting just outside. He gave her a shy smile and led her into the restaurant.

Inside, it was a no-frills affair, with cedar-planked walls, a worn wooden floor, ancient water-spotted ceiling tiles. A row of chipped and cigarette-scarred orange melamine tables occupied the lion's share of the restaurant space. A long, narrow picture window along the top of the right wall admitted a blush of dying light. A navel-high counter ran across the back of the room, with an open kitchen area behind it.

Two men sat together at the table closest to the counter, industriously levering forkfuls of meatloaf into their mouths. One was broad-shouldered and thick-necked, wearing a sloppy handlebar mustache, a Dickies insulated jacket, and a dirty green John

Deere cap. The other was skinny, with a meticulously groomed Zorro mustache and straw cowboy hat.

An old man sat alone at a second table. He wore thick glasses and a plaid hunting hat with ear flaps. Patches of white hair dotted his face, bearing witness to a lack of shaving precision. His purple-veined nose indicated poor blood circulation and perhaps a drinking habit. A fork was pinched awkwardly in his calloused hand. He was slowly and methodically working through his plate of food, bits of which were spilling onto the table as he shakily brought the fork to his mouth.

The restaurant's final patron also sat by himself, at the table furthest from the others. He was young, in his late twenties, dressed in a San Francisco State sweatshirt and jean jacket. He had pale skin and startlingly blue eyes, with the longish light brown hair and delicate bone structure of an eighteenth-century Romantic poet. He ate silently, engrossed in a dog-eared textbook.

"Teddy," called out a woman behind the counter. She waved her arms, setting off a cacophony of clatter from various bangles on her wrist.

"Evening, Mrs. P," Teddy said. "That's

Mrs. Patterson," he whispered to Helen. "She runs the place."

Teddy headed for the counter, with Helen trailing behind.

"Who do we have here?" Mrs. Patterson asked.

Helen estimated Mrs. Patterson to be in her mid-fifties. She had a thick mop of curly red hair and sharply penciled eyebrows, and wore a generous application of eyeliner and crimson lipstick.

Helen was acutely aware that all eyes in the restaurant were on her.

"This is the US Marshal up from Sac," Teddy said. He nodded to the two men seated together as he passed their table. "Gents."

"Deputy Dawg," the big one said.

"You know I don't like that."

"I know." The man grinned at Helen. Something green was lodged in his teeth. "I'm Frank." He nodded at Zorro. "This is Mike. What's your name?"

"My name is Deputy Marshal."

Frank laughed.

"That's a real pretty name for a real pretty lady."

"This the Frank and Mike you were telling me about?" Helen asked.

"Yeah," Teddy said.

Frank's grin dropped off his face.

"What you been telling the pretty marshal about us, Teddy?"

"Her car won't start. She wants to know if maybe you and Mike can take a look."

"Is that so?" Frank said, turning to Helen.

"Yes," she answered. "Please. It's important I get back on the road as soon as possible."

"Okay." Frank resumed smiling. "We'll get that fixed up for you. Soon's we finish our dinner. Right, Mike?"

"Sure thing." Mike touched a finger to the brim of his cowboy hat.

"Not to be a pain, but I'm in a bit of a hurry," Helen said.

"Just give us a few minutes, all right?" Frank said, peevishly.

Helen didn't want to start off on the wrong foot. She needed Frank and Mike's cooperation. "Sure."

"Can I get you all some coffee or something?" Mrs. Patterson said.

"Coffee would be great, Mrs. P," Teddy said.

"How about you, dear?"

"Yes, please." Frank and Mike looked to be halfway through their meal. Helen hoped they were fast eaters.

"I'm Alice Patterson, by the way."

"Helen Morrissey."

"A pleasure."

Mrs. Patterson was wearing a brightly colored, body-clinging dress that extended down past her knees. As she bustled around behind the counter, Helen noted her nicely proportioned hourglass figure — apart from her breasts, which appeared two cup sizes too large for her frame. And they were hard to miss, given the dress's plunging neckline.

When Mrs. Patterson leaned over to pour coffee into two mugs, the rounded globes of her bosom threatened to burst forth like the brown waters of the Mississippi breaching a New Orleans levee. Helen concluded they were fake.

In addition to the colorful dress, Mrs. Patterson wore an eclectic jumble of jewelry. A triple loop of necklaces, multiple bracelets, long dangling earrings, rings on eight fingers. Her taste ran toward the talismanic. Helen spotted a crucifix, an ankh, a variety of gemstones, a Star of David, and a variety of other symbols she didn't recognize.

"Sugar or cream?" Mrs. Patterson asked.

"Neither, thanks," Helen said.

"Both," said Teddy.

"I know how you like your coffee, Teddy," Mrs. Patterson admonished. She poured a slug of cream and spooned sugar into his cup. She set the two mugs on the counter.

Helen sipped. "Mmm. Good."

"Of course, dear. Life is unpredictable and capricious. But in those areas where we have control, we should pursue perfection. Like our coffee." She winked.

Helen smiled. "Are you from here, Mrs. Patterson?"

"Oh, good lord, no." Mrs. Patterson's earrings tinkled like tiny wind chimes as she shook her head. "I'm from southern California, originally. But that was many miles traveled and lifetimes lived ago." She rolled her eyes dramatically.

"What brought you to Kill Devil Falls?"

"I suppose it was the beautiful scenery. And fresh, crisp mountain air. A welcome change from the Valley."

"San Joaquin Valley?"

"San Fernando."

"Ah."

"I used to be in the pictures. That's where I met my husband, Jesse. He was a director."

Teddy took his cup of coffee and walked off toward the tables. Mrs. Patterson prattled on.

"It was fun and glamorous, in the beginning. Bright lights. Parties. Handsome men. Lots of cocaine. Oops!" Mrs. Patterson slapped a hand over her mouth. "Please don't arrest me!"

Helen laughed. She wondered what kind of "pictures" Mrs. Patterson was referring to. San Fernando was synonymous with the porn industry, and Mrs. Patterson certainly had the physical attributes of a retired XXX starlet.

"Anyway, the good times eventually came to an end, as they are wont to do." Mrs. Patterson picked up the coffee pot and topped off Helen's cup. "The industry changed, times got tougher, profits became deficits. The air got smoggier, people meaner, and eventually Jesse and I decided to get far, far away from it all."

She placed the pot back in its cradle.

"And you can't get much farther away from it all than this."

"No, that's for sure," Helen said.

"We've been here fifteen years now, if you can believe it. We arrived just before the county condemned the land."

"The deputy told me about that. So you were one of the residents who sued the county?"

"Honey, it was Jesse and me who *started* the whole lawsuit. And won it, on behalf of all these folks." She leaned in and whispered, "I mean, take a look. You think any of these country bumpkins had a clue about how to fight city hall? Most of them can barely read a bubble gum comic strip." She tittered.

Helen nodded, turned to have a quick glance around the room. Mike was licking remnants of meatloaf off his fork. Frank poked at his teeth with a toothpick. Teddy sat silently next to the old man, staring off into space. The old man dozed, his chin propped on his hand. Young Byron in the far corner, engrossed in his textbook, seemed the only relatively urbane person in the restaurant.

"You gentlemen about ready?" she said to Frank and Mike.

"We're finishing our drinks." Frank held up a beer bottle.

Helen held her temper in check. She turned back to Mrs. Patterson, sipped from her coffee mug.

"Where's your husband now?" she asked.

"Upstairs having his late-afternoon constitutional."

"Constitutional?"

"He's napping. Jesse's getting a bit up there in years. He likes to take a nice siesta before dinner. He should be down in a minute or two."

"A nap sounds pretty good."

"In lieu of a nap, how about some meat-loaf? I make the best in town."

"I'm sure you do. But I need to get back to the jail."

The young man in the jean jacket appeared at her elbow, empty plate in hand.

"Thanks, Mrs. Patterson."

"Sure thing, Lawrence."

Lawrence placed the plate on the counter, stole a glance at Helen, quickly looked away. The textbook under his arm was titled *The Complete Guide to Small Game Taxidermy.*

"Do you have cherry pie tonight?" Lawrence asked.

"Sure, Lawrence. I've got it all ready for you." Mrs. Patterson set a foil-wrapped paper plate on the counter.

"Thanks."

He laid a ten on the counter, smiled awkwardly at Mrs. Patterson, nodded shyly at Helen, hurried away.

"What's his story?" Helen asked, after Lawrence had disappeared through the door leading to the market.

Mrs. Patterson shrugged.

"He's only been up here a few weeks. His grandma owns a house at the end of the road. She finally up and left a year or so ago, shut up the house, probably didn't bother to inform the county. Suddenly,

Lawrence appears out of the blue. He says he's from the Bay Area, is an artist, up here to work without any distractions. Real quiet, keeps to himself, eats dinner here every night, otherwise doesn't talk much or socialize. Takes his dessert to go." She leaned in closer to Helen and whispered, "I'd swear every time he comes in, he reeks of booze, though."

"Did you see what he was reading? A taxidermy book."

"Well, I guess it takes all kinds."

Mike approached the counter with his and Frank's dishes.

"That was real good, Mrs. P. How about some of that famous pie for dessert?"

"You bet, Mike."

Helen watched incredulously as Mrs. Patterson cut two generous slices of pie, laid them on plates, pushed them across the counter. Mike set one of the plates in front of Frank.

"How about you guys have dessert after looking at my car?" she asked.

Frank shoved a forkful of pie into his mouth, sprayed pie crust as he answered.

"Two minutes. Give us two minutes."

"You boys make it quick now!" Mrs. Patterson said. "The marshal's our guest, and she's got a job to do."

"All right, all right." Frank waved his fork in sullen agreement.

"You sure you don't want a slice, dear?"

"I'm sure, thanks."

Helen looked over at Teddy. The old guy at Teddy's table was awake and making a mess of a homemade cigarette. As she watched, Teddy reached out, took the paper and tobacco, carefully rolled a cigarette, handed it back for the old man to lick.

Mrs. Patterson followed her gaze. "That's Mr. Yates. Third of his line to live in Kill Devil Falls. His grandfather came over around the turn of the century. From Wales, to work the mine."

Yates's desiccated tongue poked between his chapped lips like a turtle's head, ran along the edge of the cigarette paper.

"The industry was pretty much done by the 1920s, certainly around here," Mrs. Patterson continued. "Mining was in the Yates' blood, though. After Yates's grandfather retired, his father kept chipping away at the mountain, even when the operation was officially closed. And it's an open secret that until a few years ago, Yates was still regularly digging at night. Always looking for that vein of gold — the motherlode, the one that went undiscovered. He and his father are probably single-handedly responsible for half the holes running beneath town. Yates's father was even caught with a load of dynamite once."

"Lucky he didn't blow himself up."

"Yes, but let me tell you, if the entire mountainside caves in one day, it'll be the Yates's fault. All three generations of them."

"What about those two?" Helen whispered, nodding at Frank and Mike.

"Quite a pair, aren't they? You know, there's about twenty-five empty houses on this street, most of them don't have electricity or water, but still, plenty of space available. And those two squeeze themselves into a double-wide trailer like a couple of hamsters in a cage."

"Are they . . . ?"

Mrs. Patterson giggled.

"Lovers? No. I've never seen one of them with a girlfriend, but that's just because they have no social skills, not because they're gay."

"What do they do? I mean, for a living?"

"Mainly odd jobs around town. Electrical work, mechanical work. Kind of the local handymen. I don't think they have a lot of expenses beyond video games and a little . . ." She pantomimed smoking a joint.

"I see."

Helen knew she couldn't leave Rita alone

in the jail for any longer. She set her mug on the counter.

"How much for the coffee?"

"On the house, dear."

"I couldn't."

"I insist."

"Well . . . thanks."

"Don't mention it."

Helen walked over to Teddy.

"Deputy," she said. "I'm going to head back to the jailhouse and wait for you there."

"I'll go with you," Teddy said. He stood up, fingered the skeleton key dangling from his belt. "Can't get in without this, anyway."

Helen nodded and headed for the market, Teddy at her heels. Frank and Mike would be along in their own good time, no sense in breathing down their necks, getting herself worked up.

She halted when she heard a muted rattle, crash, and thump coming from behind the counter. She turned, exchanged a confused look with Teddy. There was a closed door, one Helen hadn't previously noticed, in the back corner of the restaurant.

Mrs. Patterson hurriedly tossed a dish-towel on the counter, reached for the door-knob.

Frank's chair scraped on the floor as he rose for a better look. Yates coughed out a

lungful of blue smoke. Mrs. Patterson
opened the door.

And let out a piercing shriek.

6

Frank and Mike helped carry Jesse Patterson into the restaurant. The man was limping badly and wincing in pain. They lowered him into a chair. Helen saw that his cheek bore a long, angry welt, and a trickle of blood ran from his hairline.

"I'll get the first aid kit," Teddy said.

"What happened?" Mrs. Patterson wailed.

"I fell down the goddamn stairs, that's what! Where's my cane?"

"Are you okay?"

"No, I'm not okay! I just told you I fell down the goddamn stairs!"

Jesse looked to be around seventy. Once handsome, and still with a thick head of curly white-gray hair, a neatly tended salt-and-pepper beard, a silver hoop in his left ear.

"Goddess! You're bleeding!" Mrs. Patterson wrapped her arms around his head and pulled him into her breasts.

"All right, stop fussing," he said, pushing her away. "No sense in ruining your dress." He seemed to notice Helen for the first time. "Hi there. If *you* want to fuss over me, I won't object."

Helen smiled. "Is your vision blurry? Any nausea?"

"No, but I must be hallucinating. I'm seeing angels."

Mrs. Patterson punched the old man's shoulder. "Ass."

Teddy brought over a first aid kit.

"Okay, let's have a look." Teddy opened the kit, pulled on a pair of latex gloves, began dabbing at Jesse's scalp with a gauze pad.

Yates tottered over.

"Took a tumble, did ya?" he said.

"Your powers of observation are, as always, nothing short of astounding, Mr. Yates," Jesse said.

Mike slipped through the back door, reappeared with a cane.

"Don't think you need stitches," Teddy said. "Just some gauze and a butterfly bandage."

"I prefer butterfly kisses," Jesse said, and winked at Helen.

If he had been twenty years younger, she would have found his flirtation disgusting, but he was at that age where it seemed harmless, if not charming.

"I got your cane, Mr. P," Mike said.

"Michael, you're a prince."

"I'll take that," Mrs. Patterson said. She lay the cane on the table. It was black and glossy, with a brass tip and wooden derby handle.

"Your legs and arms okay?" Teddy asked. "Nothing busted?"

Jesse lifted his feet, rotated his elbows.

"Perhaps just my cultivated air of nonchalance."

"You really should get those stairs fixed," Teddy said.

"Why? I've only fallen down them three times in the past decade. The odds are quite good, all things considered."

"He's got a bum knee," Mrs. Patterson said to Helen, by way of explanation.

"Do not call my knee a bum," Jesse said. "It's more of a trickster. Or a rapscallion, if you will."

"I'll fix up those stairs for you, Mr. P," Frank volunteered. "For one month's free dinners."

"Help, police, I'm being robbed," Jesse said. "One week."

"Deal," Frank said.

Jesse turned to Helen.

"So I take it you are the detective dispatched to toss Rita Crawford under the wheels of justice?"

Helen caught a whiff of a tart odor, thought at first it was something Teddy was using to clean Jesse's wounds, then realized it was booze. Whiskey, perhaps. Coming off the old man in waves. Perhaps it wasn't the stairs that were at fault after all.

"I suppose that's one way to put it. I'm not a detective, I'm a Deputy Marshal. And yes, that's why I'm here."

"May I ask what will happen to her?"

"That's for a jury to decide. Unless she cuts a deal and pleads guilty. Either way, I imagine she'll spend some time in prison."

"What about her partner, what's-is-name?" Mrs. Patterson said. "Any information on his whereabouts?"

Helen had no idea. Before noon today, she'd been running down unregistered sex offenders, not working the Most Wanted list. But when interacting with civilians, her policy was to give the impression that the US Marshals were always on top of everything.

"Larimer?" Helen said. "We have leads. Won't be long before he's in custody."

Mrs. Patterson nodded. "Good."

Teddy applied a bandage to Jesse's scalp

wound. He soaked a pad in rubbing alcohol, dabbed at an ugly round purplish mark on Jesse's neck.

"Ouch!" Jesse complained.

"Sorry," Teddy said.

Helen noticed that Teddy worked quickly and efficiently.

"It's strange, though, for Rita to show up in Kill Devil Falls," she said. "I mean, why such an out of the way, isolated place?"

Teddy's hand froze. "Guess you really didn't get a chance to look at that paperwork," he said.

"What do you mean?"

"Rita's from here," Mrs. Patterson said. "This is her hometown."

"Oh." Now Helen felt stupid.

"Her dad run off when she was a young kid," Teddy said. "Her mom and my dad got married a few years later.

"So he's . . . you're her . . .".

"Yeah," Teddy said. "Big Ed's her stepfather. And that makes me her stepbrother."

Teddy and Helen trudged down the center of Main Street toward the Old Log Jail. Mike and Frank had promised to head back to their trailer to collect tools, after which they would be along to look at the Charger.

"I woulda mentioned it," Teddy said.

"But, I don't know . . . it's kinda weird."

Helen nodded. It was weird. But ultimately, Teddy's family situation was immaterial. She was here to do a job, not get involved in people's private lives. *Still* . . .

"I suppose it must have been hard arresting your own sister," Helen said. "Stepsister."

Teddy shrugged. "Not hard, exactly."

"No?"

"She ran away when she was sixteen. To be honest, we wasn't sure if she was alive or dead until we heard about her on the news. That was a shock, let me tell you. Well no . . . not a shock. I mean, to hear she was alive was a shock. But to find out she was into armed robbery and all that . . . coulda seen it coming."

"She was a troubled kid?"

"My dad was real hard on her. He used to . . ." He fell silent.

"Used to what?"

"When we was growing up . . . sometimes, you know, he'd smack us around a bit. More Rita than me, 'cause she was always so damn mouthy. Didn't know when to quit. I got pretty good with the peroxide and bandages, let's put it that way."

Helen's blood simmered. It was an old story. A heavy-handed, abusive father. A damaged child. Rita may have broken the law, but the sheriff was equally culpable for her crimes.

Dusk now blanketed the town. A line of street lamps dotted Main Street, the last of them standing guard beside the jail, its crooked neck casting a yellow ring of light on the edge of the access road. Beyond it, the only illumination came from a rising moon and brightening stars.

Helen observed that the window of the jail was pitch black.

"Did you turn off the lights when we left?"

"Don't think so," Teddy said. "Maybe the electricity went out?"

"The street lamp is on."

"Could be the bulb in the jail popped, or a fuse blew."

"Rita must be freaking out, locked up in the dark."

"She may as well get used to it," Teddy said. "They ain't going to leave a night-light on where she's going."

As they got closer, Helen saw the front door was open.

"See that . . . the door?" she said.

"Maybe my dad's back already," Teddy said. "I don't see the Explorer, though."

The only vehicle parked in front of the jail was Helen's sickly Charger. Her heart flipped. Leaving Rita alone was against procedure. More than that, it was just plain irresponsible.

She broke into a run. After a moment's hesitation, Teddy followed, his boots clomping loudly on the pavement behind her.

Helen took the porch steps two at a time, calling out: "Rita? Hello?"

No answer. The door yawned on its hinges, its open mouth black as an empty well.

Helen reached an arm inside, patted the wall, searching for a light switch. Teddy plodded up the stairs of the porch, breathing heavily.

"Where's the switch, Teddy?"

"Let me get it."

He squeezed past her. After a few seconds, the overhead light flickered to life.

Helen stepped into the room, saw that Rita's cell door was open. And the cell was empty.

"Christ on a cracker," she muttered. "Where is she?"

Teddy poked his head into both cells. "Let me check in back."

He hurried around the corner, into the guard room. His voice echoed hollowly as he called back to her.

"She ain't in here, either."

Helen glanced at the hook on the wall

where she'd seen Teddy hang the cell door key. The hook was bare. She swung the door to Rita's cell shut. The key dangled from the lock.

"You put the key back on the wall when we left, right?" she yelled.

Teddy emerged from the hallway. "Yeah." He looked up at the empty hook, down at the key in the door. "I think I did."

"You still have the one for the front door?"

He jangled the keys on his belt. "Right here."

Helen stepped out onto the porch.

If anyone was moving out there, across the road or beyond the reach of the street lamp, Helen couldn't see them in the gloom.

Stupid, stupid, stupid . . . leaving Rita alone like that. Helen looked up at the sky. Saw-toothed pine trees ringed the rapidly darkening horizon like a snaggle of teeth. Her breath steamed in the frosty air. She corralled her rising panic.

"We'd better start searching. Maybe she's heading for her car," she said.

"I'll run down the road a ways."

"You have a flashlight?"

"Yeah." He pulled a compact black tactical flashlight out of a loop on his gun belt.

"Hold on, let me check something," Helen said. She trotted over to the Charger, opened the passenger door, checked inside the plastic bag. "Her car keys are still here."

"Huh," was Teddy's comment. "Maybe she just run off in a tizzy."

"But how could she have gotten out of the cell while handcuffed?"

"I really don't know, Marshal."

"What if she had help?"

"What help?"

"Maybe . . . Lee Larimer," Helen said. "Or somebody else we don't know about." *Like a guy in camo, driving a brown Honda.* "And maybe whoever broke her out has another car stashed somewhere."

"So what should we do?"

If Rita had escaped, Helen was finished in the marshal's service. She could imagine the look on her father's face when she gave him *that* news. Worse would be the jibes from Chowder and her fellow deputies. But if she got Rita back into custody, she might just be able to save her job. And her reputation. The problem was, if Rita had an accomplice, and he was armed, there was a decent possibility someone was going to get shot or maybe even killed.

Helen looked at Teddy. He seemed in no way prepared for a gun fight. But she didn't have a lot of options.

"Can you run down the access road, like

you said?" she asked. "Just be careful. If she has an accomplice, assume he's got a weapon. If they have a car, try to stop them from getting away. Shoot out the tires or put a few rounds in the engine. But don't engage them directly."

"What are you going to do?"

"Look around here. We weren't gone *that* long. Rita couldn't have gotten far."

"Okay. Holler if you find her, Marshal."

"You, too."

Teddy loped off down the road. His keys jingled so loudly, she figured if Rita and Lee Larimer or whoever had sprung her from the jail were out there, they'd hear him coming long before he ever saw them. He was like a baby rabbit sent to take down a Rottweiler. She felt guilty. But she *had* to get Rita back. *Had* to.

Helen leaned back into the Charger and removed a pocket-sized flashlight from the glove compartment. She flicked it on and then made a quick circuit of the jail. She inspected the structure's foundation and saw a series of rectangular air vents, but no cellar door or possible hiding places. She crisscrossed the grassy lot behind the jail, searching for foot prints, found nothing.

She climbed into the tree line, pushed aside a tangle of underbrush, plunged into the forest. She breathed in the scent of fresh pine. The ground was pleasantly spongy, yet treacherously rutted and tangled with roots and undergrowth.

"Rita? This is Deputy Marshal Morrissey. Come out with your hands in the air."

An insect buzzed, attempted to burrow in her ear. She waved it away.

"And if Larimer is with you, he'd better come out, too. I'm armed and backup is on the way."

Helen swept her flashlight back and forth as she moved forward.

"You can forget about that cheeseburger! And cigarettes!" she yelled.

Long fingers tugged her hair. Helen whirled, raised the flashlight.

A skeletal branch, extending sidewise from a pine tree, vibrated softly. Helen touched her hair, picked out a scatter of pine needles. Black patches of sap oozed from the tree's bark, like blood from old gunshot wounds.

"*Suck* it," she muttered.

She turned away, continued deeper into the forest, struggling to remain calm. Losing a fugitive in her custody . . . she'd never work in law enforcement again. All the time invested, the hard work, the bullshit she'd waded through. Up in flames.

"Ritaaa!"

114

This was ridiculous. If Rita was hiding in the forest, Helen was unlikely to find her without the help of twenty more officers and a police dog. And involving a bunch of cops was the last thing she wanted. Her best bet was to find Rita herself. Keep things contained. Fix the problem before anyone else found out about it.

She halted, leaned against a tree, squeezed the flashlight under her armpit, rubbed her chilled hands together.

Initially, the forest seemed deathly quiet. But as Helen stood motionless, a multiplicity of sounds crept into her awareness. Insects chirping, whirring, clicking. A light wind rustling above. The occasional patter of pine needles dropping to the ground. Distant cracking and scratching noises.

A wet, hacking cough.

Helen yanked the flashlight out from under her arm.

"Rita?" She cocked an ear. "If that's you, Rita, get your ass out here right now."

No answer. Helen drew her Glock, held the flashlight above and to the left of her head. She took a step forward, squeezed past a shrub, tripped on a hidden root, almost sprawled onto her face.

The cough, again, to the left. Helen descended into a narrow gully. Her foot bumped against something solid, but yielding.

The thing at her feet, whatever it was, wiggled.

Helen retreated, pointed her light downward. Within the circle of illumination lay a zombie. That's what it looked like, anyway. Black with blood splatter, white eyes, mouth open, gasping like a dry-docked fish.

Helen's lungs quit drawing air. Fear slammed down on her like an icy wave. She fumbled with the Glock. But then she recognized the leather jacket. The ripped-kneed jeans. The dark, hollow eyes.

Rita.

She sank to her knees. "Rita! What happened?"

Rita coughed, a liquid rattle in her throat.

"Let me see," Helen said.

There was a deep cut across Rita's neck, from carotid to windpipe. Blood pumped sluggishly, keeping time with her slackening pulse.

It looked bad. Really bad.

"Help!" Helen yelled. "Help!"

She holstered the Glock, searched her coat pockets, came up with a wad of tissue, pressed this to Rita's neck.

"I need some help here!" Helen screamed.

Rita's lips moved. A bubble of blood

leaked from her mouth, a trickle ran from her nose.

"I can't hear you." Helen leaned close.

Rita coughed blood into Helen's face.

Something large and moving fast crashed through the forest, breaking twigs, snapping branches. Helen turned, shined her flashlight in the direction of the noise.

A figure dropped into the gully. A man. Helen couldn't see his features, just that he was big. And carrying a shotgun.

"Show me your hands!" the man barked.

7

Rita died in Big Ed's arms as he carried her out of the forest. She panted, her sides heaved, she twitched, and then she was gone.

Some folks believe the soul had a calculable weight. Twenty-one grams. Which means a dead person should be a titch lighter than a living one. Big Ed's experience was quite the opposite. Dead bodies, by virtue of their utter slackness, were heavier than a barrel of wet cement. He felt it when Rita passed, an extra ten pounds suddenly added to his load.

Frank and Mike appeared, tool boxes in hand, just as Big Ed and Helen emerged from the trees. Teddy was already waiting beside the Explorer, now parked next to the Charger in front of the jail.

"Take this," Big Ed said to Teddy, indicating the shotgun held awkwardly in his right hand.

"Is that Rita?" Frank asked. "Goddamn! Is she dead?" His voice cracked. At first, Helen thought he was scared. But then she decided he was keyed up.

"You boys go on home and stay there," Big Ed wheezed.

"We're supposed to fix the marshal's car," Frank said. He couldn't take his eyes off Rita.

"Just do as I say," Big Ed growled.

Rita's head dangled off one meaty forearm, her legs the other. Helen almost admonished him to lift Rita's head in order to keep the throat wound closed, but looking at Rita's sightless eyes, her head lolling like a flower with a broken stalk, she knew it didn't matter.

When they reached the red farmhouse, Teddy held the door open for Big Ed as he carried Rita inside. Helen squeezed through behind him, found herself in a hallway, a closet to the left, a staircase straight ahead, a waist-high cabinet on the right, and an arched doorway leading to the living room just beyond it. She followed Big Ed into the living room, Teddy bringing up the rear.

The house smelled like musty curtains, damp furniture, cigarette smoke, old fireplace ashes. But it was clean and orderly, and the threadbare but tasteful furniture, needlepoint wall hangings, and lace chair covers indicated a woman's touch.

A generously stuffed couch sat in the center of the room, facing a pair of matching upholstered chairs.

"Get a blanket from the hall closet," Big Ed ordered.

Teddy disappeared into the hallway. She heard a closet door opening.

"Hurry it up," Big Ed said. "She ain't as light as she looks."

Teddy came back with a blue quilt.

"Not that one. Her blood's gonna get all over it. Something old, that we don't need no more."

Teddy returned to the hallway.

Big Ed huffed. "Let's go, Edward!"

"Sorry!" Teddy brought out a tattered Indian blanket, laid it out on the couch. Big Ed grunted as he laid Rita on top of it. He looked down at his uniform jacket, brushed drying blood from the star on his left breast.

"This ain't coming out in the wash."

He unzipped the jacket, pulled it off, turned it inside out and draped it over the arm of the couch. He wiped his hands on the Indian blanket, walked over, and sank heavily into one of the upholstered chairs.

"Shouldn't we get her to a hospital?" Helen asked.

"She's dead. Only man I ever heard of who can fix *that* is Jesus. And he don't spend much time in these parts. Edward, you want to tell me what happened?"

Teddy leaned the shotgun against the wall, stuffed his hands into his coat pockets, eyes on the floor.

"The deputy marshal here, her car wouldn't start, so we went to the Trading Post to get Frank and Mike. When we got back to the jail, the door was open and Rita was gone."

"I leave you alone for two goddamn hours —"

"Whoever killed Rita is still in those woods, Sheriff," Helen said.

Big Ed's muddy brown eyes swiveled over to Helen.

"I'll get to you in a minute."

"The killer might be getting away right now."

"I'm not a US Marshal or anything, but I know a *little* something about policing. So, do you mind if I get the facts straight before I break out the bloodhounds?"

Helen returned his glare but didn't answer. She wondered if he actually had bloodhounds.

"Edward," Big Ed said. "I thought I told

you to stay with Rita till the marshal arrived."

"She did arrive! And her car wouldn't start!"

"At which point you decided a slice of Alice's famous cherry pie would just about hit the spot."

"No, sir! I took the marshal over to ask if Frank and Mike would have a look at the vehicle. We wasn't there long. Maybe, I don't know, five minutes?"

Helen figured it was more like fifteen or twenty, but she didn't contradict Teddy. She was developing a strong dislike for the sheriff.

"And you locked the jail door?" Big Ed asked.

"Yes, sir. Rita was in the cell, all secure, and the key was on the wall. And I locked the front door, too. Here's the key."

He showed Big Ed the key dangling from his gun belt.

"Who cuffed her?" Big Ed nodded at Rita's body.

"I cuffed her and put her in my car, which, as the deputy mentioned, wouldn't start," Helen said. "When I tried to return her back to the cell, she ran for it. So I left the cuffs on. We only intended to be at the Trading Post long enough to grab Mike and

Frank. But when we got there, they were finishing dinner. So it took a bit longer than expected."

Big Ed shifted in the chair, adjusted his gun holster, settled into a more comfortable position.

"The extra key in the drawer, Edward?"

"Let me check."

Teddy returned to the hallway. Helen heard the sound of a drawer being opened, items shifting.

"It's gone!"

"You're sure?"

"Yes, sir!"

"For God's sake!" Big Ed muttered. He rubbed his eyes with a thumb and forefinger.

"Let me get this straight," Helen said. "You keep an extra key to the jail in your house?"

"That's right," Teddy said, coming back into the living room. "Just in case."

"In case of what?"

"In case the historical society loses *their* key."

"I see. And who has access to the extra key? The one not on your belt?"

"Me. The sheriff." Teddy nodded at Big Ed. "I think pretty much everyone in town knows we have one, even if they don't know it's in that particular drawer."

Helen suddenly felt bone tired. She walked to the second upholstered chair, lowered herself into it.

"Take care you don't get that chair dirty," Big Ed said.

"Your stepdaughter's dead, there's a killer on the loose, and you're worried about your upholstery?"

Big Ed took a pack of Camels from his breast pocket, lit one with a cheap plastic lighter.

"My late wife bought these chairs. They were her pride and joy. Edward, pour me a whiskey. You want one, Marshal?"

A drink. God, yes, she needed a drink.

"Please. Thanks."

Teddy avoided looking at Rita's body as he squeezed past the couch. Toward the back of the living room was a dining area with an oval mahogany table and six chairs, and beyond that, a door leading to the kitchen. A heavy oak credenza sat against the far wall. A tarnished silver service tray holding half a dozen bottles and a set of drinking glasses was on top of the credenza. Teddy unscrewed the cap on a bottle and poured amber liquid into two tumblers. He carried them over, handed one to Big Ed and another to Helen.

"Thanks," she said. Teddy nodded. He resumed his place in the living room doorway. His eyes flickered toward the couch, away again. Helen sipped from the tumbler. After the initial burn, a pleasant warmth spread through her chest and stomach.

"Who was at the Trading Post when you were there?" Big Ed drank from his tumbler, rested it on his knee, took a drag from his cigarette. Apart from the uniform, gun, and lack of social graces, he resembled a country aristocrat discussing the price of agricultural commodities over brandy cocktails.

"Let's see. Mrs. P, me, the marshal, Frank, Mike . . . uh . . . Mr. Yates . . . Mr. P . . . and Lawrence."

"In other words, everyone."

"Lawrence left before the rest of us."

"How long before the rest of you?"

"I don't know. Maybe five minutes."

"I thought you were only in the place for five minutes."

"Coulda been a bit longer than that."

"Wait a minute," Helen said. "Are you suggesting this guy Lawrence stole the key from your house and dragged Rita out into the woods to kill her?"

"He's the only newcomer to town," Big Ed said. "The Pattersons have lived in Kill Devil Falls for fifteen years. The others were born and raised here. It doesn't make sense for any of them to up and murder her."

"Lawrence has only been in town a few weeks, from what I understand," Helen said. "Does he even know who Rita is? And how would he know about the jailhouse key?"

Big Ed sucked on his cigarette, stubbed it out in an ashtray sitting on a round table between the two chairs. "Maybe he heard about the key from one of the others."

"But why, Sheriff? What would be his motive?"

"I don't know. I think I'll ask him."

"Have you considered the most obvious explanation?"

"Which is?" He swallowed the rest of the whiskey in his tumbler.

"Rita's partner killed her. Larimer. And while we're sitting here, he's making his escape."

"Why would he do that? Weren't they two peas in a pod? Robbing banks, sticking it to the man? Bonnie and Clyde, all that crap."

"Well, she got caught, didn't she? Maybe he killed her for expediency's sake."

"Seems a bit extreme, don't it?"

"It makes more sense than a random stranger who's never met Rita killing her."

"We're gonna take this step by step, Marshal, and do it my way. In fact, since your prisoner is now dead, you're pretty much free to go home at any time."

Helen couldn't believe her ears. What an asshole.

"Well, Sheriff, for one thing, my car isn't working."

"Right. We'll see to that in a bit. First, Edward, go raise dispatch on the car radio and get some more bodies up here. And an ambulance for Rita. Then we'll head over to grab Lawrence for a chat."

"Yes, sir."

Teddy left, leaving the shotgun propped against the wall. Helen heard his heavy boots clumping down the hallway, the sound of the front door opening and closing.

Well, that's it, she thought. *I'm toast.*

Rita had been murdered on her watch. Now that the sheriff was involved, there was no way to spin the story, no chance of damage control. She was going to be thrown out of the marshal's service.

Helen could picture Chowder's wet smirk. His unspoken taunt: *Maybe if you'd been nicer to me, I could have helped you out . . .*

No. Even Chowder couldn't do anything for her in a situation like this.

Big Ed sighed. He pushed himself up from the chair, walked toward the dining area.

"You want another whiskey?"

"No."

"Suit yourself." He took the bottle from the silver service tray, came back to his chair, sat down. He seemed unaffected by the presence of a dead body on his couch.

"You don't seem too upset about Rita," Helen said.

He paused mid-pour, squinted at her.

"What am I supposed to do? Have a good bawl?"

"She was your daughter."

"Stepdaughter." He set the bottle down, sipped from his tumbler. "And she left home a long time ago. She was always a handful, even at sixteen." He nodded at the couch. "I can't say I'm surprised at how it ended for her."

"That seems . . . pretty cold."

"It may surprise you, Marshal, but your opinion don't mean squat to me. And by the way, that was quite a show you put on in the woods, screaming your head off."

"I was trying to get help. I thought we might be able to save her."

"Maybe. Maybe you were just scared shitless."

"Hey, here's a thought. Why don't you go fuck yourself?"

He cracked a crooked smile.

"Okay. Fair enough."

He polished off the whiskey, set down the tumbler. He stared at Rita's body for a moment, then got up and went over to the couch. He tugged a corner of the Indian blanket free and laid it over her face. He turned to look at Helen.

"I meant what I said about you heading back to Sacramento. Once your car is running, there's no need for you to stick around."

Rita's knees showed through the holes in her jeans. They were black with forest grime. She had begged Helen not to leave her alone in the cell. As if she knew her life was at risk. But Helen had to be a hard-ass, punish Rita for running. She'd abandoned Rita in jail, wrists cuffed. Like a trussed Thanksgiving turkey.

Well, if she couldn't save Rita, or her own career, there was one thing Helen could do. Help catch the goddamn killer.

"Sheriff . . . if you don't object, I'd like to assist with the investigation."

"How?"

"Just . . . be an extra pair of hands."

"Why?"

"Because . . . I feel responsible."

Big Ed nodded. "You shouldn't have left her alone in the jail, that's for sure."

"I'm well aware."

"Anyways, Edward will get some other deputies up here in the next hour or so. You'd probably just be in the way. Better you head home."

"Respectfully, Sheriff, I'd like to stick around."

"No."

"No?"

"My town. My jurisdiction. My investigation."

"You're right. It's your jurisdiction. I'm not looking to interfere. Or step on any toes. But Rita was my charge. And now she's dead. I want to help apprehend her murderer."

"That's real nice, Marshal, real commendable. But like I said —"

Helen stood up.

"You actually don't have the authority to kick me out of Kill Devil Falls. I may not be officially part of your investigation, but I'll remain here till I'm good and ready to go. You can bitch and moan about it. You can ignore and exclude me. Or you can make use of the fact that you have a federal law enforcement agent right here on your doorstep. Who knows? I might even prove useful."

Big Ed puffed out his cheeks and looked

up at the ceiling.

"And let's not forget, Sheriff. Rita was your stepdaughter. It's going to look a bit odd to the FBI and marshal's service, don't you think? I mean, she was locked up in an old museum, for God's sake. Where you left her, guarded only by her stepbrother. The whole thing is just . . . very peculiar."

"What are you saying, Marshal?"

"I'm saying, you could probably use an objective witness such as myself to dispel any rumors of improprieties before they get started."

The sheriff glared for a moment, then cracked another one of his crooked smiles.

"You're a sharp one, now, ain't you?" he said.

"Is that a bad thing?"

"Just remember who's the boss."

"I will."

"I call the shots."

"Got it."

"You'll follow my orders."

Helen mentally crossed her fingers behind her back.

"Yes."

Big Ed looked down at his dirty pants.

"I'm going to go upstairs and wash up. You might want to get some of that blood off your face. There's a bathroom down the hall, back of the stairs."

"Thanks."

Helen trailed Big Ed into the hallway. He pointed to a door, then trudged up to the second floor.

Helen walked down the hall, opened the bathroom door, flicked on the light. The claw-footed tub, squat toilet, and cracked porcelain sink were all vintage, circa 1940s. A radiator hissed testily in the corner.

Helen removed her coat and hung it over the side of the tub. She turned on the faucet, waited a long while for the water to heat up, washed Rita's blood from her hands and face. A yellow embroidered hand-towel, which may have once been white, hung on a ring set into the wall beside the sink. She decided against using it, instead dried off with wadded-up toilet paper. She gathered another handful of toilet paper, ran a little water over it, wiped down her coat.

She checked her phone when she sat down to pee. No service. She flushed, washed her hands, shook them dry, and was reaching for her coat when everything went black.

Helen felt her way to the bathroom door, slid her hand along the wall until she located the light switch. She toggled it up and down to no avail. She opened the door, poked her head out. The lights in the hallway and living room were off as well. She fumbled for her coat, slipped into it, remembered the flashlight in the pocket. She turned it on, stepped into the hallway.

"Sheriff?"

She heard his boots coming down the stairs and flicked the beam of the flashlight up to his face. He threw a forearm across his eyes.

"You mind?"

"Sorry." She lowered the light. "What happened?"

"Electricity went out."

"You don't say," she muttered under her breath.

Big Ed opened the hall closet, started rattling around inside.

"Dammit," he barked. "I told that idiot . . . here they are."

He removed two halogen lanterns, switched one on, set it on top of the cabinet. It provided a bright circle of illumination. He pulled a down jacket from the closet, shrugged into it. He'd changed his pants but was still wearing the gun belt.

He switched on the second lantern, and without saying a word to Helen, opened the front door and went outside. Not sure of what else to do, she followed.

Big Ed descended the porch steps, walked a half dozen yards down the street. Teddy approached from the direction of the jail, flashlight in hand. They met in the middle and had a brief conversation. Teddy trailed the sheriff back up to the porch.

"Looks like the power's out all over town," Big Ed said.

"That happen often?" Helen asked.

"Now and then. Edward, go fetch my shotgun."

"Yes, sir."

Helen moved aside to allow Teddy through the front door.

"So what now?"

Big Ed set his lantern on the porch, pulled out his pack of Camels, lit a cigarette. "Same as before. We grab Lawrence."

They paraded down Main Street, the sheriff with a lantern in one hand and a shotgun in the other, like a trio of cowpokes heading for a shootout.

"What did dispatch say?" Big Ed asked.

"A tractor trailer overturned on 89 and some passenger vehicles were involved," Teddy said. "It's gonna take a while to sort that out."

Big Ed grunted. "If the goddamn bikers weren't causing such a ruckus in town, we'd

134

have more deputies to spare."

"What about that shooting in Sardine Valley?" Teddy asked.

"Nobody knew a thing about it," Big Ed said. "Prank call or misunderstanding, I really don't know. A long goddamn drive for no good reason."

They passed the Trading Post, the last of the commercial buildings, and a scatter of abandoned houses, all shadows in the night. Eventually they came to a double-wide trailer parked on a grassy lot. A gasoline-powered generator hooked up to a side panel chugged noisily, providing electricity.

Frank stood in the front yard, a can of beer in his hand.

"Real nice night for a walk!" he yelled. "What happened to the lights?"

"Hell if I know," Big Ed said.

"You want me and Mike to take a look at the marshal's car now?" Frank asked.

"Not now, Frank," Big Ed shouted. "Go on inside. We'll come get you in a bit."

Frank raised the beer in a salute. "Ten-four, Sheriff!"

Another thirty yards and they approached a two-story house, one of the largest Helen had seen in Kill Devil Falls. Like most plots in town, this one was unkempt and overgrown with weeds. A dented car was parked in a carport alongside the house.

"This is Lawrence's grandma's place," Teddy said.

"Big house for one person," Helen said.

"One thing we got plenty of up here is space," Big Ed said.

"Should one of us go round back?" Teddy asked.

"We'll just call him out. If he runs, he won't get far." Big Ed turned to Helen. "He's a city boy."

Helen didn't take the bait. She side-stepped away from Big Ed and Teddy. No sense in making it easy for Lawrence if he was, in fact, a madman preparing to unleash a fusillade of bullets.

Big Ed set the lantern down on the ground in front of the porch, held the shotgun at port arms.

"Lawrence! This is Sheriff Scroggins. I need to talk to you. Come on out. And show me your hands when you walk through the front door."

Silence. No sign of movement from within the house.

"Lawrence!"

Thirty seconds passed. Sixty.

"Don't make me come in and get you!"

The front door slowly opened.

"Sheriff? What's going on?" Lawrence's

voice quaked.

"Out on the porch, hands up."

"What's the matter? Did I do something wrong?"

" 'Course not. Come on out, now."

Lawrence shuffled forward.

"Closer," Big Ed commanded. "Down here."

Lawrence descended the porch steps. He was dressed in sweatpants, a T-shirt, and the same jean jacket Helen had seen him wearing in the restaurant. His feet were sockless, in flip-flops.

"On your knees, Lawrence."

"Sheriff —"

"Shut your mouth and get on your knees." Big Ed didn't raise his voice, but the menace in his tone was tangible.

Lawrence slowly sank to his knees. Helen was uneasy. No need to treat Lawrence like a dangerous felon just yet.

Big Ed traced an arc around Lawrence and approached him from the rear.

"Cross your ankles and put your hands on top of your head."

Lawrence did as ordered.

"Edward!" Big Ed tossed Teddy the shotgun. Teddy caught it, fumbled it, almost dropped it.

Big Ed cuffed Lawrence.

"Why you are arresting me?" Lawrence protested.

"I'm not. I just want to have a talk." Big Ed pulled Lawrence to his feet. "Wait here," he instructed. He walked over to Teddy, said in a low voice, "Have a quick look inside. I'll meet you back at the jail."

"Sheriff, please, what's going on?" Lawrence quailed.

"I told you, I need a word. Now come along."

He picked up the lantern, led Lawrence away. Helen turned to follow, but Teddy reached for her arm.

"You . . . you want to give me a hand?"

Helen figured she should go with the sheriff, participate in the questioning. For all she knew, Big Ed might chain Lawrence to the cell bars and start whipping him with a cat-o'-nine-tails. But Teddy looked forlorn. Scared.

"Sure, Teddy. But let's make it quick."

"Quick's my middle name."

"No sense in advertising that fact," Helen said.

"Huh?"

"Nothing. Let's go."

8

Helen stepped through the front door, swept the foyer with her flashlight. Like Big Ed and Teddy's house, this one featured a living room to the right, a staircase straight ahead. To the left was a doorway leading to the kitchen.

"US Marshals!" she called out. "Anyone inside this house? Come out where I can see you!"

Teddy pushed in behind her. She felt his hot breath on her neck. She walked into the living room, saw that it was devoid of furniture. Not even a scrap of carpet, a picture on the wall, nothing. Teddy waved his flashlight around the room.

"Guess he don't spend much time in here," Teddy said.

"Why don't you check this floor?" Helen asked. "I'll search upstairs."

"Don't you think we should stay together?" Teddy's voice wavered a touch.

"Come on, Teddy. I don't want to be here all night." She entered the foyer, paused, turned back. "Remember, we don't have authority to do a full search. If you find something, don't touch it. We'll have to come up with an excuse to get a warrant later. You understand?"

"Got it," Teddy said.

"Okay." She started for the stairs.

"Marshal?"

"Yes?"

"Rita was alive when you found her?"

"She was." She pictured Rita gasping, her throat sliced open like an Easter ham.

"Did she . . . say anything? Something that might help us find out who did it?"

"No. I would have mentioned if she did."

"Right."

She couldn't see him clearly in the dark, but heard the sound of his fingers scratching the bristly hairs of his beard.

"What a thing," he said. "To die in the woods like that. Hands cuffed behind your back."

Helen turned away. "Let's get this done," she snapped.

She climbed the stairs, her face flushed with anger. Teddy was right. It was a horrible way to die. And she partially blamed him, for convincing her to leave Rita unattended. But really, the fault was hers. Her idiotic decision to go to the Trading Post, to leave Rita cuffed. Her fault Rita was unable to defend herself when the killer came calling.

Helen set aside her feelings of guilt and remorse. She needed to remain sharp, focused. If the perp was still in Kill Devil Falls, she was going to take him down. Failing that, however, she wanted a solid piece of evidence. The murder weapon. Bloody clothes.

But she didn't expect to find anything here. Lawrence wasn't the killer. If she was sure of anything, it was that.

She raised her flashlight, found herself facing a hallway with doors leading off to the left and the right. She started opening them, one by one: An empty bedroom. Another bedroom, containing two single bed frames and a poorly aged chest of drawers. A supply closet holding a collection of ancient cleaning supplies and a desiccated mop.

Behind the last door on the right was a bathroom, currently in use, judging from the toothpaste and other items on the sink. Directly across from it was a furnished bedroom. She decided to check out the bedroom first.

The bedroom featured a queen bed with a

nightstand along one wall, and a chest of drawers opposite. The furniture was heavy, solid wood, not the usual IKEA particleboard. Inherited from the grandmother, Helen guessed. Spread across the floor was a collection of books. Helen shoved them around with the toe of her boot, reading titles.

Thus Spoke Zarathustra, by Nietzsche. *Sun and Steel,* by Mishima. *The Collected Works of Guy de Maupassant.* A thick comic book called *Watchmen,* which Helen recalled having been made into a movie. A couple of sci-fi titles. A photography book called *Memento Mori.*

She picked this one up, leafed through it. Inside were portraits dating back to the early years of daguerreotype photography. Two little girls in bonnets posed beside their infant brother. A skinny father in a somber black coat, a Rubenesque mother wearing a high-collared Victorian dress, a child seated between them.

All the people in the book looked terribly glum. In those days, a photo required a long exposure time, so everyone had to sit completely still for several minutes. No silly poses or goofy smiles.

But it was more than that — there was something off about these portraits. Helen turned a page, saw a small girl in a white dress, a wreath of flowers around the crown of her head, lying on a daybed, three siblings standing expressionlessly around her. Another of a woman seated on a loveseat, her teenaged daughter beside her, the girl's head leaning awkwardly into the woman's ample bosom, eyes staring listlessly off into space.

Helen flipped to the back cover, read the copy:

Memento Mori — "Remember that you will die." The practice of photographing the recently deceased was popular in the nineteenth century, when death, especially that of infants and children, was commonplace. Photographs served as keepsakes of departed family members, and not only helped with the grieving process but often were the only visual representation of the deceased a family possessed. As such, they were highly valued and given a place of prominence in the household.

Eww, Helen thought. *How morbid.* She put the book back in the pile, wiped her hand on her pants.

Downstairs, in the kitchen, Teddy laid the

shotgun on a small dining table, idly riffled through cupboards. Most were bare, apart from the belly-up corpses of cockroaches and a few ancient, petrified food crumbs. A plastic dish drainer containing chipped crockery rested beside the sink. Some stained coffee mugs were in one cupboard, a rack of ancient, stale-smelling spice bottles in another. A beat-up toaster oven sat on the counter, and in front of it, a set of keys. Teddy picked up the keys, put them in his jacket pocket.

He turned from the counter, noticed a pantry door set into the wall. He opened the door, directed his flashlight inside.

He saw a shelf lined with perhaps ten cereal boxes, all of them Cheerios. Another with ten canisters of Quaker Oatmeal. A third, two cases of Campbell's alphabet soup. Five plastic containers of Slim Jims. A dozen boxes of oat and honey granola bars.

On the floor of the pantry were a dozen cases of Miller High Life and four bottles of Wild Turkey. Teddy snorted derisively. He shut the pantry door, retrieved the shotgun, continued through the kitchen to the back of the house.

Upstairs, Helen opened dresser drawers, pawed through shirts, pants, underwear,

144

jeans. Lawrence's wardrobe seemed to consist entirely of Old Navy casual apparel. She searched the closet. A coat and several button-down shirts dangled on wire hangers. She reached into the coat's pockets, came up with loose change, a few receipts from a supermarket in Donnersville, a stale piece of gum. A gym bag lay on the floor. She unzipped it, gasped at the rank odor of stale sweat. Holding her breath, Helen dumped out the contents. Dirty shirts, pants, and other clothes. Lawrence's laundry. She kicked the items back into the bag.

She opened the nightstand drawer. Inside were a pair of sunglasses, a fold-out pocket knife. A wallet. She flipped open the wallet, checked Lawrence's driver's license, took a photo of it with her cell phone. Aside from the license, there was an ATM card, a couple of credit cards, and about two hundred in cash. Neither a pittance nor a king's ransom. Helen set the wallet down. She used her phone to take a photo of the fold-out knife, then shut the drawer.

She got down on all fours and shined her flashlight under the bed. Nothing but a loose sock and lots of dust bunnies.

She crossed the hall, entered the bathroom. On the sink were toothpaste, a toothbrush, a razor, shaving cream. The edge of the tub held shampoo, conditioner. A dark ring of grit circled the bottom of the tub. She leaned into the tub, inspected the grit closely with her flashlight, rubbed it with her finger. It looked like normal, everyday dirt and grease.

She opened the medicine cabinet. And finally, things got interesting. She used a finger to pick through a dozen plastic pill bottles. Aspirin, of course. As well as buprenorphine, clonazepam, diazepam, Percocet.

Teddy's voice came from downstairs. "Marshal!"

She leaned out of the bathroom. "Yes?"

"I think you're gonna want to see this."

"Coming!"

Helen took a photo of the pill bottles, closed the cabinet. She hurried down the hallway, descended the stairs. Teddy waited below, slightly out of breath.

"This way," he said.

He led Helen through the kitchen and into another room, perhaps once used as an office but now empty, and then beyond that to a mudroom. Lawrence apparently used the mudroom as his temporary garbage dump — half a dozen bags filled with empty food boxes, crushed beer cans, and drained bourbon bottles sat by a back door leading to an enclosed porch. An ancient green washing machine squatted openmouthed in a corner like a fossilized bullfrog.

Teddy used his flashlight to pinpoint a door set into the back wall. The door was ajar.

"Cellar," Teddy explained.

"What's down there?"

"I think you need to see for yourself. I really can't . . . can't describe it."

Helen felt a prick of apprehension. And annoyance. She scowled, stepped through the doorway. Cement steps led down into darkness. She smelled boiled meat, insect spray, and an unfamiliar acrid tang.

"What's that smell?"

"You'll see." Teddy sounded almost gleeful.

Helen crept down the steps. She directed the beam of her flashlight around the perimeter of the room.

At first she saw nothing out of the ordinary. Stained cardboard boxes, a couple of old bicycles slouching on flat tires, broken furniture — the usual junk people stuff into their basements, closets, and attics.

In the room's center was a long picnic table. A collection of shiny instruments winked and glinted. Helen moved closer.

She froze when her light revealed a pair of

glowing eyes, a set of razor-sharp teeth. A woodland animal crouched on the table, looking straight at her. She slowly reached for her Glock.

The animal didn't move. Just stared. Not a twitch or a ripple of its muscles. Not a blink of its eyes. She realized it was dead. Stuffed. Is this what Teddy wanted her to see? His idea of a joke?

The creature resembled a hedgehog — bristly fur, a round snout. A pair of miniature horns extended from the side of its head, conjuring up an image of a Viking helmet from a Wagner opera. The animal's teeth were too big for its mouth — nasty-looking fangs curved downward below its chin.

"What the hell is that?" Helen said.

Teddy snort-laughed.

Another creature sat a foot away from the hedgehog-thing. This one was definitely a cat . . . of some sort. A cat standing on all fours. With a set of feathery wings unfurled from its haunches.

Helen suppressed an urge to run back up the stairs. She quickly shined her light across the rest of the cellar.

She spied a guinea pig on a folding wooden chair. Well, two guinea pigs. Joined seamlessly at the midsection, minus back legs, conjoined torsos and heads looking in opposite directions.

A Chihuahua's head atop the body of a Papillon.

A fat little Dachshund, belly up, six legs arching from its sides, spider-like, reminding Helen of the scene in the director's cut of *The Exorcist* where the little girl crab-walks down the stairs at the dinner party.

"Look here," a voice whispered in her ear. Helen jumped. Teddy pointed his flashlight at a huge mass of black rats, tangled in a ball on the ground, their tails linked together in an unbreakable knot.

"I heard about this," he said. "They call it a Rat King. The rats get all stuck together like that, try to run every which way, and eventually starve to death."

Helen felt her gorge rise.

"What in God's balls is going on down here?"

"They're all taxidermied," Teddy said.

He edged past her, focused his light on the table. Neatly laid out on its splintered wooden surface was a collection of tools, including scalpels, scissors, forceps, needles, catgut, and many other instruments that Helen didn't recognize.

"He's got all kinds of knives, needles, pliers, you name it."

Teddy spotlit a metal rack against the wall containing rows of chemical bottles, bags of stuffing, hundreds of orbs with round and slit pupils in a plastic container, boxes of fur and feathers.

"Hair, glass eyes, stuffing, chemicals for cleaning and tanning hides," Teddy said.

"Where does he get the animals?"

"I found some carriers in the corner." Teddy indicated a stack of plastic pet carriers and some cardboard boxes for transporting rodents. "My guess is he gets 'em at the ASPCA or a pet store."

"He does this to them . . . I mean . . . he brings them here, uses them for these . . . projects?"

Teddy shrugged. "Guess so."

"Let's get the hell out of here."

"Right behind you," Teddy said.

Once outside, on the front lawn, Teddy pointed at the carport.

"Think we should have a look?"

"I want to get back to the jail, see if Lawrence said anything to the sheriff." Helen kept imagining medieval torture scenes: Lawrence spread-eagled on a rack, Big Ed ratcheting the roller.

"It'll just take a sec," Teddy said. He jogged over to the car, an old Toyota,

150

opened the driver's side door. He laid the shotgun on the roof, ducked down, searched the front seats, foot wells, and glove compartment. Helen waited on the edge of the yard, hands in her pockets, huddled against the cold.

"Deputy, we need to get crime scene techs up here — let them do that."

Teddy climbed out of the driver's seat, opened the back door, crawled inside.

"If there is evidence in there, you're contaminating it!" she yelled. She disapproved of Teddy's lack of proper procedure, but figured it didn't matter much in the end. He wasn't going to find anything. Only a complete numbskull would commit murder, then toss the weapon into his own car. Especially with an entire forest in which to dump evidence.

Teddy shut the back door.

"Deputy," Helen called.

"Hold on!" He opened the driver's side door again, pulled the trunk release. He walked around to the back of the Toyota, shined his flashlight into the open trunk.

"Marshal! Come look at this!"

Helen held her irritation in check. She plodded over. On the floor of the trunk, amid old newspapers, a roll of duct tape, dirty rags, an empty water bottle, she saw a glint of metal. Teddy moved aside. Helen leaned in.

It was a hunting knife. Five-inch blade with a blood groove, a wooden handle, brass-colored accents.

"Don't touch it," Helen said immediately. "Just leave it right there."

Teddy slapped his thigh. "How about that!"

"Let's not jump to conclusions."

Teddy pointed, his finger creating a giant shadow in the beam of his flashlight. "Don't that look like blood on the blade?"

It did. Indeed it did. "We need to get techs up here." Helen took out her phone, photographed the knife, motioned Teddy back, shut the trunk.

When Helen and Teddy came through the jailhouse door, Big Ed was sitting behind the massive desk, smoking a Camel, tapping the ashes into Teddy's can-spittoon. One halogen lantern was on the desk, another on the floor across the room. Helen blinked at the sudden glare.

"Well, now," Big Ed said, his words punctuated with puffs of smoke. "I was beginning to think you got eaten by the ghost of old Stoppard."

"We found all kinds of creepy stuff,"

Teddy said. "This guy's crazier than a sack of rabid weasels."

"Shut it, Edward," Big Ed barked. He inclined his head toward the cells. Helen saw Lawrence's fingers curled around the iron slats of the rightmost door, his eye glinting as he peered out.

"You had no right to go in my house," Lawrence said. "That was an illegal search."

Big Ed tossed his cigarette in the can, stood up.

"You a lawyer?"

"I know my rights."

Big Ed crossed the room, picked the lantern up off the floor, crooked a finger at Helen and Teddy. "Follow me."

They walked down the short hallway into the guard room. Rita's body lay on the bed, still wrapped in the old Indian blanket.

"What's she doing here?" Teddy squealed.

"You rather I left her on the couch in our living room?"

"No . . ."

"What the hell is wrong with you?" Big Ed snarled shutting the door. "I know you ain't the brightest bulb in the chandelier, but you don't burst in hollering about what evidence you found when the suspect is right there within earshot."

"I'm sorry."

"You're as dumb as a pile of bricks, boy. You must take after your mother."

"Don't talk about Mom like that," Teddy muttered.

"What?"

"Nothing."

Teddy glared at the wooden floorboards.

"So go on, then. Tell me."

Teddy didn't respond. Helen was afraid Big Ed would light into him again, so she chimed in.

"For starters, I found lots of prescription drugs in the bathroom."

"What kind?"

"Some Percocets. A collection of anxiety meds. And one other . . . buprenorphine."

Big Ed chewed on that. "Junkie meds."

"We found a bunch of mutilated and stuffed animals down in the cellar," Teddy said.

"What?"

"Dog heads on cats, wings on rats, like that."

Big Ed's mouth twisted. "That don't sound right."

"And we found a knife in the trunk of his car," Teddy continued. "Possible murder weapon."

"We don't know for sure," Helen said. "It

needs to be bagged and tagged and analyzed."

"You saw those things he made," Teddy said. "There's no doubt he's sick in the head."

"Just because he has a . . . weird hobby . . . It doesn't mean he's a killer."

"But he's got cat heads on dogs, and horns on woodchucks!"

"She's right, Edward." Big Ed stuck his thumbs in his gun belt and leaned against the wall. "Did you find bloody clothes? Rita likely leaked all over whoever cut her throat."

"I found a bag of laundry, but no blood on the clothes," Helen said. She was a touch surprised Big Ed wasn't immediately stringing up a noose for Lawrence.

"No normal person does what he's been doing down in that cellar," Teddy insisted.

"That may be true, Edward, but lots of people ain't normal, and ain't killers either," Big Ed said. "Right?"

Teddy didn't answer, just resumed drilling holes in the floor with his eyes.

"Okay," Big Ed said. "We got some stuff to go on, anyway. We'll need to get a warrant and" — he held up fingers in air quotes — " 'find the evidence.' Again. Let's hope you bursting in and screaming about the cellar of horrors doesn't screw the pooch, Edward."

"We can aim for exigent circumstances, Sheriff," Helen said. "Immediate aftermath of murder. Viable suspect. Unsure if anyone else in town was missing or harmed. Something like that."

Big Ed nodded. "That'd probably do it. In the meantime, I'm gonna hold him until we get that warrant. Make sure that knife don't go missing."

"How did the questioning go, Sheriff?" Helen's eyes darted toward the body on the cot. It was creepy, the blanket-wrapped bundle of dead flesh just lying there.

"He didn't confess."

"So what did he say?"

Big Ed's imitation of Lawrence was high-pitched and quavering: "I'm innocent . . . You got the wrong man."

"Would you mind if I spoke to him?"

"What for?"

"Maybe he's threatened by you. Scared. Perhaps I'd be able to get him to talk."

Big Ed frowned. "I don't know."

"Can't hurt, can it? At worst, he just won't tell me anything."

Big Ed yawned, looked at his watch. "I'll give you five minutes."

They returned to the front room. Big Ed

set the lantern back on the desk and took a seat. Teddy leaned against a wall.

"I really hate to ask, Sheriff, but do you think Lawrence and I could speak privately?" Helen said.

"Why? You want to hold hands?"

"Please."

Big Ed rolled his eyes. "Fine. I might as well check the access road, although you can't see squat out there in the dark. Edward, why don't you get that old coffee percolator brewing on the stove? It's gonna be a long night."

They took one of the lanterns and disappeared through the front door. Helen went to the window. She watched as Big Ed took the shotgun from Teddy, climbed into the Explorer, turned on the headlights, and drove away. Teddy walked toward the red farmhouse, the lantern swinging in his hand.

Definitely some father-son issues with those two.

Helen turned, went to the wall where the key ring hung on its hook. With only a single lantern providing light, the ceiling and corners of the room were heavily shadowed. She felt trapped in a time before electricity, or rule of law, where the potential for violence lurked within every darkened doorway.

"I'm going to open your cell door," she said. "Give you some air. Keep in mind, I'm armed."

Lawrence grumbled unintelligibly. Helen unlocked the door, opened it, set the key ring on the desk. "You want some water or something?"

Lawrence sat huddled on the cot, shivering with cold.

"I could use a drink," he said, eyes glittering. "A real drink."

"Let's have a little chat first, and I'll see what I can do about that later."

Lawrence stuffed his fingers into his armpits. "I didn't kill that woman, like the sheriff thinks."

"Hold on. I'm going to advise you of your rights, okay?"

"He did that."

"Did you sign a waiver?"

"I don't need a lawyer. I didn't kill that woman."

"Okay. Well, I don't think we've been properly introduced. My name is Helen Morrissey. I'm a deputy with the US Marshal's service."

"I know. I was in the restaurant when you came in."

"Right. And you obviously are aware that Rita Scroggins was murdered this evening

158

and you are a suspect."

"I never met her. I don't even know what she looks like. Looked like."

"Can you give me an account of your whereabouts after you finished dinner and left the restaurant?"

"I went back to the house."

"Anyone see you? You talk to anyone?"

Lawrence looked at her like a poodle was growing out of her skull.

"Did I talk to anyone? No, I didn't. First of all, everyone was at the Trading Post. And second, you've met the people in this town. I never talk to any of them, except for Mrs. Patterson when I order my meals."

"Why is that, Lawrence? What are you doing up here, if you're not fond of the company?"

"I needed a place to get away, is all."

"Get away from what?"

He shook his head, didn't answer.

"I found buprenorphine in your medicine cabinet, Lawrence."

"You had no right to search my house."

"Your grandmother's house."

"Whatever."

"Are you currently using heroin?"

He sprang to his feet. She took a step back.

"No! I came up here to get as far from all that shit as possible!"

"Calm down."

"I'm calm!"

"You're shouting. Back up against that wall!"

He vibrated on the balls of his feet for a moment, like he was getting ready to run or throw a punch. Then he slumped, backed away, leaned on the wall.

"I'm sorry. I didn't mean to yell," he said.

"That's all right, I understand. This is a very stressful situation. Now . . . you are not currently using heroin?"

"No. That's what the bupreno is for. It's prescribed. I was in a program."

"Where?"

"Oakland."

"Was this a court-mandated program?"

"I entered it myself. To get clean."

"Not the result of a drug bust, something like that?" she asked.

"No, I said!"

"Do you have a record, Lawrence?"

He huffed. "I've got a couple of possession busts. Nothing major."

"No felony convictions?"

"No."

"I have to ask you about the cellar, Lawrence. The fact is, you've got some very questionable shit going on down there."

"I'm an artist, okay? That's my art. It's

what I'm working on now."

"Mixed-up animal bodies?"

"You don't have to get it. It's not for you. It's transgressive. Fucked up. That's the point. It made you feel something, right? A raw emotional response?"

"Yeah. Disgusted."

"Great. What did you feel the last time you went to an art museum and looked at some Impressionists? Like you needed a nap?"

She had to admit, he had a point.

"Okay, so you're an artist."

"Yes. Well. It doesn't pay much. But it's what I do. I paint, I sculpt, I write. The stuff in the cellar . . . it's just what I'm working on at the moment."

"Lawrence — did you kill the animals you're using in those . . . art pieces?"

"No. I'm not an animal killer. I . . ."

He paused for a long while. He approached the doorway of the cell. Shadows etched the sharp contours of his cheekbones.

"I know a guy who works at a pet store. Another one who's a tech at a vet clinic. Animals die. Usually they get cremated or dumped in a landfill or something. These guys sell them to me. It's not exactly legal, because of health codes. But it's not cruelty to animals or anything like that."

"I see. Anything else you want to tell me?"

"I never laid eyes on Rita Crawford. I didn't even know she was in town. I didn't kill her. I swear to God."

"What about the key, Lawrence?"

"What key?"

"The key to this jail."

"I don't know anything about it. I've never been in here before. I didn't even know the building was locked or that there was a key to open the door."

"Okay."

"You believe me, don't you, Marshal?"

She did. She could think of no possible motive for why Lawrence might kill Rita and considered it unlikely he knew about the key and where to find it. But, as he was still a suspect, she couldn't tell him that.

"I'm going to lock you inside again, okay? Just until we can get this straightened out."

"Don't leave me in here alone."

She thought it odd that a man who spent hours in a cellar dissecting dead animals and creating monsters out of them should be scared of being left alone, but who knew what was really going on with this kid.

"I won't," she said.

"The sheriff and deputy. They're . . . It's like they're straight out of a bad hillbilly-exploitation movie."

Helen smiled.

"Don't worry. No one's forcing anybody to squeal like a pig on my watch."

9

When the electricity died, Jesse Patterson was relaxing in his private home theater, sprawled on a leather recliner, halfway through his fourth Scotch and finally developing an agreeable buzz.

The home theater consumed the entire living room of the apartment Jesse shared with Alice on the second floor of the Trading Post. He'd installed it with his own two hands, painstakingly, meticulously, and at no small expense. It featured QuietRock soundproof drywall, a 7.1 surround-sound system, an echo-absorbing, medium-shag carpet, a ViewSonic PJD7820HK DLP projector, a 101-inch screen and, to round it all out, an Octane Turbo genuine bonded leather manual recliner.

In addition to Jesse's living room-cum-theater, the apartment included two sizable bedrooms, a kitchen/dining area, and a bathroom with an old clawfoot tub and vintage toilet powerful enough to flush down a baby watermelon. Jesse and Alice slept in the largest bedroom, on the back side of the building. By mutual agreement, the home theater was Jesse's inviolable domain, while the second bedroom belonged exclusively to Alice. She called it her "Grove." He called it "the Stygian Lair."

Most evenings, after dinner was served, the dishes were washed, and the Trading Post was locked up for the night, Jesse shut himself in here, drank Scotch, smoked a little reefer (compliments of Frank and Mike), and watched movies. Sometimes old classics, other times the subversive New Hollywood films of the early '70s, occasionally a more recent feature. But more often than not, he watched his own films.

Jesse was a graduate of the prestigious USC School of Cinematic Arts. Immediately upon receiving his diploma in 1969, he moved to France, hoping to find work with one of his directorial idols: Jean-Luc Godard, Francois Truffaut, even, in a pinch, a lesser talent like Alain Resnais. But within three years he was back in LA, penniless, without a single demo reel to his name. He was eventually reduced to second unit work on low-budget tits-and-gore flicks. When he finally received his big break, a chance to direct a film with a decent budget and production values, naturally it was for a pornographic feature. Down to his last sixty-three dollars and living in a seedy Santa Monica bungalow with three other starving artists, Jesse didn't — couldn't — turn down the opportunity.

He was lucky to catch the tail end of porn's golden age, when films played in theaters on 42nd Street and Hollywood Boulevard, stars like John Holmes and Linda Lovelace were household names, and smut flicks were reviewed, often favorably, by critics in the *New York Times*. VHS video eventually killed the celluloid starlet, however, and the industry returned to cheap, gonzo filmmaking with shitty lighting, bad camerawork, and a revolving door of forgettable "talent," for lack of a better word, in front of and behind the camcorder. Jesse hung on for as long as he could, much longer than he would have thought possible, but by the late '80s, his career was kaput.

Twenty years ago, Jesse had converted both his 35 millimeter and VHS masters to digital, eventually storing them on a laptop connected to his ViewSonic. The 35-millimeter transferred nicely, but the VHS films looked terrible in hi-def and he rarely rewatched them.

Before the lights crapped out, Jesse was viewing the lone exception — an homage to Fellini's *8 1/2,* which the studio had forced him to title *8 1/2 Inches.* An infantile, obvious name for a pornographic film, but Jesse was proud of the finished product. The budget he'd been given was unusually generous for the VHS era and every dollar showed on screen — the hair, makeup, costumes were all top-notch. His major regret, aside from the pandering title, was that the studio refused his request to film in black-and-white.

The studio head, a fat little Greek, had laughed in his face. "Our customers want to see pussy in full color," he'd said. "The redder the better."

Jesse's favorite part of *8 1/2 Inches* was his remake of the scene in Fellini's masterpiece where the protagonist, Guido, pays tribute to the prostitute Saraghina by waving his cap from afar. In Fellini's version, Saraghina smiled at him, whispering a plaintive *"ciao."* In Jesse's, she stripped, fondled herself, and crooked a finger at Guido. He ran to her and they made love in the sand. As a director, the sex was secondary, a necessary evil, for Jesse. It was there simply to justify the expense of the film. What really mattered was the unspoken emotion expressed by the actors before they got naked and rutted like animals.

The film was just about to reach this climactic scene when all went dark. Jesse panicked, thinking his projector was broken. He lurched to his feet, spilling Scotch, cursed, and felt his way over to the wall where he blindly fiddled with the View-Sonic. He couldn't see a damn thing, so he went to the door and flicked the light switch. No dice. He opened the door, poked his head into the hall. No lights working here, either.

"Alice?"

She didn't answer. Jesse shuffled down the hall to her room. His body ached from the roll down the stairs. What hurt the most, however, was the nasty little wound on his neck. God forbid he should get tetanus, or something worse — like HIV. Not that Alice cared, the old shrew. He turned the knob, gave the door a push.

Putrid-smelling air wafted across Jesse's face. He nearly gagged. Musk, shit, and rot.

Inside, a dozen thick candles on elaborate stands provided a soft, flickering light. Alice sat in the middle of the room on a woven mat. She was naked, facing a plaster statue set against the far wall. The room's radiator valve was wide open and Alice's pale skin was shiny with sweat. The floor around her undulated grotesquely, loops and coils of black and brown bodies, gliding and slithering.

Alice turned.

"What do you want?" she snapped.

"The electricity's out."

Alice glanced over at a double row of terrariums resting on racks against the wall.

"The heat lamps. My babies will freeze." She turned back to Jesse. "Did you check the fuse box?"

"Just about to."

"Well, hurry up."

"I took a tumble down the stairs today, you know. How about you go down and check the fuse box?"

"Isn't it enough that I do all the thinking for the both of us? Do I have to do the grunt work, too?"

"You think it was so easy?" Jesse said.

"I really should have known better, Jesse, because the one thing you can reliably be counted on to do is fail. You're a regular Old Faithful of fucking up."

"Go to hell, Alice!"

"I'm already there! Now go fix the damn lights!"

Jesse slammed the door.

He stomped to the kitchen, opened a

drawer, fished out a flashlight. He wasn't much of a handyman, but at least he knew how to change a fuse. Naturally, the fuse box was in the basement, which meant a trip down two flights of stairs.

He walked down the hall, turned right, descended to the ground floor. Here, there was a small vestibule with three doors. A door on the left led to the restaurant; another on the right, down to the basement. The third door opened onto the back yard.

Jesse opened the basement door, gingerly negotiated the cement steps.

The basement smelled of onions, garlic, and wet earth. Metal racks held giant cans of crushed tomatoes, olive oil, bags of flour, cases of soda and beer, coffee beans, and other foodstuffs. Broken, discarded furniture and appliances were piled to one side. Cartons of paper goods rested against a wall.

Jesse tried to remember where the fuse box was located. He waved the flashlight around, finally spied the box on the wall behind a stack of plastic-wrapped paper towels. He pushed the towels aside. The stack toppled over.

Cursing, he savagely kicked a set of paper towels across the floor. He yanked open the fuse box, inspected the fuses one by one.

They appeared to be fine. Good thing, because now that he thought about it, if a fuse needed replacing he'd have to go back up the stairs, through the restaurant, and into the market, where the fuses were stocked. Too much goddamn walking.

The bad news, of course, was that the electrical problem wasn't going to be a simple fix. Maybe a transformer somewhere along the grid blew. Who knew how long before it might be repaired? The county government didn't give a shit about Kill Devil Falls. It wanted them out of here.

And, after fifteen years, Jesse was more than ready to oblige.

He grimaced his way back up the stairs. As he came through the doorway into the vestibule, wind tickled his beard. He rounded the bannister, saw that the back door was ajar. Strange. He usually secured it before heading up after dinner. He stepped out onto the back stoop. Outside, it was as dark as only remote forest could be, just a scatter of twinkling stars and a custard-yellow moon. He shivered in the chilly night air.

Jesse went back inside, closed and locked the door. He trudged slowly up to the second floor. The glow of candlelight bled through the bottom of the door to Alice's room. He extended his middle finger as he passed.

"Hope your babies turn into Popsicles," he muttered.

Back in the kitchen, he set the flashlight sidewise on the dining table. He opened the freezer and removed a plastic ice tray. He cracked ice into a tall glass. His plan was to keep drinking until he passed out. Relegate this horrible day to a distant, hazy memory.

He picked up a bottle of Johnnie Walker and the glass in one hand and the flashlight in the other. He shuffled down the hall to the master bedroom, opened the door. He set the flashlight on Alice's vanity, picked up a disposable lighter, lit a few candles. He turned toward the big brass bed, looking forward to sinking into a soft mattress and drowning himself in the bottle of Scotch.

In a shadowed corner of the room, something moved.

"Wha—" was all Jesse managed to say before taking a hit across the temple. He saw a burst of stars. The bottle and glass fell to the floor, and Jesse crashed down on top of them.

Helen stepped out onto the porch and breathed in the sharp scent of mountain pine. There was no sign of Big Ed or the

Explorer. Just her ailing Charger.

It occurred to her that, if Lee Larimer was responsible for Rita's death, perhaps he'd disabled her car to prevent her from taking Rita back to Sacramento. But if that were the case, how could he have known she would leave Rita to go off and find a mechanic? Or was his original plan just to break Rita out by force? If so, why bother with the car? To prevent her from pursuing?

Lots of unanswered questions.

She saw Teddy approaching, a lantern in one hand and a thermos in the other. He waved. Helen waved back.

"Any luck?" he asked, clomping up the porch steps.

"Says he didn't do it."

" 'Course he does."

"How much longer for the other deputies to get up here?" she asked.

"Hard to say. Dispatch said the accident scene was just one big ol' goat rodeo."

"What about the crime scene techs?"

"Well, we don't have a crime scene unit in Donnersville. We use a team from Carson City. Probably won't be here till late morning, and that's if they don't catch any other cases."

"Great."

"We're just a small county, Marshal. Big

in area, but only a handful of people. We don't got money, equipment, resources like you all in Sacramento."

"I understand, Teddy. I didn't mean to be snarky. But . . . for God's sake. We have a fresh murder, possible evidence lying around . . . and no means to conduct a proper investigation."

"Come morning, we'll get it all sorted out."

Helen had her doubts. Teddy set the lantern and thermos down on the wooden steps and pulled a tobacco pouch from his pocket.

"I'm real sorry about how complicated this all turned out to be," he said.

"Not your fault. But thanks for saying so."

"I know my dad feels the same way, although he ain't so good at expressing himself." Teddy stuffed a wad of tobacco into his cheek. "He comes off as kind of a hardass sometimes. Okay. All the time."

Helen laughed. "He does, at that. Seems like you and he have a difficult relationship. Must be tough working with him."

Teddy shrugged. "He's good at his job."

"If you say so. He doesn't seem overly concerned with catching whoever killed your sister."

"I think he's a lot more upset about her

than he lets on."

"That wouldn't be difficult, because he doesn't seem upset in the least," Helen said.

Teddy leaned over, spat into the dirt.

"Well . . ." he started. He scratched his nose. Looked at Helen, back down at the ground. Back at Helen.

"What is it, Teddy?"

Teddy's jaw bulged as he worked the tobacco.

"You know my dad married Rita's mom when Rita was about ten. We're the same age, Rita and me. Thirty-two this year."

Helen nodded, but she was surprised. Rita had looked much older, while Teddy, apart from the beard, could pass for early twenties.

"When Rita was thirteen or so, her mom got sick. Cancer. She spent a few hard years fighting it."

Helen remembered the day her father had come to pick her up from school, three hours early. In the car on the way to the hospital, he told her about her mom's car accident. It was the only time she'd ever seen him cry. At least her mom didn't suffer — she just simply never woke up.

She pushed the memory away.

"That must have been rough."

"Well, she wasn't my mom," Teddy said.

He stopped abruptly.

"I didn't mean it like that. I, uh . . . my mom was already dead. She died when I was six."

Helen shivered, stuffed her hands into her pockets. What were the chances of the three of them all losing their mothers as kids? Astronomical. She was suddenly overcome by a crushing wave of sadness. For Rita, Teddy. For herself.

"So, yeah," Teddy continued. "I'm sure it was tough on Rita. But the thing is . . . when Rita's mom got sick, she was in and out of the hospital, and even when she was home, she was in bed most of the time. In a lot of pain, near the end. Sleeping mostly. Drugged up."

"How awful."

"And somewhere along the way . . . my dad . . . he took a shine to Rita."

Helen's stomach sank.

"What do you mean?"

"Yeah, he . . . you know."

"He molested her?"

"Oh, I don't know if I'd say it was as bad as that." He wiped his nose on the back of his hand. "Maybe just . . . grabbed her a bit, every now and then."

"Grabbed her?"

"I think it's why she run away."

"I see."

"Thing is . . . he's not a bad man. Not really. And deep down, I know he regrets what he done. And blames himself for the way she turned out. For the way she ended up."

"He regrets it."

"I believe so. Part of him probably feels like what happened to her tonight . . . It was like a, you know . . . It was a sure thing she'd end up dead or in prison."

"An inevitability."

"Right. And my dad, he knows it's partially 'cause of him. Not entirely. She was kind of a troubled kid even before her mom married him. But . . . if she hadn't of run away, maybe she could have finished high school. Even gone to college or just gotten a steady job in Donnersville. Married, had kids. Like that."

Helen clenched her fists. *If there was any justice in the world . . .*

"I don't know why I told you that," Teddy said.

"I'm glad you did."

"Don't let on to my dad. Promise me."

Helen looked up at the night sky, the moon, thinking how the sheriff should be hogtied and stuffed in a hole along with a few sacks of black powder, like the cannibal

Stoppard.

"Marshal?" Teddy said.

"Okay, Teddy. I won't say anything."

"Thanks. We should probably go on inside."

"Is there any chance of getting the electricity back on?"

Teddy shrugged. "We could ask Frank and Mike to take a look."

"Do they know what to do?"

"Better'n me," Teddy said. "They rewired the Trading Post, so maybe."

"Let's ask them."

Teddy nodded toward the jail door. "My dad wants us to stay with Lawrence."

"You stay. I'll go."

"Marshal, it ain't safe to walk around here by yourself."

"I'll stick to the sidewalk. And watch out for mountain lions."

"It ain't a joke."

"I know it's not."

Teddy sighed. "My dad won't be happy."

"I'll be back before you know it," Helen said. "Save a cup of coffee for me."

Frank and Mike's double-wide was a shrine to arrested adolescence combined with a complete lack of parental, legal, or social restrictions.

Hanging on the walls were full-color, highly pornographic spreads ripped from European adult magazines. Beer cans, dirty dishes, weed paraphernalia, potato chip bags, loose change, crumpled dollar bills, random tools, and various other bits of garbage fought for space on the dining table and kitchen counter. Mike's crossbow was mounted on the wall beside the front door.

Frank sat on the edge of a broken-down couch playing Grand Theft Auto. He paused frequently to sip from a tall can of Blue Hurricane Four Loko. Mike was smoking a joint and reading a tattered copy of *The Walking Dead: Volume 17.*

"No, you don't, motherfucker!" Frank yelled. He leaned his body precariously to one side, frantically working the controller to steer his stolen Trans Am through a busy intersection, two police cars in hot pursuit.

There was a knock at the door. Frank ignored it. Mike went to the window, looked through the cheap plastic blinds.

"Oh, shit!" he whispered. "It's the lady cop."

Frank didn't take his eyes off the TV screen. "What does she want?"

"I don't know, but we got, like, four kilos in the bedroom."

Frank's Trans Am sideswiped a fuel tanker

179

and was engulfed in a massive explosion.

"Fuck!"

Another knock, louder.

Frank tossed the controller to the floor.

"Go shut the bedroom door, then! And ditch that fatty!"

Mike trotted to the sink, tossed in his joint, ran the water.

Helen called from outside: "Frank? Mike? It's Deputy Marshal Morrissey. Open up, please."

Frank rose from the couch, waited while Mike closed the bedroom door. He waved a hand in the air.

"You smoking the Sasquatch? That shit smells to high heaven."

Mike shrugged. Frank opened the front door. He leaned against the door jamb, one hand on his hip.

"Hi."

"Frank."

"Noticed Big Ed grabbed up Lawrence. Did he kill Rita? Or was he just arresting him for being a freakazoid?"

Helen sniffed.

"You raising skunks in there?"

"Ah . . . no. That's just the smell of Mike's dirty socks." Frank laughed.

"Aren't you going to invite me in?"

"We're kind of busy. What can I do for you?"

"I'm wondering if you can do something about getting the lights back on," Helen said.

"You are, are you?"

Helen didn't like the predatory nature of his smile.

"Actually, the sheriff asked me to come over," she said.

"Is that so?"

"Why would I lie, Frank?"

"Well, I don't know." He scratched his armpit. "People lie all the time, for various reasons."

"Like when you said just now you were busy?"

"Big Ed told us to stay put."

"Well, now he wants you to check out the electricity. Can you do that, please?"

"Depends."

Helen sighed.

"On what?"

"How much does the job pay?" Frank said.

"Excuse me?"

"Seeing as how we're being asked to provide a service, and seem to be the only ones around here with the necessary skills, it's only fair that we get paid."

"Wow. I didn't realize I was dealing with a rapacious capitalist."

Frank frowned, not fully understanding the definition of "rapacious."

"How much are we getting paid?" he asked again.

"You'll have to take that up with the sheriff."

"I'm taking it up with you."

"Listen, I really don't have the patience for this. Get your ass out of this trailer and see if you can put some mother-effing lights on, or I'm coming in there on suspicion of illegal narcotics. Namely, the skunkiest weed this side of Pepe Le Pew."

Frank's eyes turned flat and cold.

"You wait right there," he said. He shut the door in her face.

"Get the tools, Mike," he said. He grabbed his Dickies jacket off the back of the couch, slipped into it. A nickel-plated .45 rested on the floor beside the can of Four Loko. Frank tucked it into the back of his pants.

After a long wait, the door opened again. Frank and Mike came out, carrying a tool box and handheld electric lanterns.

"Well, let's fucking do it, then," Frank said to Helen, stalking off down Main Street.

Helen trailed along behind. "Where are

we going?" she asked.

"Transformer," Mike said.

"Transformer?"

"If there's no electricity, first place to check is the transformer," Mike said.

"Listen," Frank said. "We know what we're doing. Don't you worry your pretty little head about it. You just follow along and try to look sexy."

Helen considered and discarded a number of responses. Right now, she badly wanted to get the electricity working. Enduring Frank's bullshit was a small price to pay.

After five minutes or so, Frank and Mike halted at a wooden pole on the edge of the sidewalk, a few buildings down and across the street from the Trading Post. Mike directed his lantern to the top of the pole, where a large metal cylinder sat beneath a crossbar, sprouting a network of cables.

"Go ahead," Frank said to Mike.

"You go ahead."

"Rock, paper, scissors."

Helen rolled her eyes while the two men pumped their fists. Frank chose scissors. Mike went with paper.

"You lose," Frank said.

"Two out of three?"

"Mike," Helen said. "Get up there and take a look. Now, please."

Mike tipped his hat. "Yes, ma'am!" He turned to Frank. "Gimmie a boost."

Frank interlocked his fingers, made a sling, spread his legs wide, and bent his knees. As he did so, his jacket rode up, exposing the .45 in his pants.

Mike put his foot in Frank's hands and stepped off the ground, holding onto the pole for support. He reached up and grasped an iron rung, pulled himself upward. He climbed quickly and nimbly. At the top, he used the lantern to inspect the metal cylinder and its components. He fiddled around a bit, clambered back down, and took a moment to catch his breath.

"What's the story?" Frank asked.

"Smashed bushing. Wires yanked out."

"No shit," Frank remarked.

"What's a bushing?" Helen said.

"It's a little doohickey that allows you to run an electrical wire through the wall of the transformer," Mike said.

"What's so special about it?"

"You don't know much about electricity, do you, Marshal?" Frank said.

"No. That's what guys like you get paid the big bucks for, Frank."

"It's insulated," Mike said. "Without the bushing, the transformer will short out. Maybe explode."

"Can you fix it?"

"Possible," Mike said. "We'd need to rig up a new bushing, with insulation, then re-run the wires."

"Okay," Helen said impatiently. "How do you do that?"

Frank and Mike had a short conversation that was rather technical, except they seemed unfamiliar with electrical jargon — there were a lot of "thingies" and "whatchamacallits" tossed around. Finally, Mike turned to Helen.

"We can make a temporary bushing with some aluminum foil and wax paper and oil."

"Do you have the equipment you need?"

"Yeah, all except the foil, paper, and oil," Frank said.

"Hilarious," Helen said.

Mike grinned his yellow grin. "We can probably find all that stuff at the Trading Post."

"How do you think this happened?" Helen nodded up at the transformer.

Mike slipped his hands into his coat pockets. "Don't look natural. Bushings are pretty sturdy. They don't just shatter for no reason. If I had to guess, I'd say someone took a wrench or something heavy to it."

A rash of goose bumps broke out along Helen's arms.

185

"Anyway, we can see about fixing this tomorrow," Frank said.

"I'd rather get it done now," Helen said.

Frank rolled his eyes. "The Pattersons are kinda old. They might be in bed already."

"This early?" Helen scoffed. "I doubt it. Aluminum foil, wax paper, and oil. Like motor oil?"

"That would do it," Mike said.

"Okay. You boys head on back to your trailer. I'll get the stuff and come find you in a bit."

"We'll just go get it ourselves, since you're in such a goddamn hurry," Frank said.

"I'd rather you stayed put. I don't want anyone running around that doesn't need to be right now."

"What are we, prisoners in our own home?"

"There's been a murder, and now it looks like someone's tampered with the electricity. This whole town is pretty much a crime scene."

Frank snorted. "This ain't no North Korea, *Marshal.* It's America. You can't tell us what to do."

"You got a CCW for that gun in your pants, Frank?"

"Huh?"

"You heard me. 'Cause if you don't,

186

you're in violation of California penal codes governing the carrying of concealed weapons. That's punishable by up to a year in county jail."

"Don't be a bitch, lady."

Helen transferred her flashlight to her left hand. She drew her Glock.

"Call me a bitch again and I'll shoot your dick off. I know it's a small target, but I'm a crack shot."

"Fuck off. You can't just shoot me."

"We're in the middle of the woods, Frank. You've got a gun in your pants. Who's to say what happened? Who's to say you didn't draw on me?"

"Mike's my witness."

"When I take out jerkoffs like you, I don't typically leave witnesses. That would be sloppy."

Mike's jaw dropped. Frank stared at Helen for a moment, then laughed.

"Don't get your tits in a wringer. We'll wait at the trailer."

"Give me the gun first. I'll hang on to it for now."

She slipped the flashlight into her pocket, held out her hand.

"Fucking bullshit," Frank said.

Helen waited.

Frank glared at her long enough to demonstrate he wasn't intimidated. Then he reached around, tugged the .45 from his waistband, and slapped it into her palm.

Yates watched from his front porch, fifty yards down Main Street, hidden in darkness. He was smoking one of his hand-rolled cigarettes and drinking a Schaefer beer. It was his eleventh can of the day.

Yates didn't sleep much — he usually woke up before dawn and had his first beer with breakfast. After that he spaced them out, one an hour or so. When he got to digging, he took a six-pack down with him, and worked till the six-pack was done. Some nights that took four hours, others, less than two. This evening, he'd climbed down into the mine after dinner, chipped away for a while, but just wasn't feeling it. It was too goddamn cold and his arthritis made it difficult to hold the drift pick.

He'd come back topside, only to discover the lights were off. That didn't trouble him much. He didn't watch TV or read before bed. And it wasn't the first time the electricity went on the fritz. But rather than sit in his kitchen, drinking by candlelight, he'd come outside to finish the remaining beers. And he'd observed silently, from the shadows, as the marshal walked down to Frank and Mike's trailer, then as the three of them made their way back up Main Street to have a look at the transformer.

Yates swallowed the rest of the beer, crushed the can, dropped it onto the floorboards of the porch. He picked up another can, the last of the six-pack, popped the tab.

He bristled at the exchange between Frank and the marshal. What in hell would induce Frank to give her his gun? She certainly had no right to be coming up here and disarming folks. Typical federal bully.

Yates, in addition to being a strong advocate for the Second Amendment, was a card-carrying member of the John Birch Society. He, like many other JBSers, believed in a global conspiracy of the rich and powerful to take away individual property rights and usher in a socialist New World Order. He also suspected the federal government was plotting to disarm recalcitrant citizens and place them in concentration camps run by the Federal Emergency Management Agency.

He took a drag on his cigarette, sucked the smoke deeply into his lungs. It occurred to him that the lady's story about coming to Kill Devil Falls to pick up Rita Crawford could be a load of crap. Maybe some shit-eating Sacramento state congressman in the pocket of the NWO had gotten wind of the mine and the marshal's real mission was to do some reconnaissance. Lay the groundwork for claiming the mine as a federal asset. Just when he was on the verge of finding the gold that had eluded him all his life. Eluded his father, too.

Well, the lady was going to find him a whole heap harder to intimidate than Frank. No way he'd just roll over like that. She wasn't taking his guns, and for damn sure she wasn't taking his gold mine. Not without a fight, anyway. Not without a goddamn fight.

Helen marched briskly to the Trading Post.

Humbling Frank like that had been a risky move, but a necessary one. She was all alone up here. Establishing authority was a must. Otherwise, she was like a zookeeper locked in the gorilla habitat, equipped only with a squirt gun.

The moon cast an anemic light over Main Street and its double row of abandoned storefronts. The temperature continued to drop. Helen zipped her coat up to her chin. Frank's .45 was tucked into her left coat pocket, the handle protruding slightly.

She stopped in her tracks when she heard a strange noise. Halfway between a snarl and a strangled cry. Her scalp tingled. Was that what a mountain lion sounded like?

She pictured an undead Franklin Stoppard watching her from a darkened window, his skin blistered and blackened, his nose and lips blown off, revealing white bone and rotten teeth.

Jesus, Mary, and Joseph. This shit-town was getting to her. She kept moving.

So, according to Mike, the transformer was purposely sabotaged. The work of Rita's killer? If so, why not just get out of town after the murder? Did he think it would be safer to make his escape under the cover of darkness?

Or was he still skulking about, looking to complete some unfinished business?

And why smash the bushing? That seemed messy. Why not just cut the wires with the same knife used to kill Rita? Unless he'd ditched the knife in the woods. Or tossed it in a car trunk?

She still didn't buy Lawrence as the murderer. Ten to one, it was Lee Larimer.

Helen reached the Trading Post and tried the front door. Locked. She knocked and waited sixty seconds. No answer. She stepped back into the street and looked up at the windows of the second floor. There was no electricity, but she was hoping to see at least the flicker of candles indicating the Pattersons were still awake. No such luck. The windows were black squares.

She walked down a narrow alley between the Trading Post and its neighboring building. Rounding the back corner, she found a small, grassy back yard, and beyond that, the edge of the forest. She swept her flashlight across the tree line. If Rita's killer was still in town, he could be hiding a mere ten yards away and she would never see him.

Helen went to the back door, tried the doorknob. Locked. She knocked.

"Mrs. Patterson? Mr. Patterson? It's Deputy Marshal Morrissey."

She listened, but there was no response. Maybe they *were* asleep. She didn't want to wake them. But she really needed the stuff for the doohickey.

After a moment's hesitation, Helen got down on her knees and examined the door panel. The lock was a standard Kwikset, nothing unusual or complicated. Easy enough to pick. Doing so was, strictly speaking, breaking and entering, but she decided to worry about that later.

She removed a key ring from her coat pocket. In addition to keys, the ring held a basic lock-pick set in a foldable frame, similar to a Swiss army knife. She worked a medium hook in the lock tumbler. It took her two minutes to spring it. She opened the door and entered the vestibule.

"Hello?" she called out, shutting the door behind her. "It's Deputy Marshal Morrissey!"

Still no answer. She opened the door leading to the back of the restaurant, poked her head through. It was empty. She turned, glanced up at the stairs. She assumed the Pattersons' bedroom was on the second floor, as Jesse had fallen down those steps after his nap. It just seemed ridiculous to wake them up for some foil and paper — better to take the things she needed and settle up later.

Helen passed through the restaurant and into the market. She scanned the aisles with her flashlight, located a box of wax paper and aluminum foil on a shelf next to cheap pie tins and tupperware. There was no motor oil, but she discovered a can of WD40, took that. She scouted around, found a package of small paper bags. She opened the package, removed a bag, put the wax paper, foil, and oil can inside, and folded down the top. She left the market, went back through the restaurant, and slipped into the vestibule.

Helen was about to sneak quietly out the

door when she heard a thump and a groan from above. She paused, listened. A moment's silence, then a yelp. Sounded like someone in pain.

She set the paper bag on the floor and went to the foot of the stairs. Could be nothing. The house settling. Jesse Patterson rolling over in bed, moaning over his injuries. Or maybe . . . maybe it was something else.

Helen tiptoed up the stairs, hoping she wasn't about to walk in on Mr. and Mrs. Patterson having kinky sex. A vision of Mrs. Patterson in leather riding a handcuffed, ball-gagged Mr. Patterson popped unbidden and unwanted into her mind.

On the second floor was a hallway with doors to either side. The door to her immediate right was closed. Another, halfway down the hall on the left, was open. Light flickered within. Helen crept forward.

"Hello?" she said, at a half-whisper.

She leaned in for a quick glance through the open doorway. It took her a moment to process the bizarre scene within.

Thick white candles on tall stands bathed the room in a soft glow.

A low table along the right wall was devoted to Mrs. Patterson's eclectic jewelry collection. Earrings were piled in a huge stone bowl. Rings were heaped in a square chest with a red velvet interior. A sturdy metal necklace stand literally drooped under the weight of dozens of necklaces, thickly clustered with charms, crystals, and gewgaws. A variety of small jewelry-making tools sat atop the table — tiny needle-nose pliers, an awl, scissors, a metal hole punch.

Along the opposite wall were racks holding a dozen glass terrariums. A heat lamp was clipped to the top of each terrarium. Minus electricity, the lamps were dark.

But what really drew Helen's attention was a plaster statue at the back of the room, positioned beneath a wooden arbor, the kind you might buy at a gardening store. The statue was about four feet tall and depicted a woman in a flounced skirt and tight bodice that covered her torso from the waist up, but left her breasts exposed. A tall crown sat atop her head. Her arms were raised, bent at ninety degree angles, each hand grasping a snake that was displayed in a zigzag posture, like a bolt of lightning. She wore another snake around her waist like a belt. Two more snakes drooped over her shoulders and encircled her breasts, each of them enclosing a nipple in their fangs. The statue was painted with bright, garish colors — red, blue, gold.

Offerings were placed at the statue's feet. Bowls of fruit and flowers. A bottle of whiskey. What appeared to be a large phallus carved of stone.

Helen stepped into the room, shined her light on the terrariums. She saw long, sleek bodies inside. Snakes. Some were small, the width of a finger. Others, thicker than a man's forearm. Helen didn't know much about snakes. Which were harmless. Which could kill you with a single bite. She wasn't particularly frightened or disgusted by them, though, like some people. Just the same, she was glad they were on one side of the glass and she was on the other. Although the radiator was turned up full blast, she figured they must be cold minus the heat lamps.

The floor in front of her rippled. Helen took a step back, directed her flashlight downward. She saw long, tubular black-and-white splotches. Turds. And slithering among them, snakes.

She scanned the floorboards quickly. Half a dozen of the snakes were loose, a couple on the move, others corkscrewed into tight little spirals.

Helen heard a muffled bang. She whirled to face the doorway on the opposite side of the hall. Another bedroom? A bathroom?

Dear God, don't let it be Mr. Patterson suffering a bout of constipation.

Helen crossed the hall, listened at the door. Nothing. She knocked lightly. "Hello?"

Another bang. A thump.

Helen drew her Glock, turned the knob, pushed open the door.

The room smelled like a cheap plastic shower curtain, piss, and sweat. She raised her flashlight, took in the porcelain sink, toilet, tub. A man in the tub. Blood splatter on his face, a cloth stuffed into his mouth.

"Jesus Christ," Helen said. She rushed to the man's side, set the flashlight down on the edge of the tub. It was Jesse Patterson, his eyes swollen, a sliver of white showing through a nasty gash across his eyebrow. She pulled a saliva-soaked wash cloth from his mouth.

"What happened?" she said.

He coughed, tried to speak. His eyes looked past her, over her shoulder. She saw the fear in them. A dog anticipating a clout from his master's shoe.

Helen turned. The bathroom door swung shut, revealing a man standing in the corner. *Stupid,* she thought. *You are so, so stupid.*

It was too dark to make out his features,

but she saw all too clearly the barrel of the enormous gun pointed at her face.

10

Helen couldn't pry her eyes away from the giant round hole at the end of the revolver. It was as large as a dinner plate. A subway tunnel. It was sucking her in, like an ocean vortex.

She raised the Glock. The man reached out and struck it from her fingers, effortlessly. One minute it was there, the next it spun away, landed in the tub on top of Jesse.

Helen froze, her brain experiencing an overload, a synaptic blowout. The one conscious thought running through her mind was *I'm going to die.*

Reflex circumvented her gray matter, hijacked her body. She watched with surreal detachment as her left hand slapped the man's gun to one side, her right catching his wrist, bending the revolver back toward his chest, twisting counterclockwise. The man cried out and the revolver joined the Glock in the tub.

The intruder wrenched his hand free, shoved Helen into the edge of the sink. He swung a fist. She ducked, felt the edge of his knuckles skim the top of her head. The mirror in the medicine cabinet shattered.

Helen lunged, driving a shoulder into the man's solar plexus. They both careened into a wall. The man bent over, wrapped his arms over her back and around her waist, levered her off the ground, threw her into the tub on top of Jesse. Helen scrambled for the Glock, Jesse flailing beneath her. The intruder reached out, grasped the front of her coat, tossed her sideways through the air. She hit the bathroom door, heard a crack as the cheap wood splintered. The man lifted a foot, kicked her. Helen managed to turn and block the brunt of the blow with her arm, but the force of the kick smashed her straight through the door, particles of wood flying across the hall. She plopped onto the floor.

She rolled to her elbows and knees, scrambled to her feet, sprinted for the stairs.

The intruder snatched a glass candleholder from a shelf above the sink, stepped out of the bathroom, hurled it. It struck Helen in the back of her head. She stumbled, danced on chicken legs, tumbled down the stairs.

She came to a stop halfway to the first floor, sprawled on her back, head pointed down, feet up, like St. Peter inverted on the cross. She lay stunned, unable to move.

The intruder stepped around the bannister at the top of the stairs. He was breathing heavily. And he was carrying her Glock. She registered the military fatigues, the clipped, gray-speckled hair. Sgt. Fix-it.

Now, suddenly, she could see the mug shot resemblance. Same crooked nose. Same heavy brows, deep-set eyes. Lee Larimer. Of course.

She struggled to sit upright. Lee aimed the Glock at her face.

Helen patted her hip holster by reflex, even though she clearly saw her gun in Lee's hand. Shit. Unarmed, ass-backward. About to be murdered by her own service weapon.

Her left hand brushed something solid and heavy. In her pocket. Frank's .45. She tugged it out.

Lee squeezed the Glock's trigger.

Glock firearms had a reputation for safety, especially with regard to preventing accidental discharges. For that reason, most Glock enthusiasts kept a round in the chamber, eliminating the need to cock before firing.

Not Helen. She was never comfortable going about her daily business with a loaded and cocked gun. So when Lee squeezed the trigger, nothing happened. He lifted the Glock to his face, glared at it, furious at its obstinacy.

Helen transferred the .45 to her right hand, fumbled for the safety.

Lee racked the Glock's slide, aimed, and pulled the trigger in one motion. A flash of light, a roar of gunfire. Splinters of wood exploded from the stairs inches to the left of her temple.

Helen had never shot another human being. Never been in a gun fight.

As a kid, she'd been as obsessed with guns and cowboys as any boy. And one of her fondest memories was digging into old leatherette-bound Time Life encyclopedia sets her dad owned, especially the one about the Old West, which featured volumes on cowboys, Indians, and scouts. By far, her favorite was *The Gunfighters,* with its tales of Wyatt Earp, Bat Masterson, Billy the Kid. Among the revelations contained in the book was that the prototypical cinematic scene in which our hero and the bad guy meet at high noon for a quick-draw duel virtually never happened. More often, someone just walked into a bar and shot someone else in the back.

One of the few gunfighters who *had* fought such a duel was Wild Bill Hickok. By his own admission, he wasn't the quickest draw. Instead, he took his time. While his opponent got off two, three rounds, Wild Bill methodically drew, aimed, and fired a single bullet. The difference was, his opponent missed and Wild Bill didn't.

Ironically, despite his calm nerves and steady hand, Wild Bill met his end the same as most other gunslingers when a man with a grudge snuck up behind him during a poker game and put a round in the back of his skull.

Helen rolled as Lee fired again. She felt a tug at her left ear, knew the bullet had either creased it or blown a ragged hole through it.

Resisting the urge to shoot in a panic, she leveled the .45, exhaled, gently squeezed the trigger. The .45 kicked hard. The top of Lee's head exploded. He swayed, slowly tipped backward like a felled tree, and dropped onto the landing, coming to rest in a sitting position.

Helen lay still for a moment, gathered her wits. Her ears pealed like a church bell signaling mass.

After a moment, she scooted around, sat upright. She saw stars, felt sick, almost passed out.

She took a few deep breaths, and her vision cleared. She stood, still holding the .45, and leaned heavily on the railing as she descended the stairs. She felt a trickle down her neck, touched it, saw blood on her fingers. She wobbled on rubbery legs through the restaurant and into the market before remembering that Jesse Patterson was still upstairs. Badly in need of medical attention. She couldn't stomach the thought of retracing her steps. Best to roust the sheriff and Teddy, let them handle it.

Helen unlocked the front door from the inside, emerged into the cold night air. She staggered down the sidewalk, Frank's .45 still dangling from her hand.

After a seemingly endless walk, she passed Big Ed and Teddy's red farmhouse, its windows dark. Not much farther now. She wanted to vomit and curl up in the dirt for a long nap, but instead focused on putting one foot in front of the other.

The Explorer was back, parked beside her Charger outside the jailhouse, but Helen barely took note of the fact. When she reached the jail's wooden porch, she climbed halfway up the steps, then collapsed in a heap.

Helen came to, face against a thin, scratchy mattress. She groaned, lifted her head, took in the brick walls, the door constructed of iron slats. She was in Rita's cell, on the cot. A halogen lantern sat on the floor.

She touched the back of her head, felt gauze and tape. The room started spinning. She lay back down until it stabilized. Then she slowly sat up.

Next to the lantern on the floor was an open first aid kit. Helen riffled through the kit until she found some aspirin. She tore open the package with her teeth and dry-swallowed two pills.

She shivered, cold, and realized she wasn't wearing a shirt. Just her bra, a lacy lavender number with a little bow between the two breast cups. She wondered where her shirt was, who had undressed her, treated her head wound.

"Marshal?"

A whisper came out of the darkness.

"Hello?"

"It's me. Lawrence."

Of course. She mentally slapped her forehead with a palm. She rose from the mattress. Her shirt was on the floor, crusted with partially dried blood. Her coat was lying across the foot of the cot. She left the shirt where it was and gingerly slipped into her coat, wincing at the pain in her knotted muscles, the burn of fabric rubbing against her cuts and bruises. She picked up the lantern, walked out of her cell, peered through the iron slats of Lawrence's cell door.

"Are you okay, Lawrence?"

"Can you let me out?" Lawrence said. "Please?"

"Not just yet. Soon."

"I'm cold. My feet are going numb."

She remembered he was just wearing flip-flops.

"I'll see about getting you some socks and shoes."

"What happened? Are you hurt? There was a lot of commotion but nobody would tell me what's going on."

Helen pictured the dead man at the top of the stairs, the contents of his skull dripping down the wall. She didn't have the energy to explain.

"It's a long story. For now, sit tight, okay?"

She was heading for the door to return to the Trading Post when it suddenly banged open. Teddy entered, supporting Jesse

Patterson with a hand around the old man's waist.

"Put him in there," Helen said. Together, they escorted Jesse into Rita's cell, laid him on the mattress. Jesse groaned.

"How are you doing, Mr. Patterson?" she said. He was a mess. Bruised, battered, bloody. A ragged cut in his eyebrow, swollen lips, a nasty hematoma bulging from his forehead.

"Tip-top!" Jesse snapped. "Aside from the fact that a crazy man just tried to beat me to death."

"Where's Mrs. Patterson?" Helen asked.

"Still upstairs at the Trading Post," Teddy said. "She's okay. My dad's there now. Said to bring Mr. P over here, see what I can do for him."

"You shouldn't have moved him," Helen said.

"My dad wanted to clear the scene," Teddy said.

"I'm fine," Jesse said. "I just need some aspirin. And a drink. Scotch would be good. And a little grass might help with the pain."

Helen looked quizzically at Teddy, but he was busy poking through the contents of the kit. Its assortment of Band-Aids and gauze seemed inadequate for the damage to Jesse's face.

"Did you bring me in from the porch?" she asked. "Patch me up?"

"Yes," he said. "Me and my dad, we heard you drop out there. When we found you, you was babbling, but after a minute, we got the picture." He was holding a bottle of peroxide in one hand, sterile pads in the other. "Holy gosh, I don't know where to start."

Jesse's teeth started chattering.

"Got any blankets?" Helen asked.

"At the house."

"That'll take too long. Lend me your flashlight."

Teddy slipped the flashlight out of the loop on his belt, handed it over. Helen left the cell, rounded the corner, entered the guard room. As before, Rita's corpse lay on the bed, still wrapped in the Indian blanket. Helen mouthed a silent apology to her, tugged at the blanket. It was glued to Rita's skin with dried blood. Rita's dead eyes watched as Helen gently peeled the blanket away.

She carried the blanket back into the cell, laid it over Jesse's legs and belly. Teddy recognized the blanket, glanced up at Helen with raised eyebrows. Helen shrugged. Teddy shrugged back, sponged blood off Jesse's face.

"How can I help?" she asked.

"Maybe just clean these cuts while I start on that eyebrow."

"Sure." She took a package of sterile pads, ripped it open. "Mr. Patterson, can you tell me what happened?"

Jesse snored.

"He's out," Helen said.

"Probably got a concussion."

The old man shifted, muttered under his breath.

"What's he saying?" she said.

"I don't know, can't make it out."

"Mr. Patterson, can you hear me?" she asked.

Jesse's eyes popped open. He spoke clearly.

"Where is it, you cunt?" he said.

His eyes closed and he resumed snoring.

Helen frowned at Teddy. "Did you hear that?"

"Sure did. Like I said, he must be out of his head. Wake up now, Mr. P!"

"Let him sleep," Helen said. "That old wives' tale about keeping a concussion victim awake isn't true."

"Really?"

"From what I understand. But we should get him to a hospital."

"As soon as my dad's done at the Trading

Post, one of us will run him down to Donnersville in the Explorer. For now, let's do what we can."

Helen helped wipe the blood off Jesse's face while Teddy applied a butterfly bandage to his eyebrow. Then Teddy found ice packs in the first aid kit, popped them, laid one on Jesse's forehead, the other on his cheek. Helen pulled Jesse's collar aside to clean his neck — she saw a spherical purplish wound marking the skin.

"Is that a bite mark?" she asked.

Teddy shrugged. He pulled the blanket up to Jesse's chin, tucked it around his body.

"I don't think he's as bad as he looks, but let's keep him warm. Oh, here." Teddy pulled something from his coat pocket, handed it to her. It was a black shirt, orange stripes on the upper sleeves, a rectangle across the chest that read *Harley Davidson*, spelled out in glittering sequins, most of which had long ago fallen off. "After I bandaged you up, I stopped by the house and got you a clean shirt before I headed over to help my dad."

"Thanks." She removed her coat, turned her back to Teddy, slipped the shirt over her head. It fit almost perfectly, just a tad snug. She shrugged back into her coat.

"Don't tell me this shirt used to be yours

and you outgrew it," she said.

"Uh, no . . . Rita left it here. When she run off. I always thought she'd come back, you know? So I saved some of her stuff."

"Oh." Helen didn't know how she felt about wearing a dead woman's discarded T-shirt. But it was better than nothing. "I'm going to head over to the Trading Post."

"My dad said you should stay here."

"Did he, now?"

"You're part of the investigation. What with . . . the shooting."

"That's ridiculous."

"I'm just telling you what he said."

"Well, I want to have a look at the . . . the body. And we need to get your dad back here so you can run Mr. Patterson down to the hospital. Can I hang on to this flashlight for a bit?"

Teddy shrugged. She took that as a yes.

"Marshal," came Lawrence's voice.

"Right. Teddy . . . How long are we going to keep Lawrence in the cell?"

"Until my dad says he can come out."

"I'm pretty sure I just killed the guy who killed Rita."

"Lawrence is still a suspect, till my dad says otherwise."

Helen went to the door of Lawrence's cell. "Be patient, Lawrence. We'll have this cleared up as soon as possible."

"But it's dark in here. Marshal, I'm cold!"

Helen pushed the front door open and entered the night.

Helen walked along Main Street, giving wide berth to the sinkholes, feeling weak and jittery. She patted the holster on her belt. Empty. Last she'd seen the Glock, it was in Lee Larimer's hands.

Empty buildings to either side loomed menacingly, their derelict shells possible havens for more knife-wielding murderers, mutilated animals, cannibalistic mountain men.

Helen heard the crunch of boots on gravel, jerked her head around — but the street was clear. Just her nerves.

As she shuffled along the sidewalk, breath steaming, she listened to a cacophony of hoots and chitters, buzzes and croaks. Why were people always talking about going to the mountains to get away from it all? It was noisy as shit out here.

She reached the Trading Post, tried the front door. Locked again. She went down the alley, crossed the yard, entered through the back door.

The smell hit her immediately. Meat. Feces. She covered her nose and mouth with her hand.

"Sheriff?"

She moved around to the foot of the stairs, glanced upward.

Lee Larimer still sat slumped against the wall on the landing. Someone, presumably Big Ed, had covered him with a tarp. Larimer's muddy shoes protruded from the tarp's bottom.

Helen began to shiver violently. An adrenaline rush. The cold, hard realization she'd killed another human being. She closed her eyes, tried to picture sunny green meadows, frolicking lambs, kittens in Easter bonnets.

Rat kings and spider-dachshunds invaded her thoughts.

She shook the images from her head and ascended the stairs, using Teddy's flashlight to ensure she wasn't stepping on anything of importance — a spent shell casing from Frank's gun, some other piece of evidence. She reached for the tarp.

"I wouldn't do that!" a voice barked.

Helen flicked the flashlight upward. Big Ed was standing on the second floor, staring down at her.

"You shouldn't sneak up on people," Helen said.

"You shouldn't be doing what you're doing."

"What's that?"

"Tampering with a crime scene," Big Ed said. "I thought I told Teddy to tell *you* to stay put at the jail."

"You did. But I don't work for you, Sheriff."

"No. But I will put in my report that I caught you here fussing with the body."

Helen kept her cool. "Mr. Patterson needs to be looked at by a doctor. As soon as possible."

"Well, I needed to deal with things here first."

Big Ed came around the bannister. He was carrying the second halogen lantern, which he now switched on, and a cloth-wrapped bundle.

Helen switched off the flashlight she'd borrowed from Teddy and put it in her pocket. "Why are you skulking up there in the dark?"

He motioned her down the stairs. She turned and descended. He followed.

"I was with Alice when I heard a noise. So I turned the light off and came out real quiet. Two deaths in one night. Makes a man cautious. Hold on!"

Big Ed stopped two-thirds of the way down the stairs, sat on a step, set the lantern and bundle down. He took a knife from a sheath on his belt, folded the blade out.

"This is one of his, I assume?" He touched a splintered hole in a stair step with the tip of the knife. "How many shots he fire?"

"I don't know. Two, I think."

"And you? How many?"

"Just one."

Big Ed folded up the knife and slid it back into its sheath. He removed a pen from his pocket and circled the bullet holes. "Tell me what happened."

"I came in here to grab some things Frank and Mike need to repair the transformer." Helen elected to omit the part about picking the door lock.

"And who asked you to tell Frank and Mike to look at the transformer?"

"No one."

"You were supposed to stay at the jail."

"I had a crazy idea it might be nice to have some fricking lights!"

Big Ed sighed. "That your bag down there on the floor?" He pointed to the paper bag at the foot of the stairs.

"Yes."

"Okay. Continue."

"I heard a sound upstairs. Like someone in pain. I went to the second floor. It was coming from the bathroom. I opened the door, saw Mr. Patterson. When I went in to help him . . . he popped out from the corner." She nodded at Lee. "Carrying this enormous horse gun. We fought. Both of us lost our guns. I ran out here. He must have thrown something at the back of my head." She touched the bandage. "I fell down the stairs. He had my Glock, shot at me. I shot at him."

"With what? That .45 you dropped on the jail house porch?"

"Yes."

Big Ed got to his feet, lifted the lantern and bundle. "Well, looks like you were the better marksman. Good work."

Helen nodded. It didn't feel right, being congratulated for killing a person.

Big Ed said something, but she couldn't catch the words. Her eyesight dimmed, shrank to a pinhole. She felt herself falling.

Next thing she knew, she was sitting at one of the restaurant tables, head down on her forearms.

"What happened?"

"You passed out."

"God. Sorry."

"Nothing to be sorry for. You took a wallop to the head. Surprised you're able to stand at all."

Big Ed's lantern was resting on the counter, along with the cloth-wrapped bundle.

He bustled around the kitchen area. After a moment, he came out carrying two mugs, set one in front of Helen.

"Drink."

She lifted the mug, sniffed. Coffee. She swallowed a mouthful.

"Christ on a coat hanger. That's good."

Big Ed smiled his crooked smile.

"It's just instant, is all. With no electricity, all I could do was boil a pot of water."

"Well, I don't think I've ever tasted better." Helen sipped, grateful for the warmth. "Frank and Mike said the transformer was sabotaged. The bushing was smashed. On purpose."

"No doubt by . . ." Big Ed jerked his chin toward the vestibule.

"Lee Larimer."

"Guess you were right, Marshal. About him and Rita. I suppose I owe you an apology."

Helen was touched. And he was right, he did owe her an apology. But she didn't want to rub it in.

"How's Mrs. Patterson?" she asked.

"Larimer had her tied up in the bedroom. She was in quite a state. Naked as a jay bird, for one. I cut her loose. She apparently twisted her ankle or something when Larimer got ahold of her, can't really walk. I gave her a couple of aspirin and a Valium, told her to sit tight for the time being. I don't want her to see the body, if that can be avoided. She's an old hippie, you know, into nature and tree spirits, all that crap."

"So why did Larimer break in here? Why assault Mr. Patterson?"

"No idea." Big Ed slurped from his mug, pulled out a Camel, lit it.

"Where's my Glock?"

"I have it. And Larimer's gun. Right there." He nodded at the bundle beside the lantern. "You always carry two guns, by the way?"

"The .45 is Frank's. I confiscated it from him."

"For what?"

"For being a dick."

Big Ed laughed. "Wouldn't think it to look at you, but you got some pair." He sucked in a lungful of smoke.

"Can I have the Glock back?"

"No. Larimer fired it, it's evidence."

"It's my service weapon."

"You shot a man with a gun that didn't belong to you. Meanwhile, a suspected killer fired yours. It's a bit of a mess. You see what I mean? For the moment, I'm going to secure all the weapons in my vehicle. And until the scene is processed, I don't want anyone, especially you, traipsing through here."

"What about Mrs. Patterson?"

"I'm going to let her rest in her own bed for now. After we get Jesse sorted out, I'll move her over to my place."

He tapped ashes on the melamine table, brushed them onto the floor with the heel of his hand.

"I saw him earlier today," Helen said. "When I stopped for a bite on the way up here."

"Larimer?"

Helen nodded. "I didn't recognize him at the time. The . . . the glasses and haircut."

"Uniform was a nice touch," Big Ed said.

"I'm ninety-nine percent sure he tampered with my car. At the diner. And maybe after I arrived in town, which is why I couldn't get it started and take Rita down to Donnersville right away."

"Why would he do a thing like that? I can understand messing with it once you got here, but why at the diner?"

"I guess he figured me for law enforcement."

"How? Did you flash your badge around? Tell people to stub out their funny cigarettes and get a haircut?"

"I don't know. Some criminals — they

have instincts. Or maybe he saw the cage in the Charger."

Big Ed tipped his mug to his mouth, wiped a trickle of coffee off his chin.

"In any case, Rita must have come here alone," Helen said. "Without Larimer. I mean, it makes no sense for him to drive up with her, then head down the mountain, only to turn around and drive right back up again."

"True."

"So he was following her. Pursuing her. But why did he free her from the jail only to kill her?"

Big Ed shrugged. "He might've figured, since she was caught, she'd testify against him. To get a reduced sentence."

"That was my thought, too. Although he could have just as easily taken her with him and left town."

"If they came up separately, like you said . . . maybe they had a falling out."

"So he killed her over a lovers' spat?"

"Who the hell knows why these types do what they do?" Big Ed said. "Half the time they're so hopped up on booze and drugs, they're no better'n animals. Oh . . . here."

He pulled a flashlight out of his pocket and set it on the table.

"This was lying on the bathroom floor. Yours?"

"Yes. Can I have it back?"

"As long as you didn't use it to kill anybody."

"Ha ha." She put the flashlight in her pocket. "Was Larimer carrying a knife?"

"No. That don't mean anything. He could have ditched it anywhere. And that's another thing. I'm still curious about the knife in Lawrence's trunk. You don't suppose he and Larimer knew each other? Were in it together, somehow?"

"Seems unlikely. Maybe Mrs. Patterson can shed some light on things?"

"How?"

"Perhaps she can tell us why Larimer broke in and beat the tar out of her husband."

"Mmm." Big Ed took a last drag from his cigarette. "No, I think we should let her rest for the time being. Plenty of time to talk to her later."

"But —" Helen's protest was interrupted by the sound of the back door slamming open. Teddy barged into the restaurant.

"It's Mr. P!" he gasped. "He ain't breathing!"

11

Teddy and Big Ed ran to the Old Log Jail, Helen trailing behind at a slower pace. By the time she got there, the sheriff was sitting on the cot next to Jesse, ear to the old man's chest. After a moment, he turned and glared at Teddy.

"What happened?"

"He just stopped breathing. I didn't do nothing!"

"I didn't do nothing!" Big Ed mimicked. He got up, kicked the brick wall of the cell.

Helen was feeling faint. She sat on the edge of the desk, caught her breath. "You should have put him in a car as soon as you found him in the bathroom," she said.

Big Ed didn't answer. He ran his hands through his hair, wiped them on his pants. He pulled out his cigarettes, lit one, exhaled twin jets of smoke from his nose.

"Where the hell is that backup, Edward? You called more than an hour ago."

"Dispatch said —"

"I know what dispatch said," Big Ed said. "Go out there and radio again. Tell them to get someone here, right fucking now."

"Yes, sir."

"Hold on." Big Ed handed Teddy the cloth bundle. "Put these in the SUV's gunbox. Make sure you don't touch them with your fingers. Got it?"

"Yes, sir."

Teddy rushed out the door. Big Ed clomped to and fro across the wooden floor. Helen went into the cell, covered Jesse's face with the Indian blanket. When she came out again, Lawrence whispered to her.

"Marshal!"

"Not now, Lawrence."

"Until we get some more deputies up here, I want you to stay right here in the jail, Marshal," Big Ed said. "I'm getting tired of tracking bodies all over town."

"What are you going to do?"

"Get some lights on, for starters."

Helen pulled her phone out of her coat pocket, checked the time. Jesus, it wasn't even midnight yet. She wanted a long soak in a hot tub, a warm meal, clean sheets. To not feel like a rat trapped in the bilge of a sinking ship.

"Sheriff," she whispered. "Why don't you

223

let Lawrence out of the cell?"

"Because, Marshal, as we discussed, I'm not sure of the facts yet," he answered. "And until I am, nobody goes anywhere. Everyone just stays put." He tossed his cigarette on the floor, picked up one of the halogen lanterns, pushed through the front door.

Helen followed him out onto the porch and down the steps, looking to continue the conversation.

Teddy was inside the open cab of the Explorer, radio microphone in his hand.

"Dispatch, come in. Dispatch, come in."

"What's the problem?" Big Ed said.

"I can't seem to raise them."

"Give me that, goddammit." He walked to the vehicle, roughly pulled Teddy from the cab, took the microphone from his hand.

"Dispatch, respond. This is Sheriff Scroggins. Dispatch respond."

Big Ed set the lantern on the seat, reached over and fiddled with some knobs.

"The hell?"

"What's going on, Sheriff?" Helen asked.

"Just a minute!"

He spent another few seconds messing with the receiver before hurling the microphone down onto the cab floor.

"Sonofabitch!"

"Sheriff?"

"It's not fucking working, Marshal. Edward, did you do something to it?"

"Radio was fine earlier. I don't know why it won't work now!"

Helen's heartbeat quickened. "Is there any other way to reach your dispatcher?" she said.

"Not unless we drive about thirty minutes down the road and pick up some cell reception," Teddy said. He turned to Big Ed. "What should we do?"

Big Ed puffed steam into the cold night air.

"*I'm* going to get that bag from the Trading Post and fix the lights so we can stop running around holding our dicks in the dark. You two" — he said, jabbing a finger at Helen and Teddy in turn — "are staying right here. Understand? If the other deputies arrive, you can fill them in on the situation, but don't none of you go anywhere. When I get back, I'll get everyone organized."

"Maybe one of us should take the Explorer and try to pick up a phone signal," Helen said.

"No," Big Ed said. "Between the three of us, this is the one working vehicle we got in town. It's not going anywhere. Just in case."

"In case of what?" Helen said.

Big Ed shrugged.

"How about my Glock?"

"How about it?"

"I want it back."

"Told you. It's evidence."

"Listen, Sheriff," Helen said. "You said yourself, we don't know all the facts yet. Have you considered the possibility that someone's been monkeying with your radio? Given all the weird shit that's been going on, I'm not going to sit around here armed with nothing more than my razor-sharp tongue. You want me to stay put? Fine. I want my gun back."

Big Ed glared.

"Pretty please," Helen said.

"No. You can't have the Glock. But I have something I can lend you."

He went around to the back of the Explorer and opened the lift gate. He spun the combination dial on a sizable metal gunbox on the floor of the rear compartment and removed a Taurus PT940 pistol. He shut the box, rotated the dial again.

"Here, this is my backup weapon." He handed her the gun, butt first. "I'll be back in thirty minutes."

Helen slipped the Taurus into her hip holster. Big Ed picked up the lantern, closed and locked the doors to the Explorer, trudged off down Main Street.

Inside the jail, Teddy brought the lantern out of Jesse's cell, placed it on the desk, and sank into the wooden chair. He took a wad of tobacco from the pouch in his pocket, stuffed it into his cheek.

"I don't think this night is ever gonna end, Marshal."

"I'm beginning to think you're right."

Lawrence stood at the door of his cell, one eye peeking through the iron slats.

"You can't keep me in here," he whined. "It's not right. It's not legal."

"Sheriff says you stay locked up," Teddy said.

"Marshal . . ." Lawrence pleaded.

"It ain't up to her," Teddy said.

Helen scowled at Teddy. He met her gaze for a few seconds, then leaned over and spit in the coffee can.

"I'll open the door, Lawrence," she said. "Give you some air, but you have to remain in the cell for now."

"Marshal —" Teddy mumbled.

"We can't hold him in there indefinitely," she snapped. "These cells aren't up to modern standards. Let's give him a little break."

She went to the wall, took the key ring off

the hook, unlocked the cell door, swung it open. Lawrence poked his head out, blinking rapidly like a coal miner emerging from a cave-in. Helen hung the key ring back on the hook.

"My dad is gonna get pissed when he sees that," Teddy said.

"Honestly, I don't care anymore," Helen said.

Teddy shrugged. He chomped tobacco for a bit, then asked, "So it was Larimer?"

"What about him?"

"You shot."

"Yes," Helen said.

"But why would he . . . ?" Teddy made a wet sound and drew a line across his throat.

Lawrence stood on the threshold of the cell, arms folded, shivering. "Does this mean I'm no longer a suspect?"

"No, it don't, Lawrence," Teddy said. "Not until we check out that knife in your car."

"Knife? In my car? What are you talking about?"

"The knife in your trunk. Like you don't know."

"What kind of knife?"

Teddy shrugged. "I don't know. A hunting knife."

"I don't hunt, Deputy."

"You got a thing for knives, though, don't you?"

"I use them for my work!" Lawrence said.

"Work?" Teddy said. "That what you call it?"

"If there *is* a knife in my car, you put it there!"

"Why would I do that?"

"To frame me!"

"Why would I want to frame you? You only been up here a few weeks, I barely know you!"

Their discussion dissolved into a shouting match.

"Boys!" Helen yelled. "Boys! Enough!"

Teddy, red-faced, spat into the coffee can. Lawrence spread his hands.

"I didn't put a knife in my trunk, Marshal. I just didn't."

"Okay, Lawrence," she said. "Take it easy."

Lawrence huffed, retreated into the darkness of his cell.

"Oh," Helen said. "Here." She handed Teddy back his flashlight.

He slipped it into the loop on his gun belt, rubbed his eyes. "Man, what a day."

Helen resumed her seat on the edge of the desk. "I need some hot chicken soup."

"And a beer," Teddy said.

"I could go for a beer," Lawrence chimed.

"Judging from your pantry, you could go for a beer, a jug of whiskey, maybe a bottle of mouthwash if things get desperate."

"Fuck you, Deputy!"

Teddy abruptly lurched to his feet, gripped his baton.

"What'd you say?"

"Sit down, Teddy," Helen said. "Sit down. That's enough."

"You heard that?"

"I heard it. You said something, he said something back. Now, sit down. Lawrence — don't speak to the deputy like that, understood?"

After a long moment, Lawrence's voice emerged from the cell: "Fine."

Teddy slowly sank back into the chair. "He's got some mouth."

Helen went to the window, peered out. She longed for the lights to come on again. She drew the Taurus from her holster, turned it over in her hands, ejected the magazine.

"Are you shitting me?"

"What?" Teddy asked.

"Your dad gave me an unloaded gun."

Teddy chuckled. "Always got a trick up his sleeve."

"You knew about this?"

Teddy held his palms up. "No! Don't look at me."

Helen fumed. The sheriff was becoming a real tyrant. Ordering her around. Leaving her defenseless. Restricting her to the jail.

Speaking of the jail, it was fast becoming a mini-morgue.

"Teddy?"

"Yeah?"

"I don't know about you, but I find it creepy to have Mr. Patterson's body lying right there in plain sight. Why don't we move him to the back room?"

"Okay. Sure."

Inside the cell, she and Teddy rolled Jesse's body over and slid the Indian blanket under it.

"You grab the corners by the head and I'll get the feet," Helen said.

"Wait a sec," Teddy said. "What about Lawrence? Who's to say he don't just run out while we carry Mr. P into the back?"

"I won't," Lawrence said, from next door.

"He won't," Helen echoed.

Teddy didn't look convinced. "Fine. Whatever you say, Marshal."

"Ready?" Helen said.

"Yes." They lifted Jesse. "Wait."

They set the body back down onto the mattress.

"What now, Teddy?"

"We need a light. It's dark back there."

"Right." Helen took the flashlight from her pocket, switched it on, put it in her mouth. "Okay?" she asked, voice garbled by the flashlight.

"Yeah."

They carried Jesse into the guard room, rested him on the floor beside the bed where Rita's corpse lay.

"Good enough," Teddy said, anxious to leave.

"I want to have a look at something real quick," Helen said. "Be there in a minute."

"Suit yourself." Teddy retreated to the front room.

On the surface, the events of the night appeared to be straightforward. Lee Larimer freed Rita from the jail, dragged her into the woods, killed her. He then sabotaged the transformer and broke into the Trading Post, where he attacked the Pattersons. But the how and why of it troubled Helen. How did he get into the jail? Why did he kill Rita? Why attack the Pattersons?

She was tired of playing catch up, bouncing from one predicament to another. And she didn't want to just sit around, waiting for a passel of country cops and a crime scene unit that might or might not arrive in

232

the morning.

Even though a corpse could not speak, it sometimes had secrets to tell.

Helen shined her flashlight across Rita's face, skin, hair, and scalp. Lots of dirt and dried blood. Rita's glassy eyes reminded Helen of the bucket of disembodied orbs in Lawrence's cellar.

She peeked down her collar, rolled her over. Rita's hands were still cuffed, wrists bent at awkward angles. Helen removed the key ring from her coat pocket, unlocked the cuffs, dropped them on the bed.

She took a close look at Rita's throat wound. It extended directly across the neck, right carotid artery to windpipe. The cut was moderately deep, with clean edges. Produced by a sharp blade. The one Teddy had found in Lawrence's car would fit the bill. As would any well-maintained kitchen knife. Even the fold-out knife Big Ed had used to dig at the bullet in the stairwell of the Trading Post.

Helen searched Rita's pockets. Empty. All of Rita's possessions were in the plastic bag on the passenger seat of the Dodge Charger.

Helen finished her examination without having gained any insights. She rose from the bed, turned to leave, but then paused. Might as well check out Jesse Patterson's body, too. She crouched down, shined a light on the old man's damaged face. His injuries were the result of three or four pounds of solid gunmetal against flesh and bone. Why the vicious beating? What was Jesse's connection to Rita and Lee Larimer?

Helen closed her eyes, mentally ran through scenarios:

Rita knows the heat is on. She ditches Larimer, flees to Kill Devil Falls.

But Kill Devil Falls is the one place where Rita was sure to be recognized by almost everyone, even after sixteen years away. She must have had some *reason* for coming here, other than seeking a place to hide out.

Okay. Rita heads to Kill Devil Falls with some plan in mind. But before she can complete it, she's discovered, placed in custody. Larimer follows. Fearing that she will testify against him, he springs her and kills her.

But then, afterwards, why doesn't he just leave?

Helen dug through Jesse's pockets. She examined his hands, his shoes, inside his shirt. That mark on his neck was bizarre. Two hemispheres, purplish punctured flesh, definitely looked like a bite. Was Larimer a biter? There were no similar bite marks on Rita's body. Weird.

She sat on the edge of the bed by Rita's feet. *Think.* Why did Larimer go to the trouble of dragging Rita into the woods instead of just killing her in the jail? Did he mean to take her with him, but she fought and *then* he killed her? Maybe.

Or maybe he was buying time. A few minutes with Rita, without the threat of being seen.

Yes. That made sense.

Helen left the guard room, closing the door behind her.

Teddy was sitting behind the desk, boots propped next to the lantern. Lawrence sat cross-legged in the doorway of his cell.

"What were you doing in there?" Teddy asked.

Helen opened the front door. "Just a sec."

"Where you going?"

She descended the porch steps, walked to the Charger. She opened the passenger's side door, retrieved the plastic bag from the car seat. She carried it back into the jail, shut the door, dumped the contents of the bag onto the desk.

Marlboro Reds; a cheap lighter; a gold ring; a gold crucifix on a chain; a Samsung cell phone; a pair of sunglasses; a watch; a small plastic flashlight; a roll of bills held together with a rubber band.

"This is what she had on her when you caught her?"

"That's right. You and I filled out the paperwork together."

Helen removed the rubber band from the roll of bills, fanned the cash.

"About eight hundred bucks," she said. "No more?"

"That's it."

Helen pushed the bills together into a stack, rolled them up, slid the rubber band around them again. She put everything back into the bag.

"Let's say you're Rita. If you're going to run out on your robber boyfriend, with whom you've stolen thousands of dollars, do you just grab a wad of eight hundred bucks before you head out the door?"

"Hell, no," Lawrence said. "You take it all."

"No one asked you," Teddy growled.

"He's absolutely right," Helen said. "You take it all. What have you got to lose?"

"Nothing, I guess," Teddy said.

"So where's the money, then?"

Teddy shrugged. "In her car?"

"I think Rita came up here to hide it," Helen said. "To stash it where she figured it would be safe. And she did just that. But

236

then got caught before she could get out of town."

"Maybe. Could be." Teddy scratched his beard. "So then, Larimer follows her —"

"He's after the money."

"Right." Teddy said. "And when he gets here and finds Rita locked up, he hauls her off into the woods to smack the location of the money out of her!" Teddy popped up from his chair, bobbed with excitement. "Then he kills her and cuts the electricity so he can grab the money under cover of darkness."

"A logical scenario," Helen said. "Except that Rita wasn't beaten before she was murdered."

"Okay," Teddy said. "Maybe Larimer still had a soft spot for her and couldn't bring himself to hit her. Or maybe she told him right away, so he didn't have to."

Lawrence chimed in. "If she told him where the money was, why didn't Larimer just go get it? Why'd he make a detour to beat on Mr. Patterson?"

"Shut up, Lawrence," Teddy said. "This is official police business."

"He's right again," Helen said. "I have the exact same question."

"Well . . ." Teddy shrugged.

"Do you think . . ." Helen started. "Is

there any way Mr. Patterson might have known Rita and Lee Larimer? Any possible connection?"

Teddy snorted. "No way. Not that I can think of, anyway. I mean . . . far as we know, Rita ain't never been back since she left sixteen years ago. And Larimer . . . well, don't think he's ever been to Kill Devil Falls before today."

"There's obviously something linking them," Helen said.

"I don't believe so, Marshal. Can't see how that's possible."

"One way to find out. Let's go ask Mrs. Patterson."

Teddy sighed. "My dad told us to stay here."

"Aren't you getting sick of not knowing what the hell is going on? Don't you want some answers?"

"I doubt Mrs. P has any answers for you, Marshal."

"Worth a try," Helen said.

"I really wish you wouldn't."

"I'm doing it anyway."

Teddy spat in the can, wiped a dribble off his beard. He drummed his fingers on the desk.

"If you're going, I need to go, too."

"Why? To keep watch over me?"

"If my dad catches us running around, I'll catch hell. But it'll be lots worse if he finds out I let you go alone."

"My goal isn't to get you in trouble, Teddy."

"It's gonna happen anyway." He pushed himself up from his chair. "I'm gonna insist, if we ain't here to watch him, we lock Lawrence in the cell."

Helen looked at Lawrence. Back at Teddy. Teddy was not going to budge on this one. "Okay."

"No, no way!" Lawrence protested.

"I'm sorry, Lawrence. We won't be long," Helen said.

"You're gonna leave me here with two dead bodies?"

"Easy, Lawrence."

"No!"

"Take a deep breath."

"No fucking way!"

"Tell you what." This was a horrible idea, but Lawrence appeared on the verge of completely losing it. "You wanted a drink, right? We'll get you one. Something to calm your nerves."

The fear in Lawrence's face shifted to something else. A lean, predatory look.

"Can you get . . . can you get some Wild Turkey?"

Helen turned to Teddy. "Teddy . . . Could you grab a bottle from your house?"

"Are you serious?"

"Yes. Please."

"We don't got no Wild Turkey."

"Whatever you have is fine," Lawrence said quickly.

"Marshal . . ." Teddy said.

"Please, Teddy," she said.

"Good lord!" Teddy drew the flashlight from his belt, opened the front door, slammed it behind him.

"Go sit on the cot, Lawrence."

"Don't lock me in! Not until I get that bottle."

"I won't. Promise."

Lawrence went into the cell and sat down, the springs on his cot squeaking.

"And don't leave me in the dark. Let me keep the lamp."

"Deal. But it has to stay outside the cell."

Helen moved the lantern to the floor in front of the cell door. After a long wait, Teddy returned, his fingers curled around the neck of a Jack Daniel's bottle. He brusquely handed it to Helen.

"Here."

"Thanks."

She gave the bottle to Lawrence. "Let me get you a cup."

"I don't need a cup," he said, hugging the bottle to his chest.

"All right."

She took the key from the wall, closed the cell door, locked it. She hung the key back on its hook.

"Lawrence wants us to leave him the lantern," she told Teddy.

"We're supposed to walk around town with just our flashlights?"

"Pretty much."

Helen picked up the plastic bag with Rita's belongings and they went out onto the porch. Teddy locked the jail door, snapped the key back onto his gun belt.

"Think you could open up the lockbox in the Explorer?" Helen said. "I'd really like to get some ammo for this gun."

"Sorry, Marshal. If my dad wanted you to have the ammo, he'd have given it to you."

"Come on, Teddy. What's the use of having a gun if you don't have any bullets?"

Teddy shrugged.

"Teddy . . ."

"Don't worry, Marshal." Teddy patted his revolver. "I got you covered."

"Great," Helen said through clenched teeth.

She returned the bag to the passenger seat of the Charger. She tossed her cell phone

241

on the seat next to it. The phone was of no use up here. She and Teddy set off down Main Street.

The jingling of Teddy's keys was beginning to wear on Helen's nerves. She fumed silently about his refusal to let her load the Taurus during the long, cold walk to the Trading Post. When they reached the entrance, she flashed her light across the street, up and down the length of the transformer pole.

"Wasn't your dad supposed to be working on the electricity?"

"Yeah."

"I don't see him. Or Frank or Mike."

"Maybe they finished."

"If they were done, Teddy, the lights would be on."

"Well . . . got me."

Helen tried the front door of the Trading Post. As before, locked.

"I'm going to go in through the back. Why don't you wait here while I talk to Mrs. Patterson — see if your dad or Frank and Mike show up?"

Teddy tugged at his chin. "We should stick together."

"Suit yourself. Hope you like dead bodies. Lee Larimer's sitting right at the top of the stairs, reeking like a county fair porta-potty after a chili cook-off."

"Ugh."

"Just warning you."

"I'll wait here. Be quick."

"Will do."

Helen trotted down the alley, around to the back door. She slipped inside the vestibule. As she started up the stairs, her foot brushed across an object on the floor. It was the paper bag, filled with the items for the bushing. The sheriff hadn't even come by to collect it. What was he doing if not fixing the lights?

Helen climbed the stairs, skirted Larimer, stood at the end of the hall. Candlelight glowed from the open doorway of Mrs. Patterson's room on the left. Broken bits of bathroom door still littered the floor. Helen knocked lightly on the closed door to her right.

"Mrs. Patterson?" She opened the door.

A shapeless lump lay on a sagging brass bed. Candles flickered.

Helen tiptoed over to the bed. Mrs. Patterson was tangled in the coverlet, dressed in a white gown. She snored softly. A line of drool trailed from the corner of her mouth.

"Mrs. Patterson?"

No reaction. Just snoring. Helen saw a nearly empty glass of wine and pill bottle on the nightstand. She picked up the bottle, read the label. Valium, as the sheriff had mentioned.

She set the bottle down, leaned over, pressed two fingers against Mrs. Patterson's neck. She felt a strong, rapid pulse. The old gal was out cold but seemed to be fine.

She jiggled Mrs. Patterson's shoulder. No response.

"Mrs. Patterson?"

It was useless. Short of having a bucket of cold water dumped on her face, Mrs. Patterson wasn't going to be answering any questions for quite some time.

Helen left the bedroom, shut the door behind her. She navigated around Lee's body, back down the stairs. She passed through the restaurant and market, unlocked the front door, exited onto the sidewalk.

"How is she?" Teddy asked.

"Sound asleep. But listen — I found the bag of stuff I collected for the transformer. I don't think your dad bothered to come by here at all."

"That's strange. Where is he, then?"

"Let's go ask Frank and Mike if he stopped by."

Teddy bit his lip. "I think we should get back to the jail."

"Aren't you worried? What if something happened to him?"

Teddy hitched his gun belt. "All right, Marshal. Let's talk to Frank and Mike."

As soon as Helen left, Alice Patterson sat up and wiped the drool from her chin. She'd been fully conscious the whole time the marshal was poking and prodding her. Just didn't feel like talking.

She picked up the bottle of Valium, tapped two tablets into her palm. Her hands still trembled. She'd lived anything but a sheltered existence, but Lee Larimer's attack was by far the most terrifying experience of her life. She upended the tablets into her mouth, washed them down with the dregs of her wine.

She opened the bedroom door, checked to make sure the coast was clear. She couldn't help but glance at the landing where Lee Larimer's body sat, head covered with a tarp, blood and brain matter crusted against the wall. Goddess, what an ordeal. The house was ruined now. Tainted.

She made her way down the hall, poked her head into the second bedroom.

"I'm sorry, my loves," she told the snakes on the floor. "Give me just a moment and I'll have you back in your homes."

Alice shut the bedroom door and continued on to the kitchen. She peered out the front window, just in time to see Helen and Teddy walk off down Main Street.

She should have considered the possibility that Larimer would know where to find Rita and come after her. But she hadn't, and now it was chaos out there. Big Ed, Teddy, and the marshal scurrying like rodents around in the dark; Frank and Mike unsupervised, like a couple of dogs who'd dug their way out of the kennel and were too dumb to stay off the highway; Jesse pistol-whipped and carted away.

She was troubled that it was Helen and not Teddy who'd come to see her. That meant one of two things. Either Teddy did not have sufficient control of the situation. Or he was winging it.

In Alice's opinion, Teddy was about as sharp as a marble. If he was putting himself in the driver's seat, it was only a matter of time before the bus went over a cliff.

As Helen and Teddy marched toward Frank and Mike's trailer, breath steaming in the cold, a suspicion began to take root in Helen's mind. She glanced at Teddy. He kept his eyes focused on the circle of light from his flashlight playing along the ground in front of his feet. He wasn't going to like it.

The generator outside the double-wide trailer chattered noisily and a bright light leaked through the window blinds. Teddy halted.

"Hey, give me a second with them, okay? Can you wait here?"

Given their last interaction, Helen assumed Frank would be less than pleased to see her.

"Okay," she said.

She stood with her hands in her pockets while Teddy walked over to the trailer, banged on the door. She heard him say, "It's Teddy." The door opened. Frank looked out, glared at Helen, down at Teddy. They had a quiet but intense conversation. Mike appeared in the doorway over Frank's shoulder. They spoke for a long while. Teddy hitched up his belt, looked back over his shoulder at Helen, then shook hands with Frank. Frank shut the door and Teddy trudged back.

"My dad didn't come by here," Teddy said.

"It took you five minutes of discussion to find that out?"

"They wanted to know what was going on."

"Did you tell them?"

"Not much. Just enough to convince them to stay in the trailer for now."

"So where do you think he is, Teddy? Big Ed?"

"No idea. I hope nothing bad . . ." His voice trailed off.

Helen took a deep breath. This was going to be tricky.

"Teddy, let's think about this. Right now, we've got two suspects for Rita's murder. Lawrence and Lee Larimer."

"Yeah. And you don't believe Lawrence did it."

"No, I don't."

"What about the knife in his car?"

"Until we get forensics to test it, we don't know anything about the knife."

"He says it ain't his. That's kinda suspicious, right?"

"Yes, it is. But what if . . . whoever killed Rita planted it there? As a red herring."

This was met with silence.

"You know what a red herring is?" she asked.

"Yes, Marshal. I ain't stupid."

"I know you're not stupid, Teddy." She rubbed her hands together nervously. "I just don't think Lawrence had sufficient time or motive for killing Rita. And aside from the knife, we didn't find any evidence implicating him. So let's put him aside for a moment."

Teddy zipped up his jacket, shuffled his feet in a bid to stay warm.

"Now, if Lee Larimer was the killer, how would he know to plant the murder weapon in Lawrence's car?" Helen continued.

"Maybe he saw Lawrence leave the Trading Post before the rest of us and thought he could pin it on him," Teddy said

"Possible. That's a good thought. So how did he get into the jail when it was locked?"

Teddy shrugged. "Key's missing."

"Yeah, but it's unlikely either Lawrence or Larimer had any idea where to find the key."

"I don't know the answer, Marshal."

"Maybe it wasn't Lawrence," Helen said. "And it wasn't Larimer. Maybe it was someone else. Someone who was aware Rita was in town, had access to the jail key, knew Lawrence well enough to set him up as a potential suspect. Someone who wasn't present at the restaurant when the murder occurred."

"But we was all there, except for Lawrence, Larimer, and . . . uh . . ."

She let him process it.

"No," Teddy said. "No way."

"It fits the facts, doesn't it?"

"No!"

"Sure it does."

"I met him on the access road while you was searching in the woods. He was on his way back from Sardine Valley."

"He could have easily parked outside of town, snuck in, snatched Rita while we were gone, and headed back to his car to make it look like he was just then returning from the shooting call."

"It's just . . . that's crazy. Why? Why would he do it?"

"The money, Teddy. It's an almost perfect crime of opportunity. Rita is wanted for a string of bank robberies, right? When he hears Rita is in Kill Devil Falls, he figures she must be here to hide money. Why else come up here? But then it gets complicated. If Rita goes to jail, she'll get out eventually, and when she discovers the money is missing, she'll know who took it. She might tell the authorities. What's she got to lose? She's already done her time. But if she's dead . . . You know the saying. Dead men tell no tales. He can keep the money and no one will ever be the wiser."

"*Damn*, Marshal! That's my dad you're talking about."

"I know."

"The *sheriff,* for goodness' sake!"

"I know, Teddy."

Teddy shook his head, kicked at the pavement.

"I may be wrong," Helen said. "It's just a theory. But there's one way we can prove it."

"How's that?"

"Well, if it is the money he's after, he's probably trying to retrieve it right now, before reinforcements arrive. If we catch him doing that . . ."

Teddy turned away.

"Teddy," Helen said. "If you were Rita, where would you hide the money? Some place where no one would just randomly happen upon it. Where it's safe from fire, water, beetles and worms. Do you know a spot like that? One you think Rita might have used?"

Teddy puffed out his cheeks. "Yeah. I know a place. A place she used to go. And my dad knows it, too."

"Where?"

"The mine."

Near the edge of town, past the double-wide trailer, beyond Lawrence's house, pavement gave way to packed dirt. Straight ahead, Main Street quickly devolved to a narrow hiking trail and disappeared into the forest. Helen followed Teddy as he turned left, downhill, taking a narrow track, one riddled with potholes and pools of muddy water, crisscrossed with fallen tree limbs and partially blocked by growths of twisted, leafy vines that looked like creeping tentacles.

Eventually, they turned left again, emerged from a scatter of trees into a long, broad clearing with a granite-faced ridge to the left. To the right were more trees, gently descending to a valley hundreds of feet below.

"God, it's beautiful," Helen said. There were no lights in the valley, just a wide trench of velvety darkness, above which stars twinkled like diamond chips.

"Makes you feel pretty small, don't it?" Teddy said. "Like you're just a little speck in the universe. Like your life don't really mean much, one way or the other."

The bulk of an enormous wooden building dominated the clearing. Helen shined her flashlight on it. "What's that? A barn?"

"Stamp mill."

"What's a stamp mill?"

"In the old days, miners dug ore out of the mine, carted it up here, and dumped it on these conveyor belts inside the mill. The belts ran under huge posts with metal heads, called stamps. The stamps went up and down, crushed the ore to little bits, like a hammer smashing a walnut shell. After that, the bits were spread on a copper sheet coated with mercury. Gold sticks to mercury, you see? Miners would sift out the rock and other stuff they didn't want and collect the gold left behind. And that's why we got toxic soil up here. All the mercury they used."

"You know your stuff."

"Hard not to pick it up, growing up right next to the mill. Also, I did some mining myself before joining the sheriff's department. Not gold. Sand and gravel, mostly, for cement."

"So . . . we go inside the mill?"

Teddy shook his head. "Into the mine."

"I see. And once we're inside, do you know where Rita would have put the money?"

"Uh . . ." Teddy scratched his cheek. "Not really. I mean, I know she used to hide out in there, but I don't know the exact spot. I didn't go into the mine as a kid. Don't much care for tight spaces."

"Didn't you just say you used to be in mining before you became a sheriff's deputy?"

"I didn't sling a pick underground, Marshal. I blasted rock topside."

"But wasn't this mine worked for decades?

There must be miles of tunnels down there!"

"Not miles. Maybe two, three hundred yards. Most of 'em is just dead-ends. We'll take the main tunnel, go in a ways, and listen. If my dad's in there, I think we'll be able to hear him."

Helen would have preferred to just wait at the entrance for the sheriff to emerge, rather than go into the mine. But if her suspicions were correct, she wanted to catch him in the act.

She waved Teddy forward. "Lead on."

Teddy led her past the stamp mill, across rutted ground dotted with scrub brush, to the wall of the granite ridge. Tucked between an outcrop and a stunted tree at the base of the ridge was an iron gate, and beyond this, a rectangular opening wide enough for two men to enter side-by-side.

Teddy opened the gate, shined his light inside. Helen saw walls of solid rock, squared off and pitted with the scars of a thousand pickaxes and drills, and a set of wooden reinforcement posts topped by a wooden wedge placed every ten feet or so.

"Old man Yates's grandfather came over from Wales to work this mine," Teddy said.

"Mrs. Patterson told me Yates's father continued digging for gold even after it shut down. And Yates himself is still at it."

"Yeah. My dad caught Yates coming in and out of here a few times, but that hasn't happened for three, maybe four years. I think he's just too old for that nonsense now."

"Does your dad know his way around the mine?"

"I don't think so. Like me, he ain't fond of tight spaces."

Helen peered into the entrance. The wooden support posts bracing the tunnel looked like ridges on a trachea, descending down a human throat.

"How safe is it?"

"Not very. Those timbers could give way any second."

"That's reassuring, Teddy."

"Trust me, Marshal, if anyone's nervous about going in there, it's me." He motioned with his flashlight. "Ladies first?"

Peering into the maw of the mine, Helen began to feel claustrophobic herself. But if Teddy was game, she wasn't going to be the one to chicken out. She stepped through the doorway.

12

The air inside the mine smelled stale, musty, and slightly acrid. Helen pictured an old-time prospector, a carbide lamp protruding from the center of his steel hardhat, holding a birdcage with a dead canary inside.

"Should we be worried about poisonous gasses?"

"Don't think so. Otherwise, Yates would've croaked a long time ago."

Helen started walking. There were piecemeal remnants of ancient metal tracks on the ground, like a miniature railroad. She glanced over her shoulder, saw Teddy still standing in the mouth of the entrance.

"You coming in?"

She shined her light in his face. He blocked it with his hand. Sweat beaded his forehead.

"Maybe I'll wait out here."

"Come on, Teddy."

"I don't like tight spaces."

"Me either. We'll be okay."

"I — I couldn't never bring myself to go in there."

"Teddy . . . I can't do this without you. I need your help. Please. Take a deep breath. I'll be with you every step of the way."

Teddy sucked in a lungful of air, exhaled with a whoosh.

"Do you think . . . maybe . . . you could hold my hand? Just till I feel a little calmer?"

Christ in a bumper car.

"Sure, Teddy."

Teddy took another couple of deep breaths, stepped into the tunnel. He shined his light up at the ceiling, touched it with his fingers as if checking for stability.

Helen walked back, grabbed his hand. "Let's go."

She tugged him along. The ceiling was low enough that even she, at five feet five inches, had to duck her head under each wooden ceiling wedge. Teddy's hand was hot and unpleasantly moist. She wanted badly to let go, wipe her palm on her pants.

Water dripped from the ceiling or ran in trickles down the walls, pooling in nooks and crannies on the ground. Helen felt the pressure on her eardrums increase as they slowly descended deeper into the mine.

"You doing okay?" she asked Teddy. Her voice sounded harsh and hollow in the enclosed space.

"Okay," he said, breathlessly. "Just . . . you know."

Helen tried not to think of the millions of pounds of rock and earth pressing down just inches above. "Focus on what's directly in front of you."

The tunnel doglegged and they came to a square chamber, about ten-by-ten feet. Bits of wood and rusted metal lay scattered on the ground. A wooden chair, possibly decades old, tilted on three legs. Dozens of ancient, crushed beer cans were piled in a corner. The black mouths of two tunnels, one directly across the chamber and another carved into the wall on the left, led off into darkness.

Helen shined her light on the tunnel to the left. A few badly weathered plywood sheets were nailed slantwise into the wooden posts on either side of the opening. She examined the other tunnel. It was clear.

"You hear anything yet?" Helen said.

They listened. Water plopped. Teddy breathed loudly through his nose.

"No," Teddy said after thirty seconds.

"Let's keep moving." She relaxed her hold on Teddy's hand. He held on for a bit, then let go. She waited long enough to not be obvious, then surreptitiously wiped her palm on her coat.

They entered the mouth of the open tunnel. This one was narrower than the first, with curving walls, narrow bottlenecks and passageways extending off to the side that appeared to have been abandoned after only a few yards. As she penetrated deeper into the mine, Helen caught herself fixating on the slowly constricting space. Her heart beat faster. She began to worry she wasn't getting enough oxygen.

Calm down! Focus!

It wasn't working. She reached back, found Teddy's hand, squeezed. He squeezed back. The touch of another human being, even one with a clammy palm, was comforting. Helen breathed easier.

After minutes that seemed like hours, she felt a rush of cool air caress her skin.

"Feel that?" she said.

"Oh, yeah."

They emerged into a cavern with a fifteen-foot ceiling. Fresh air wafted down from above. Helen tilted her flashlight up. She saw a long shaft drilled into the ceiling, and at the top of the shaft, a metal grate with fan blades lazily rotating behind thick iron bars.

"Ventilation shaft," Teddy said, letting go of her hand. "I know exactly where we are now. Right behind Yates's house. There's a brick well just inside the forest with a grate on top. Been there since long before I was born. The miners drilled a few of them over the years. One here, another closer to my place, a couple the other side of Main Street. We used to piss down them for fun."

"Sounds like a hoot."

"Ain't much to do in a small town," he said defensively.

"Teddy, I don't care if you used to take a dump down these things. What matters is that I can breathe air that doesn't smell like the earth's asshole."

Teddy snort-laughed. He directed his flashlight around the room.

"Lookit this stuff."

His light washed across a set of arcane mining tools: picks and shovels, a broken-down wheelbarrow, some kind of machine-gun apparatus with a large pointed tip extending from its barrel, which Helen took to be a portable drill; more beer cans; and stacked against the wall, a half dozen wooden crates and a yellow plastic box.

Teddy lumbered over, lifted the lid off one of the crates.

"Oh, man. Yates, you crazy old coot."

"What is it?" Helen looked over Teddy's shoulder. Inside the crate were paper-wrapped cylinders in a thick bedding of sawdust.

"Is that —" she started.

"Dynamite!"

Long, coiled fuses extended from the tips of the cylinders, just like sticks of dynamite she'd seen in old movies featuring cowboys and train robberies.

"Jesus on a jukebox," she said.

"There's enough dynamite in here to bring down the whole mountainside."

"He's been using this to mine for gold?"

"Looks pretty old," Teddy said. "Maybe it belonged to Yates's father. He did a six-month stretch once for possession of explosives."

"What's it doing down here after all these years?"

Teddy shrugged. "We've heard rumbling from time to time over the years. Figured it was the mine settling. But maybe Yates still blows a bit of rock, now and again."

"I thought you said he was retired."

"As far as we know, he is. But . . ." He waved at the crates.

"Let's not mess with it," Helen said.

"Don't worry. I ain't touching this stuff. Dynamite's real unstable. And the longer it sits, the more unstable it gets." Teddy replaced the lid on the crate, crouched down by the plastic box. "Can you give me a light?" Helen held his flashlight for him as he opened the box. Inside were coils of blue tubing.

"Oh gosh."

"What is it?"

"Det cord."

Helen was familiar with detonation cord. It was a thin plastic tube filled with pentrite — basically, nitroglycerin. Given its flexible structure, det cord had a thousand and one uses. It was employed as a precision cutter to remove cables, pipes, wiring, and other structures by wrapping it around a target. It could be lowered vertically into a well to destroy obstructions to the water flow. She'd even heard of people wrapping it around tree trunks and blowing them in half. And it was perfect for stringing together multiple explosive charges and igniting them all at once.

"Maybe you should shut that lid."

"Det cord's pretty safe, not like the dynamite," Teddy said. "Here." He pulled an object that resembled a video game controller from the box. It had a long handle, shaped like a pistol grip, and a rectangular unit on top with a thick black antenna.

"Transmitter."

He rummaged around some more in the box.

"Teddy, I don't think you should be doing that."

He removed another object, square, with dangling wires. "Receiver. Hook this up to the det cord, get yourself a safe distance away, and squeeze the trigger on the transmitter. *Ka-Boom!*"

"Put that stuff back," Helen said.

"Sure thing." Teddy laid the receiver and transmitter in the box, shut the lid.

Helen searched the perimeter of the cavern, noted four tunnels. One appeared ancient and abandoned. Another two looked more recent. They were narrow, roughly hewn, with wooden supports that were relatively new. The fourth was the one they had just come through, leading back to the square chamber and the main entrance.

She also discovered an electrical wire strung with naked light bulbs. It emerged from one of the newer tunnels, ran partially around the ventilated chamber, and disappeared down the other recently carved passageway.

"Look," she said to Teddy, showing him with her flashlight.

"Yates strung lights down here," Teddy

remarked. "Must be a generator at one end. Maybe we should try to get 'em switched on?"

"If your dad's here, that will just tip him off that we're down here, too."

"Right."

Helen considered her next move. It seemed unlikely a sixteen-year-old girl would penetrate this far into a dark and dangerous hole in the ground, even to avoid the unwanted sexual attentions of her stepfather. Maybe this was all a wild goose chase.

"Do you think Rita could have come all this way?" she asked Teddy. "As a teenager, I mean?"

"I don't know about when she was a teenager, but it does seem a long ways to carry a load of money. For someone as skinny as Rita."

Helen flicked her light across the crates of dynamite. She hadn't counted on finding a stockpile of explosives down here.

"What if we're barking up the wrong tree?" she said.

"I'm happy to get the heck out of here, if you want."

"Yeah. Maybe —"

Clink!

Helen froze. "Did you hear that?"

Teddy shook his head. "I didn't hear —"

"Shh!" *Clink.* "There is it again. Someone's down here."

"Where?" Teddy asked.

Helen inspected each tunnel in turn. Inside the mouth of the old, seemingly abandoned tunnel, she spied a cigarette butt lying among splinters of old wood. She picked it up, sniffed it, rubbed it between her fingers.

"Marlboro Red. Fresh. Your stepsister's brand, if I recall correctly."

"Good call. So she went that way."

"I'm guessing." Helen motioned with her flashlight. "You want to take the lead, since you have the big gun?"

"Not really."

"Come on, Teddy."

He swallowed, his dry throat clicking. "All right."

He squeezed past her. Helen caught a whiff of rank body odor. She didn't judge. She probably smelled like a boxcar hobo herself.

They moved forward. Helen didn't hear any further sounds and began to worry she'd imagined them. The tunnel veered upward. Helen gradually became aware of a dim glow ahead.

"Shut off your flashlight," she whispered.

She slipped hers into a pocket. Teddy slid his flashlight into the loop on his gun belt, unsnapped his holster, put his hand on the butt of his .357 revolver.

They came to a bend. Teddy was making a racket, his heavy boots scraping the ground, his labored mouth breathing, his keys clinking. Helen worried he would ruin the element of surprise. She tapped him on the shoulder, edged past him to take the lead.

Ahead was a final section of tunnel, about twenty feet long, leading to a narrow opening, and beyond, some sort of cavity. Alternating shadows and light came through the opening. Someone was moving to and fro in front of a light source.

She turned to Teddy. She could just barely make out his features in the weak light. She gave him a thumbs-up. He nodded.

Helen scooted along the wall, slowly approached the opening. She heard boots scuffling on rock. A man grunting with effort. She risked a quick glance into the cavity.

It was a sizable room, dug from solid rock and earth, with a ceiling that descended at a sharp angle on the right side to a narrow point on the left, creating an interior space shaped like a tipped-over slice of cake.

A halogen lantern rested in the middle of the floor, providing a bright nimbus of illumination, although the chamber's numerous cracks, nooks, and crannies remained deeply shadowed. Faded graffiti drawn in magic marker streaked the walls: crude drawings, curse words, meticulously sketched metal band logos. Old, melted candle wax puddled on the ground, dripped from rocky outcrops. Dozens of ancient cigarette packs and damp, mildewed paperback books were scattered about.

A large man was on his hands and knees, facing away, digging at the wall where the ceiling met the floor. Big Ed. His jacket and shirt rode up, exposing a generous expanse of plumber's crack.

Helen withdrew her head, nodded at Teddy. Teddy slipped his revolver out of its holster. Helen shook her head, put her hand on the gun, lowered it to his side. A bead of sweat dangled from the tip of Teddy's nose.

Helen risked a second glance. Big Ed was now reaching into a crack in the wall, tugging. Helen heard canvas rasping against stone. Big Ed grunted with effort, yanked a dusty duffel bag out of the crack, dumped it in front of the halogen lantern.

He squatted in front of the bag, his back to Helen. She heard him pull the zipper.

And whistle. He zipped the duffel closed. As he started to get to his feet, Helen backed further into the tunnel.

A sudden shove from behind propelled her into the room, face to face with Big Ed as he turned.

Startled, he dropped the bag, reached for his gun.

"Easy, Sheriff!" she said.

"Christ, you about gave me a heart attack. What are you doing down here, Marshal?"

Helen angrily shot a glance at Teddy. He put a finger to his lips, moved a few steps down the tunnel, disappearing into shadows.

"Who's with you?" Big Ed said. "Don't tell me it's Edward. Boy's scared shitless of the mine."

Big Ed seemed calm, unabashed. Strange behavior for a man busted in the act of committing a crime.

"Is that Rita's money?" Helen nodded at the duffel.

"Guess it is."

Was he confessing? So easily?

"So you . . . you came down here to take it?"

"Why the hell else would I be in the mine, Marshal? For the scenery?"

"As soon as you heard Rita was in town, you knew. Why she'd come back."

"Not right away, no. I figured she was just desperate, hiding out. But then I got to thinking. Same as you, I guess. Otherwise, you wouldn't be down here."

"You insisted Teddy and I stay at the jail. So you could search for the money."

"Well, Marshal, I told you and Edward to stay at the jail because things are confusing enough around here without you two bumbling around. And I wanted to see if I was right about this before someone else had the same bright idea and decided to find the cash and keep it for themselves. Understand?" He hoisted the strap of the duffel over his shoulder again. "Now, if you don't mind, I'd like to get the hell out of this hole."

"How could you do it, dad?" Teddy called out. He remained in the tunnel, out of Big Ed's sightline.

"Do what?" Big Ed said.

"Kill Rita."

Big Ed's mouth dropped open.

"What in the hell are you talking about?"

"You know exactly what I'm talking about, you sonofabitch."

Big Ed's face turned an alarming shade of crimson. Helen, acutely aware that she was playing monkey in the middle with two armed men, took a step toward the tunnel entrance.

"I didn't kill Rita, dummy," Big Ed growled.

"Yes, you did. You killed your own step-daughter for a bag of stolen money. And tried to pin it on Lawrence."

"Teddy . . ." Helen warned.

"Is that really what you think?" Big Ed growled. "Come on out of there and talk to me face to face, boy."

"You're sick, Dad. You need help."

"Teddy," Helen hissed.

"You're out of your fucking dimwit mind," Big Ed said. He let the duffel bag fall to the ground.

"You can plead insanity," Teddy continued. "It doesn't have to be prison. Maybe a mental hospital. Someplace nice, where you can sit outside and smoke your Camels and talk to pretty nurses."

"Jesus, Teddy," Helen said.

"The marshal knows it was you, Dad."

"Everyone take a deep breath." Helen said. "Teddy, you shut up."

"We get it, you had to kill Rita," Teddy continued. "So's no one would know about the money. If not for the marshal here, you probably would've gotten away with it."

Big Ed shook his head, ran his hands through his hair, leaving it sticking up at odd angles.

"You can't believe that, Edward," he said. "We got our differences, you and me, but you can't believe I'd hurt Rita like that."

"I can and I do."

Helen didn't want to be sandwiched between their guns and decades of pent-up hostility. She took another step toward the tunnel. Teddy remained in the shadows, but held out a hand to block her.

"Teddy!" she protested.

"Answer me this, boy," Big Ed said. "How did *you* know where the money would be?"

"Same as you," Teddy said. "This is where Rita used to come . . . when she couldn't stand your fat, sticky fingers grabbing her tits and reaching down her pants no more."

Big Ed's face twisted.

"You little shitheel. That's what you been telling the marshal, huh? Why don't you tell her the goddamn truth?"

"Shut up!" The .357 appeared in Teddy's hand. He moved forward, leveled it over Helen's shoulder.

"Teddy —" she said, ducking her head to one side.

"We caught you red-handed, dad."

"You didn't catch me doing nothing."

"Goddamn murderer, is what you are!"

"You're the sick one, boy. I always knew

it, but never did nothing about it."

"He's gonna draw!" Teddy yelled.

The barrel of his .357 roared. The sound of the gunshot rammed through Helen's right eardrum like an ice pick. She clapped her hands to her head and fell to the ground.

13

Big Ed doubled over, clutching his side.

Teddy fired again. Big Ed's shoulder exploded, spraying meat, blood, and bone. Feathers from his down jacket drifted like snowflakes.

Teddy fired a third time, punching a hole through Big Ed's neck. Big Ed pressed his fingers to the hole, black blood spilling down the front of his shirt. His eyes rolled up and he collapsed.

The chain-saw buzz in Helen's ear felt like an animal trying to gnaw its way out of her skull. She squeezed her eyes shut, tears running down her cheeks.

After a moment, the throbbing in her head subsided, and Helen opened her eyes. Teddy leaned against the tunnel wall, revolver at his side, chest heaving. Helen crawled on all fours across the rocky ground to Big Ed. He stared up at the ceiling, unblinking. She touched his wrist, felt for a pulse. There wasn't one.

"What did you just do?" she said.

"He was gonna kill us," Teddy said.

Helen shook her head. "No."

"He was gonna kill us!" Teddy repeated. He choked out a sob. Covered his face with his hand and began to weep. "Oh, Lord."

She let him cry, too tired, too aghast to comfort him. She slowly got to her feet. She needed air. Open space. The walls were closing in. Priority one was getting out of the mine. There would be time to deal with the circumstances of Big Ed's death later.

"Teddy. Let's go."

He wiped his face, sniffled. "I had to."

"Let's go, I said."

Teddy holstered his gun. "He's dead, right?" He wouldn't look at Big Ed's body.

"Yes."

More sniffles. He wiped his eyes with the heels of his palms, brushed tears off his beard. "Well, we can't just leave the money here."

She thought it strange he would have the presence of mind to think of the money minutes after killing his own father. But she agreed. They couldn't leave it here. As for the sheriff — no way the two of them would be able to carry him out of the mine. Someone from the ME's office would have to collect him later.

"I'll get the lantern," Helen said. "Grab the bag."

Teddy shuffled over to the duffel. Helen lifted the lantern. The excruciating ringing in her head was slowly receding.

Teddy slung the strap of the duffel bag over his shoulder. He nodded at Helen. She started down the tunnel, the lantern lighting her way. Teddy followed, boots crunching, keys jingling. He panted with the effort of carrying the money.

"You don't believe him, do you?" Teddy asked after a dozen steps.

"What?" Helen said.

"My dad."

"Jesus, Teddy."

"It was him. Who, you know . . . did those things to Rita. Not me."

"I just want to get out of here."

They continued walking. *Crunch-jingle. Crunch-jingle.* Teddy's marching tune.

One thing Helen knew for sure, the sheriff wasn't reaching for his revolver when Teddy shot him. Did Teddy really think he was? Or had the years of mental abuse, belittlement, seething anger reached a climax, compelling Teddy to kill Big Ed in cold blood?

She felt Teddy's fingers dig into her shoulder.

"Helen." It was the first time he'd used her name and it sounded strange in his mouth. She turned.

Teddy's face was a jarring landscape of jagged lines. His eyes glimmered inside cratered sockets. He looked . . . unhinged.

"You think I'm lying."

"Teddy . . . I . . ."

He lifted his gun, pointed it at her face.

"Be honest, now, Helen. I mean, it don't really make a difference either way, but be honest."

Christ in a coma. "Teddy . . . listen. All I care about is getting above ground." She took a step backward. "Really."

Teddy cocked the hammer. The metallic click echoed resoundingly off rock walls.

"I believe you, Teddy. I do. He was the one . . . with Rita . . . not you."

"Now who's lying?"

"I know you wouldn't do such a thing. You cared for her. I mean . . ." She pulled on the fabric of her shirt. "You even saved her clothes. You would never hurt her."

"That's right, Helen. I loved her."

"I know you did." *Eww.* "Now let's just . . . keep moving."

Teddy lowered the hammer. Hung his

head. "I'm sorry."

"It's okay. We're . . . we're all under a lot of pressure here. Doing the best we can, right? Please put the gun away."

"Okay." Teddy dropped the gun by his side, but didn't holster it.

Helen took a few more steps away from him, slowly turned, resumed walking, faster now.

"Slow down, Helen," Teddy whined. "This bag is heavy."

"Sure, Teddy."

She didn't slow down. She felt Teddy's eyes drilling a hole in her back. Imagined his gun aimed between her shoulder blades, his finger on the trigger.

In the past five hours, Helen had weathered enough unmitigated terror to last her several lifetimes. The tire blowout on the mountain; finding Rita blood-splattered and dying in the woods; the shootout with Lee Larimer. But a psychotic Teddy? Hapless, sad-sack Teddy? Truly the last person in Kill Devil Falls she'd expected to be a threat.

Clearly, he was deranged. And obviously, he'd been lying to her about Rita and the sheriff. Maybe the sheriff had slapped Rita and Teddy around as kids, and he definitely regarded Teddy with a cold callousness, but she didn't believe he was a child molester, not anymore. Helen thought back to the tense exchanges between Rita and Teddy in the jail. The contempt and scorn Rita displayed for her stepbrother.

Teddy could easily kill her down here. He had plenty of motivation. In order to spin whatever story he wanted to regarding Big Ed's death. To prevent her from revealing the truth about him and Rita. Perhaps most of all, the same reason she'd suspected Big Ed murdered Rita: the money. With Rita, Lee Larimer, and Big Ed dead, the only two people who knew about the stolen cash were Teddy and Helen. If she was out of the picture, it would be his, free and clear.

So what was he waiting for? Why didn't he just get it over with? Shoot her in the back? She resisted the urge to turn around. Afraid of what she might see. That big .357, rising up to blow her brains all over the ceiling.

Helen mentally ticked off options. Run? In a narrow tunnel? It would be like shooting fish in a one-gallon bucket. Fight? With an unloaded gun, against an armed man who outweighed her by ninety pounds?

She knew her only chance of survival was to catch him by surprise.

They were approaching the large ventilated chamber. Helen felt the whisper of cold air on her face. She breathed deeply, savoring the fresh oxygen. The halogen lantern swayed in her hand. She stepped across the threshold into the chamber, Teddy's *crunch-jingle* right behind her.

She whirled, swung the lantern against the side of Teddy's head. There was a satisfyingly meaty *thunk!* Teddy yelped, fell backward. The lantern spun from her grasp, bounced off a wall, hit the rocky ground.

The chamber was plunged into darkness.

Helen ran blindly, aiming for the tunnel leading toward the mine exit. Her palms struck a wall and a shooting pain traveled up her arms. She moved to the left, patting the unevenly carved rock face, searching for the opening. A shot boomed. Granite shards sprayed her cheek. She scrambled to the right. A second shot, the muzzle blast lighting up the chamber for a split second like the flash of a strobe light.

Helen dropped onto all fours, crawled on the floor. Her hands touched wood, a handle, a tool, a possible weapon. She snatched it up, kept moving. Another shot rang out. Teddy was tracking her position with each muzzle flash.

Her outthrust arm plunged into empty space. A passageway. She squeezed through, got to her feet, and ran, one hand in front, the other dragging the tool. More shots echoed from the chamber behind her.

She tasted salt, realized she was crying. Her forehead smacked into a wooden support wedge set into the ceiling. She fell on her butt, stunned. She shook the cobwebs clear, turned to look behind her. A flicker of light stabbed through the mouth of the tunnel.

"Helennn!" Teddy screamed.

Helen fumbled the flashlight out of her pocket, switched it on, raced forward.

After fifteen more yards, the tunnel sloped upward, then bent sharply. The beam of her flashlight revealed an opening straight ahead. Another chamber. She prayed for an exit.

Helen burst into the chamber. It was rectangular, perhaps eight feet by ten. She turned in a circle. Wall. Wall. Wall. No connecting passageway, apart from the one she'd just come from.

A dead end.

14

No!

Helen rested her forehead against the cold rock, tears spilling down her cheeks.

After all she'd been through, to have it end like this. In some godforsaken pit, buried beneath tons of rock and dirt.

A simple fugitive transport, Chowder said. Up the mountain and down again by dinnertime. She pictured his idiotic grin, the detailed stitching on his ridiculous snakeskin cowboy boots.

Helen wanted to live. For so many reasons, but not the least of them to make it back to Sacramento so she could slap that grin off Chowder's face.

Jingle-jangle. The sound of Teddy's keys.

A weapon. She needed a weapon. She shined her light on the ground, at the tool she'd taken from the ventilated chamber. It was a pickaxe. A long shaft, topped by a metal blade with two wickedly sharp points extending to either side.

Deadly, if she were to sneak up behind Teddy and bury it the back of his skull. But face to face, against a .357 revolver, not so much.

She ran her flashlight along the walls, hoping against hope for a door, a crack, anything. But they were solid, carved directly from rock. She looked up at the ceiling.

It was a different color than the surrounding walls, a different texture. It took her a moment to realize that while the walls were of rock, the ceiling was constructed from cement. Man-made. A cement slab with a square wooden panel set into its center.

A trap door?

Helen extended her fingertips toward the ceiling. But it was beyond her reach.

She put the flashlight in her mouth, lifted the pickaxe, held it vertically, placed the head lengthwise against the trap door. She pushed, raising the door a few inches. She lowered her grip to the bottom of the axe shaft, gave a mighty heave. The door flipped open a third of the way, then crashed back down.

"Helen!!" Teddy's voice reverberated down the tunnel.

Helen regripped the axe handle, bent her knees, heaved again. The trap door flipped up, hung in mid-air, started to fall. She turned the pickaxe diagonally, laid it across the corner of the opening. The trap door slammed down on top of the pickaxe blade.

The beam of Teddy's flashlight licked the edge of the tunnel entrance.

Helen slipped the flashlight into her pocket, wiped her hands on her pants. She reached up, took hold of the dangling axe handle, pulled herself upward like a monkey climbing a coconut tree. She inched to the lip of the opening and slid her left hand through, beneath the trap door, the skin of her knuckles shredding like a banana peel.

Helen removed her right hand from the axe shaft, jammed it under the door also. She hung there in space, shoulder joints stretched to their limits.

Clomp-jingle. Clomp-jingle.

She lifted her torso upward until the tip of her head touched wood. She thrust her right arm deeper, scrabbled for a handhold through the opening. Her fingers touched something cold, metallic. She gripped it, pulled her head sidewise through the trap door.

Fingers snatched at her pants.

Helen screamed, kicked, felt impact. She wrenched herself upward, squeezed her shoulders, waist, legs through the trap door, rolled into the space above.

"Wait!" Teddy shouted.

She turned, wrapped her hands around the head of the pickaxe, still wedged beneath the trap door, and tugged it up and out. The door shut with a sharp *THWACK!*

She collapsed on the cement, gasping for breath, her shoulders aflame.

A sharp rapping came from below. The trap door popped up and down. Helen scooted away, panicked Teddy would crawl up from below like a gigantic malevolent spider.

The door continued to jiggle violently and she heard Teddy grunt with effort. But after a few moments, the jiggling stopped. Teddy was taller than her by five or six inches. But she guessed he was too heavy, and lacked the upper-body strength to lift himself through the door as she had done.

Helen reached into her coat pocket for her flashlight, quickly scanned her surroundings. A large room, cement walls, wooden support beams across the ceiling. Stairs leading up in one corner. Spools of electrical wire, woodworking tools, and machinery she could not immediately identify was shoved into corners. A basement. Probably beneath one of the empty houses on Main Street.

The trap door opened a few inches, a yellow glow from Teddy's flashlight bleeding through the crack. Helen saw the long barrel of his .357 snake under the door.

She dropped the flashlight, snatched up the pickaxe, swung it across the gun. Teddy yelped in pain. The gun disappeared below and the trap door slammed down.

Helen retrieved the flashlight. She needed something heavy to block the door. An aluminum ladder rested against the wall. Not weighty enough. She rejected the tools and machinery as too unwieldy. But there — the object she'd used as a handhold to pull herself into the cellar — a portable generator, on wheels.

She attempted to move the generator, but it wouldn't budge. She kneeled down, inspected its wheels, saw that the front two wheels were fitted with friction locks. Helen disengaged the locks, rolled the generator on top of the trap door. She engaged the right wheel lock.

Teddy banged anew on the door, rattling it on its hinges. Helen reached for the left wheel lock. A hole exploded in the wood, ten inches from her fingers. She reared back, flattened herself on the cement.

There were no more shots from below. After a cautious wait, Helen crawled back to the generator, engaged the wheel lock, then scrambled away.

No telling what Teddy was doing down there. Grabbing one of those crates to boost himself up? Running for the mine exit? Whichever, Helen assumed it wouldn't be long before he was topside again.

She collected the pickaxe and climbed the basement stairs, encountering a closed door. She turned the knob, pushed the door open.

Beyond was a short hallway. The house was silent, dark. It smelled like stale tobacco, sour milk, burned coffee, and old carpets.

Helen crept down the hall and found herself in a small foyer. Behind her, stairs rose to the second floor. Directly ahead was a door leading outside, with a pair of old leather boots on the floor in front of it and a coat dangling from a precariously tilted coat rack to one side. On the left was a doorway — Helen shined her flashlight inside, saw that it was a kitchen. Empty cereal boxes, milk cartons, and dozens of beer cans littered the counter.

The old guy, Yates, must live here.

Helen was surprised Teddy's gunshot hadn't woken Yates up, but he'd seemed old and doddering in the restaurant — perhaps half deaf. She considered running upstairs, rousing him from bed, asking for his help. But she quickly discarded the idea. He was probably too infirm to be of much assistance. And she didn't want him getting caught in the crossfire between her and Teddy.

She thought about searching the house for a firearm but decided not to waste time. Teddy might, this instant, be coming through the trap door, or nearing the mine exit. She needed to hurry — get to the jail, free Lawrence. Maybe warn Frank and Mike. Get her hands on a loaded gun.

As she grasped the knob to the front door, it occurred to her why no one had seen Yates enter the mine for the past few years. The old nut had built himself a secret shaft, leading to the mine, right in his own basement. *Bless you,* Yates, she thought. *If you weren't such a lunatic, I'd be dead now.*

She went outside. She found herself on a moonlit porch bordering a small front yard choked with scrub and weeds, and beyond it, a low wooden fence. She heard the distant rattle of the generator powering Frank and Mike's trailer. Otherwise, Kill Devil Falls was dark and still.

Helen walked down the porch steps, carrying the pickaxe over her shoulder. *Woof-woof-woof-woof!* A dog lunged around the side of the house, mouth wide, teeth snapping.

Helen dropped the axe, sprawled on the grass. The dog sprang forward, in kill mode. But his snout jerked to a sudden halt, just inches from her throat. She scrambled away. The dog strained to reach her, his front legs furiously peddling in midair. Helen saw the leather collar around his neck, the sturdy chain holding him back.

She retrieved the pickaxe, ran for the fence gate, pushed it open, ran down the sidewalk.

The dog didn't quit barking until she was well past the Trading Post. Exhausted, she slowed to a walk. Her head was beginning to throb again, but the cold night air was bracing after the stuffy, underoxygenated air of the mines.

She passed vacant storefronts, derelict houses, Big Ed and Teddy's red farmhouse. The jail was straight ahead, its single window dully glowing with lamplight, her Charger and Big Ed's Explorer parked in front.

When she reached the porch of the jailhouse, she leaned the axe against it and took a moment to catch her breath. Then she limped over to the Explorer, tried the door. It didn't open. Of course it didn't. She'd watched, earlier, as Big Ed locked it.

She assumed both Big Ed and Teddy had a set of keys. Teddy's were probably snapped into that loop on his gun belt. And Big Ed's were with his body down in the mine.

Helen shined her flashlight through the window of the Explorer. She spied the shotgun Big Ed had been toting around earlier, set upright into a stand between the two front seats. She considered smashing the window with the pickaxe, but even if she managed to get the door open, she'd still need keys to start the engine.

Maybe there was spare key in the red farmhouse. But it would take time to find it, and she didn't want Lawrence sitting in a cell, helpless if Teddy arrived. One such murder in a single evening was enough. She decided to free Lawrence, then search the house.

She plodded back to the porch, hefted the pickaxe, climbed the steps. Now, facing the jail door with its thick strips of reinforcing metal, she remembered that Teddy had locked this one, too. And *that* key was also on his gun belt, too. *Suck it!*

She heard the low murmur of a voice from inside. A male voice. Lawrence? Or was there someone in there with him? Couldn't be Teddy. She slipped her flashlight into her pocket, put her hand on the wrought-iron thumb latch, pressed down. The latch clicked. The door wasn't locked after all. She entered.

The halogen lantern had been shifted from the floor in front of Lawrence's cell to the mahogany desk. Both cell doors were closed, and she could see nothing of their interiors through the crisscrossed iron slats. It occurred to her that Lawrence might be dead drunk by now. Another complication she didn't need. Perhaps providing him with that bottle hadn't been the best idea, after all.

She sniffed. Smelled skunk weed.

The front door swung shut behind her. Frank emerged from the shadows.

"Hey, pretty lady," he said.

Mike rose from where he'd been sitting on the floor beneath the front window. He touched the brim of his cowboy hat.

"Marshal," he said. "You partners with old Yates now?" He nodded at the pickaxe in her hand.

Helen never expected she'd be glad to see these two, but she was. Overjoyed.

"Oh, thank Jesus, Mary, and Joseph," she said. "Teddy . . . he's . . . he just killed Big Ed. And he tried to kill me!"

Frank laughed and shook his head. He took a seat on the corner of the desk. Helen noticed a .12 gauge shotgun lying beside the lantern.

"You don't believe me?" she said.

"Oh, I believe you. Where is he now?" Frank asked.

"I don't know. In the mine. But he'll be above ground soon. We need to get the hell away from here."

Lawrence whispered hoarsely from the darkness of the rightmost cell. "Don't trust them."

"Pay him no mind," Frank said. He held a fat joint between his fingers. "He's wasted on that bottle of booze you give 'im."

"They're part of it," Lawrence said. "They're in it together, with the deputy."

Mike walked over and planted himself in front of the door. Helen saw a pistol sticking out of his pants.

Helen read it in their faces. What Lawrence said was true.

Frank exhaled smoke, tossed the joint on the floor, went for the .12 gauge.

Teddy quickly realized he wasn't getting through the trap door. Not without a stepladder. And shooting the crap out of it wasn't going to accomplish a darn thing.

Okay, no big deal. The marshal wasn't going anywhere. He and his dad had the only keys to the Explorer. Her Dodge Charger was out of commission, as was every other vehicle in Kill Devil Falls apart from Lawrence's car. And he'd already snatched Lawrence's keys when he and the marshal were searching the grandmother's house earlier.

That left Rita and Lee Larimer's cars. Probably hidden in the brush off the access road. Hard to find in the light of day, let alone the dark of night. If the marshal was going to leave town, it would be on foot. Plenty of time to deal with her later.

He retraced his steps down the tunnel to the ventilated chamber.

If the Lord Jesus had appeared in his dreams, green laser lights shooting from his eyes, and said *"GET READY"* because *"A CHANGE IS A-COMING,"* well . . . Teddy would've woken up laughing into his pillow.

And yet . . . here he was. Rita dead. His dad dead. With a bag of cash. In the span of less than twelve hours, his whole world turned upside down.

He dropped the duffel bag on the floor of the chamber, took a seat on it, rested his legs. A bottle of water would be nice. Even better, a cold Coors Light straight from the fridge, condensation beading on the can. His dad always had a six-pack or two chilling at home. He'd grab a few when he got back to the red farmhouse.

It didn't seem real yet. All the years of yes sir, no sir, the comments about his weight and intelligence, the disrespect, the jeers, from his *own* father. Big Ed had it coming, nobody could argue that.

Teddy wiped his hands on his pants, pushed himself to his feet. He marched over to the stack of dynamite crates. The Coors Light would have to wait. There was lots of work to do.

Helen dropped her pickaxe and drew the Taurus. "Don't move!"

Frank's fingers halted inches from the shotgun.

"Whoa," he said.

"They were talking about what they wanted to do to you," Lawrence said.

"I told you, he's drunk," Frank said.

"They said they were going to rape you, both of them at once," Lawrence hissed. "They argued over who was going to take which end."

"Shut your trap," Frank snarled.

Mike slid his hand closer to the pistol in his waistband. Helen tracked left with the Taurus.

"Hands on your head. Both of you. Right now."

Frank slowly complied. Mike put his fingers on top of his cowboy hat, as if to keep it from blowing off on a windy day.

"You killed Rita," Helen said.

"How could we?" Frank said. "We was all in the restaurant. With you."

True. Teddy, Frank, Mike — they'd all been at the restaurant. Still — they were after the money. And somehow or another, they had a hand in Rita's murder. She was sure of it.

"How did you get in here?" Helen asked.

Obviously, they had a key. Perhaps the one that had gone missing from the cabinet in the red farmhouse?

"Just put down that gun," Frank said. "Before you do something you're gonna regret."

"Marshal, my arms is getting tired," Mike said.

"On your knees," she said.

"Is that how you like it?" Frank said. "A man on his knees? You're a real ball-buster, ain't you? You one of those man-hating bull dykes? What do you think, Mike?"

"Don't know, Frank. Sounds about right."

"Down!" she yelled in her best cop-voice. "Right fucking now!"

"Or what?" Frank said.

"Or I'll shoot."

"I'll tell you something funny, pretty lady," Frank said. "Before, when Teddy and you stopped by the trailer? He told us you was putting it all together. About Rita, the money. And because of that, we was gonna have to make sure you didn't leave town. You know. Ever."

Mike took his fingertips off his hat, started to drop his arms.

"He told us something else, too," Frank said. "Want to know what it was?"

"No," Helen said.

"He said you ain't got no rounds in that gun."

15

Helen hurled the Taurus at Frank. He raised a meaty forearm, a split-second too late. The gun bounced off his forehead.

She leaped at Mike. He fumbled for the pistol in his pants. Helen hit him with a right cross, jarring her wrist. Mike fell back against the jailhouse door. Blood poured from his nose.

Helen pressed her shoulder into him, trapping his right hand, the one grasping the pistol, between their two bodies, preventing him from pulling it free of his pants. She aimed a fist between his legs but he shifted, so her fist bounced off his thigh.

Frank attacked from behind, wrapping a forearm around Helen's neck, pulling her away from Mike. She fought Frank's wrist to prevent him from locking on a choke, but he was much too strong. She struggled, feeling Frank's breath on her wounded ear, the scratch of his stubbly chin on the nape of her neck.

Mike wiped his nose, looked at the blood on his fingers.

"You fucking bitch."

His hat was on the floor. He bent down to pick it up. Helen kicked him in the face. Frank hauled her two steps backward, squeezed her neck more tightly. He didn't know how to properly apply a blood choke, but the edge of his forearm dug painfully into her windpipe. She flailed.

"Mike don't like to bleed," Frank hissed. "Now, you're gonna get it."

Mike, crimson with rage, cocked a fist. Helen kicked him in the stomach as he stepped forward. Her windpipe was on fire. She needed a weapon to free herself from Frank's grasp. She dropped her right hand to her waist, reached under her coat. Her fingers touched a cylinder on her belt. She tugged it out.

Mike spat blood on the floor, drew his pistol, leveled it at her face. His knuckle was white on the trigger.

Frank's head was directly behind Helen's, in the line of fire.

"Don't shoot, dumbass!" Frank yelled. He leaned to the side, away from the gun muzzle, forcing Helen to lean with him.

Mike's mouth and nose were a red wet

mess. His eyes bugged from their sockets. He was beyond reason. He continued to track Helen with the pistol. She sensed he would pull the trigger, Frank be damned.

She lifted the cylinder, shot a burst of pepper spray into Mike's face. He immediately clapped both hands over his eyes. Helen turned the nozzle, directed it over her shoulder, shut her eyes tightly, fired off another burst. The canister was nearly empty and produced only a small puff of spray, but it was enough. Frank released her, roared.

Helen coughed as pepper particles irritated her throat.

Mike was on all fours, gun dropped and forgotten. Helen picked it up, whirled.

Frank raised the shotgun, one-handed. His left eye was swollen, gluey tears leaking down his cheek. His right eye sighted down the barrel.

Helen jumped. The shotgun roared, blowing a chunk of wood from the jailhouse door. Helen took cover behind the huge mahogany desk. Mike continued to sputter on the floor.

Helen raised the gun blindly over the top of the desk, pulled the trigger. She heard metal shriek as the bullet hit the iron slats of one of the cell doors. Lawrence screamed.

Frank dived behind the opposite side of the desk.

Helen huddled there, watching Mike retch.

"Well, this is one hell of a pickle!" Frank yelled.

She and Frank were separated by five feet of solid wood, but she was on the side facing the front door, through which she expected Teddy to enter at any moment.

"Throw out that gun," Frank said. "And I'll let you run for it."

Helen didn't reply. She examined the bottom of the desk, hoping it was raised off the floor on legs so she could aim a bullet underneath it. No such luck.

Mike coughed and spat, wiped at his swollen eyes with a sleeve. Helen aimed the pistol at him.

"Frank, toss the shotgun or I'll shoot Mike."

Mike glowered at her through puffy lids, resembling a boxer after a twelve-round ass-kicking.

"Can't do that, Marshal," Frank said.

"I'm not bluffing, Frank."

"I believe you. Go ahead and shoot, but you ain't getting my gun."

"Frank!" Mike croaked.

"Sorry, buddy. If I toss her the gun, we're

done for. If I don't, only you are done for."

Helen heard the *clomp-clomp-clomp* of boots on the porch.

"Mike," she said. "Get up and bolt the door."

Mike dabbed at his eyes. "Fuck you."

"Now," she said. "Or you're dead. This gun is loaded."

Heavy footsteps stopped outside the doorway. Mike flipped Helen the bird.

Helen aimed at the door, fired. A bullet thudded into the oak.

Mike scrambled to his feet, ran for the hallway leading to the guard room. Helen squeezed off a round, hit him between his shoulder blades. Mike lurched, fell onto his face.

Frank popped up, blasted the corner off the desk just above Helen's head. A slug ripped a deep divot into the floor. He resumed his cover behind the desk. Helen pulled her legs in, squeezed herself into a little ball.

If Teddy came through the door, she'd be caught between his .357 and Frank's .12 gauge.

She inched over, fired a round down the front side of the desk. She heard Frank's boots scrape as he shifted away. She quickly rolled to the opposite side of the desk.

300

Frank was a big man, and although the desk was five feet long, it wasn't particularly deep from front to back. As she peered around the desk corner, she spied the edge of Frank's boot poking out. She lined the toe of the boot up in her sights.

The jailhouse door popped open, admitting a rush of cold air. Helen stayed focused on her target, squeezed the pistol's trigger. Leather exploded. Frank screamed.

Helen spun around to cover the door. She saw only an empty rectangle of nighttime sky. No Teddy. But he was there, probably skulking just to one side or the other. She couldn't stay here. Had to make a move. Take a chance.

She got to one knee, hand touching the floor, a modified sprinter's stance. She pushed off, sprinted for the hallway leading to the guard room. Frank, cursing, scrambled to get a shot off. A lead slug cut across the shoulder of Helen's coat, blew a crater in the wall. She jumped over Mike's body and turned the corner, out of Frank's line of fire.

She pressed herself flat against the hallway wall, took a breath, focused on slowing the runaway freight train in her chest. She looked down at the gun in her hand, seeing it clearly for the first time. It was a Sig

Sauer, .380 automatic. A clip capacity of just six bullets. She wasn't sure how many she'd already fired. Was it four? Five?

From this vantage point in the hallway, she had a visual of the window, which was directly opposite Lawrence's cell. Anyone looking through the window could see her, unless she retreated toward the guard room, into the shadows where the halogen lantern's light didn't reach.

"You out there, Teddy?" Frank called. Helen pricked her ears. She heard Teddy's voice coming from the porch.

"Yeah, I'm here."

"She shot me in the foot."

"Coulda been worse."

"Fuck you! She shot Mike, too!"

"Dead?"

There was a beat, then Frank said, "Looks like. She's around the corner, by the guard room."

Glass shattered and a gun barrel poked through the metal bars of the front window. Helen sprang down the hallway as Teddy fired. A bullet thumped into the wall.

"You get her?" Frank yelled.

"Don't think so. Can't see, too dark."

"Sonofabitch!"

"She ain't going nowhere, Frank. We got her trapped."

"Why don't you limpdicks come and get me!" Helen yelled.

"I ain't sitting here all night, Teddy!" Frank said. "I'm leaking all over the floor."

"I got an idea."

"What's that?"

"Walk out the door."

"What?"

"I'll cover you through the window. She'll have to show herself to get you. If she does, I'll shoot her!"

Helen's mind raced, seeking a way, no matter how slim, to turn the tables on Frank and Teddy. With one bullet versus whatever arsenal Teddy might bring into play, the odds sucked. But if Frank ran out onto the porch, she might be able to get the door closed and either lock it from the inside or block it with something heavy, like the mahogany desk. The jailhouse was a solid piece of architecture. Short of a sledgehammer or dynamite, once the door was secured she could hold any number of attackers off, indefinitely.

Unfortunately, she happened to know where Teddy might get his hands on enough dynamite to level the entire structure, but first things first. Survive the next five minutes. There'd be plenty of time later to worry about all the other ways Teddy and

Frank could kill her.

She heard a clatter and an uneven stomp-drag as Frank left the cover of the desk and limped across the wooden floor. She knew Teddy would be gunning for her, but it was hard to hit a moving target with a pistol, especially when it was poking through metal bars with a narrow range of fire.

She jumped from the hallway, shot at the window, sprinted for the open door. Teddy's return fire whizzed through the air a few feet behind her. She reached the door, slammed it shut, felt a body thump against it from the outside. She frantically searched the back of the door, discovered a sturdy slide bolt and rammed it home.

The door vibrated violently as Frank pounded on it. Helen sank to the ground, sucked in a lungful of air, choked as a stray particle of pepper spray found its way into her lungs. Even if Frank and Teddy still had the skeleton key, it would be useless now. She was safe. For the moment.

The pounding stopped. Outside, Teddy and Frank talked, their voices a low rumble.

"Lawrence," she whispered.

A muffled "Marshal?"

"Are you hit?"

"I don't think so."

"How can you not know? Either you are

or you're not."

"I'm not hit."

"Okay. I'm going to open the cell door and get you out of there."

She slithered along the wall behind the desk. She quickly stood up and lifted the key ring from its hook, sank back down again.

"Lawrence, I'm going to kill the lights so they can't see through the window."

Helen crawled to the desk, snatched the lantern off its surface, switched it off. She blinked in the sudden darkness.

More talking and stomping from outside. A flash of light and the roar of Teddy's revolver through the window. Three rounds. Helen buried her face in the floor. This was followed by the sound of Teddy and Frank laughing like a couple of teenagers blowing up mailboxes with cherry bombs.

"Lawrence!" she hissed.

"Yes."

"I'm coming."

She crept across the floor to Lawrence's cell. She reached up, felt blindly for the door lock, found it. She slipped the key into the hole, slowly turned. She pulled the door open.

"Hurry!"

She felt Lawrence's hand reach out. She

grabbed him, pulled him from the cell. They took cover behind the desk. He reeked of booze.

"For God's sake. Are you drunk?"

"Not nearly enough."

"Great timing, Lawrence."

He belched. She nearly gagged.

"Sorry," he said. "Needed to take the edge off. What do we do now?"

"No clue."

"Great. You have a gun, right?"

"Yes." She ran her fingers across the pistol, felt the open slide. She ejected the mag, inspected it with her fingers. She dropped the pistol and mag on the floor. "Unfortunately, it's empty."

"Brilliant. What if they break down the door?"

"It won't be easy. It's reinforced with steel. An axe or a sledgehammer aren't enough. It'd have to be something . . . stronger."

"Are we going to sit here all night waiting for them to find a way in?"

"There are no other exits, right?"

"How should I know?" Lawrence whined. "I've never been in here before tonight and since then I've spent the entire time in that shitty cell."

Helen already knew there was no back

door, no back window. But Lawrence was right — they couldn't just sit idly, waiting for the inevitable.

"Let's go to the room in back," she said. "Bring the lantern. Maybe we'll find something useful."

"Like a SWAT team?"

"I'm glad you still have a sense of humor."

"I want to get the fuck out of here, Marshal. And not in a body bag."

She squeezed his shoulder. "Me too. And call me Helen. No need to be so formal. Not when we're locked in an old jail with two psychos out front who are determined to kill us."

"If that's your attempt to reassure me, don't bother, because you suck at it."

"Sorry," Helen said. "Let's do this. Ready?"

She patted the floor around the desk, located the lantern. She gripped Lawrence's hand. "Quickly now."

They started for the hallway. When they were halfway across the main room, the beam of a flashlight stabbed through the window. Helen ran, pulling Lawrence behind her. Frank's .12 gauge nosed between the window bars. Frank fired. Lawrence stumbled over Mike's body. Helen dragged him around the corner. She pulled him through the door to the guard room, swung it shut. She switched on the lantern.

Lawrence huddled in a ball on the floor.

"Lawrence!"

He looked up at her, cringing in fear. She took him by the collar of his jean jacket. "Did he get you?"

He choked out a sob. She let go of his jacket, waved the lantern up and down his torso. She didn't see any blood.

"You're okay," Helen assured him. "No gunshot wounds."

"I'm not okay!" He wiped his eyes and nose on the sleeve of his jean jacket. "I'm very fucking far from okay!" He shivered. She saw that his toes, exposed in the flip-flops, were purple with cold.

She glanced over at Jesse Patterson's corpse. "Do you want to borrow Jesse's socks and shoes?"

"Hell, no! I don't want a dead man's clothes!"

Helen touched the fabric of her shirt. A dead woman's shirt. Given to her by Teddy. Preserved in his room like a holy relic for sixteen years. He'd probably sniffed it, rubbed himself on it. *Don't think about that!*

She raised the lantern, scouted out the room. Rita's body lay on the bed, crusted with blood, exposed teeth and sightless eyes,

Jesse's corpse on the floor beside it. Meanwhile, the round table with its pewter place settings and the pot-bellied stove in the corner lent a homey touch. The juxtaposition of the two was jarring.

Lawrence got to his feet, sniffled.

"God," he whispered. "Look at them."

"Yeah." She silently counted. Rita, Lee Larimer, Jesse, Big Ed, Mike. Five dead. Five dead in the space of what? Seven hours? That was less than a standard work shift at the local Starbucks. She pulled out one of the dining room chairs, sat down.

"You all right?" Lawrence asked.

"Not really, no." She set the lantern on the table.

Lawrence touched her shoulder. His finger felt like a hot poker.

"Ow!"

"You're bleeding. Take that coat off and let me see."

Lawrence helped her off with her coat, examined her shoulder. "It's not bad," he concluded. "A little groove in the skin along the top."

Helen remembered Frank shooting at her from behind the desk as she ran for the hallway. The slug must have just creased her shoulder. In all the excitement, she hadn't even noticed.

"How deep?"

"Oh . . . not very. If I had some gauze or even a big Band-Aid, I could fix you up."

She slipped her coat back on. "Never mind. We need to get our shit together. Check the ceiling and floor. Maybe there's an attic or a cellar in this place. Look around for anything we can use to defend ourselves."

A quick search revealed that, aside from a set of pewter forks and spoons, there was nothing remotely weapon-like in the room.

The ceiling, floor, and walls were constructed of flat pine boards. Some were cracked and warped, but Helen did not see any large gaps or holes that could be used to pry them loose. There was no door in the ceiling leading to an attic, no human-sized vent in the floor.

"The only way out is through the front door," Lawrence said. "So basically . . . we're stuck in here. All they have to do is wait for us to come out."

"We're safe inside."

"We're as dead as them." He nodded at Rita and Jesse. "Only our bodies don't know it yet."

Helen's eyes unexpectedly welled with tears. "Shut up."

"It's true."

She turned away, embarrassed.

"Hey," he said. "I'm . . . I'm sorry."

"It's fine." She wiped her eyes with a coat sleeve. "I don't know what's wrong with me."

Lawrence laughed.

"What's so funny?"

"Well . . . if the situation we're in isn't enough to make someone cry, I sure as hell don't know what is."

Helen smiled. "True."

She was frightened. Terrified. But that wasn't what brought on the tears. Having her back against the wall had forced her to confront a fundamental fact regarding her life. One she habitually suppressed whenever it threatened to show its ugly face.

Aside from her father, who was hardly a warm, loving presence in her life, she had no one. No boyfriend or husband waiting at home for her return, panicked she hadn't checked in, frantically calling her colleagues in a bid to track her down. Not even a close friend to share tawdry gossip and embarrassing revelations with over too many bottles of Merlot. No one loved her deeply enough to be suitably devastated when she turned up dead. She was pretty much alone in life, and would be similarly alone in death.

Helen didn't like feeling sad. Anger was better. Sadness was a downer. Anger was a kick in the ass. She slapped a palm on the dining table.

"I'm not getting killed by these shitheads."

"What are we supposed to do?"

"Fight. If we can. Take one or both of them with us."

"I'm not a fighter, Marshal. I'm a . . ." He shrugged. "I'm an artist."

"Ever hear of Caravaggio? Renaissance guy? As famous for his brawls as he was for his paintings. Even killed a guy or two."

"What happened to him?"

"Uh . . . never mind." If she recalled correctly, Caravaggio had died an outcast, penniless, at a young age. "I'm going out there to get the pickaxe. Then maybe I'll open the door and whack whoever comes in first."

"That's a . . . if you don't mind me saying . . . a ridiculous plan."

"Better than sitting around."

"And what should I do while you're whacking people?"

"Keep looking around for something we can use."

"But there isn't anything."

"Maybe you want to stand by the door with the pickaxe?"

"No."

"Stay in here and keep searching for a weapon, a tool, anything that might come in handy."

Lawrence nodded at the corpses. "Did you already check to see if they had anything?"

"Yeah. They don't. Unless you want those shoes."

Lawrence grimaced. "No thanks."

Helen put her hand on the door. "Kill the lantern."

Lawrence switched the lantern off. Helen opened the door, slipped through, closed it behind her. She edged her way along the hallway. She heard voices, footsteps, saw flashes of light through the window. She got down on her hands and knees and crawled along the floor, searching for the pickaxe.

A beam from a flashlight flickered through the window. Helen froze. The beam swept left, right, then winked out. Helen resumed searching. Her hand brushed rapidly cooling flesh — Mike — then the wooden axe handle. She lifted it, went to the front door, crouched to one side.

Now that she considered it more carefully, her plan was pretty stupid.

So she waited. For what, she couldn't say. The tattoo of boots on the wooden porch came and went. Eventually, Helen heard the sound of water splashing. Renewed laughter from Teddy and Frank.

She hoped for a miraculous rescue, a convoy of police vehicles rolling down Main Street. Instead, there was a metallic rattle, and footsteps on the roof. What the hell were they up to?

More splashing. Followed by liquid sloshing through the front window onto the floor of the main room.

Now she smelled it. Gasoline.

They were going to light the jailhouse on fire.

16

A twist of flaming paper flew through the window. A whoosh of flame erupted along the floor.

"Hey, Marshal, got any marshmallows?" Frank yelled.

Helen skirted the flames, raced down the hall and through the door into the guard room. She closed it behind her.

Lawrence was kneeling over Rita's dead body. Her sweater was pulled up to her chest.

"They're lighting up the — what are you doing?"

He sprang up. "Searching. For something useful."

"Like her tits?"

"No . . . a cell phone . . . uh . . ."

Helen waved a hand. Bigger fish to fry. "They've set the building on fire. The floor, the roof. We need to get out."

"But that's probably exactly what they

want us to do. They're standing right outside the door waiting to shoot us."

Already, white tendrils were beginning to snake across the ceiling. Helen coughed as a wisp of smoke tickled the back of her throat.

Lawrence was right. But it was either go out the front door or burn. Unless they could find another exit.

She eyed the pot-bellied stove. It sat on squat, claw-footed legs like a barrel-chested Dachshund. A metal stove pipe extended from its back, ran straight up the wall, then made a 90 degree turn and disappeared through a small round hole leading outside the building. Helen considered yanking the stovepipe out and squeezing through the hole, but it was much, much too small.

Lawrence covered his mouth with his hand.

"This place must be dry as old newspaper," he said. "It'll go up like a Christmas tree in July."

Helen opened the door leading to the hall to get some air circulating. Bad idea. The floor of the main room was burning brightly. She shut the door.

"Going out through the front is no longer an option, even if we wanted to."

She kicked one of the walls. Constructed

of logs, it might as well have been solid brick. Even with a chain saw, it would take an hour to cut through it, and they didn't have a chain saw, or an hour. More like fifteen minutes before the smoke alone killed them.

"The foundation is raised off the ground, right?"

Lawrence shrugged. Helen stomped on the floor.

"This floor is probably nailed onto a wooden frame. You can't lay a wood floor on top of dirt because it'll rot away."

Lawrence shrugged again, coughed, and wiped tears from his eyes.

"If we can get through the floorboards, there might be an open space below," Helen said.

"We'd still be trapped. The whole building will just collapse right on top of us."

Smoke billowed along the ceiling. She heard the crack and groan of the rafters above. How long before a major support post gave way?

Helen was certain there was only one way out. Not through the ceiling or front door. Definitely not through the log walls. Straight down.

She chose a spot on the floor, raised the pickaxe, slammed into a joint between two floorboards. She lifted the axe again, sucked in a lungful of smoke, doubled over. Lawrence patted her back, unhelpfully. She pushed him away, tucked her mouth and nose into the collar of her shirt, lifted the axe, chopped at the floor. Again. And again. The wood chipped. A gap between the floorboards widened, but slowly. Too slowly.

A section of ceiling above the bed crashed down, flaming bits of wood falling onto Rita's head and shoulders. Black smoke curled through the hole and a wave of heat baked Helen's face. Lawrence ducked beneath the dining table.

Helen hacked away, eyes watering, coughing steadily now. She felt a tug on the axe, resisted, realized Lawrence was offering to take over. She handed him the axe. Lawrence continued attacking the floorboards.

They alternated, a few swings each, passing off the axe when their coughing became too intense to continue working. The temperature was unbearable.

She smelled cooked hair and flesh, wondered if it was her own. She wiped away tears, saw Rita's corpse sizzling under burning debris. Human fat popped and splattered.

Christ, I'm in a living hell.

Helen took the axe from Lawrence. The

hole was now the size of two fists. She slipped the blade of the axe into the hole, attempted to pry up the boards.

"Help," she croaked.

Lawrence wrapped his hands around the handle. They pulled together. After a few seconds, there was a groan and one of the boards loosened.

Helen and Lawrence ripped and tore at the floor, half blind, each breath a searing torture. Another section of roof caved in, landing on the dining table, scattering pewter place settings and red-hot sparks.

The hole seemed too small, but the heat and smoke were overwhelming. Helen let go of the axe, gripped Lawrence's triceps, and thrust him toward the hole. He understood. He slipped his head and shoulders into the tiny space. His jean jacket bunched on the edges of the opening. He wiggled, head below and hindquarters protruding into the room like a Corgi in a badger hole.

Helen put two hands on his butt, pushed, forcing him deeper. She was going to die if he didn't get his ass through the floor. She shoved hard, not caring if she was hurting him.

Lawrence's waist, legs, and feet disappeared into the opening. Helen followed, squeezing her head and shoulders through, her back scraping painfully along the needle-like edges of the splintered floorboards. She clawed at the underside of the floor, forcing her hips and legs into the gap. She felt herself falling. She plopped into the bless-edly cool and pillowy embrace of wet soil.

She lay there for a moment, panting, body racked by deep, hacking coughs. She blinked hot coals from her eyes.

Groaning, she rolled over onto her belly. A heavy thud rattled the boards above her head. More bits of the ceiling falling in. Helen started crawling, a grub in the dirt.

She encountered a floor joist, followed it to a wooden barrier — the wall of the foundation. She skirted the wall, grit filling her mouth, until she discovered a metal vent. She pounded the heel of her hand on the vent frame, but it didn't budge. She swiveled her body around and kicked with her foot. The vent gave, just a little.

A roof support crashed through a section of floorboards five feet away, scattering sparks across Helen's face and hair, singing her skin. She brushed them away and resumed kicking the vent. On the fourth kick, it popped out of its frame.

She wormed her way headfirst through the hole. It was a tight fit. She emerged onto the ground outside the jail and lay on the ground for a moment, utterly spent, completely exposed should Frank or Teddy come around the back of the building.

Glowing embers floated from the roof, across the back yard, and into the forest like lazy fireflies. The building screeched and crackled, dying in agony.

Helen reached an arm inside the hole, felt around for Lawrence. Her hands encountered only empty air. She waited as long as she dared, then got up and stumbled across the yard into the tree line. She took shelter behind a tangle of undergrowth. The cold mountain air sizzled against her skin like water on a hot skillet.

The jail was now fully aflame, ten-foot flames shooting from its roof, dripping down the sides of the outer walls. No sign of Teddy and Frank, who she suspected were still around front, waiting for her and Lawrence to burst through the door.

And speaking of Lawrence . . . Smoke leaked from the open vent like a factory smoke stack. Helen felt a wrenching twist of guilt. She couldn't just abandon him. She left the shelter of the trees and lurched back to the side of the building.

Just as she reached the wall, a blackened hand shot through the vent. Helen grasped it, pulled. Slowly, she tugged Lawrence onto the grass. His eyes were swollen, his sides heaving, spittle dotting his lips. She got an arm around his waist, helped him across the yard and into the forest.

She leaned Lawrence against the trunk of a pine tree, massaged his chest. He coughed, shoved her hand aside.

"I thought I lost you in there," she said. "If you'd been ten pounds heavier, you would've never made it through that hole."

He wheezed, unable to speak.

Helen heard a voice, Teddy or Frank, she couldn't be sure which. She was afraid they would hear Lawrence's coughing, so she helped him to his feet and they retreated further into the forest, where they collapsed in a heap again.

Minutes passed before Helen had the strength to sit up. The night air, so refreshing when she'd first come out of the jail, was now seeping into her bones. Lawrence was lying on his side, hacking phlegm into the dirt.

"Lawrence. We have to keep moving."

He groaned, his eyes angry red slits.

"My lungs," he said. "Hurts . . ."

"I know, Lawrence. Now listen to me. Your car . . . it runs, right?"

He nodded.

"That's our way out. We need to get to

322

your house. Do you have any guns there?"

He shook his head.

"Okay," she said. "We'll stay in the shelter of the forest until we get close. Then we'll cut across Main Street, sneak into your car, get out of here."

"What if . . . Teddy blocks road . . . with . . . Explorer?"

"How about we deal with one deadly obstacle at a time?"

Frank spied the open vent, knew the tricky little bitch was free. Lawrence? If the marshal had any sense, she would've just left that useless faggot inside to burn, but even if she hadn't, Frank wasn't exactly worried about *Lawrence*.

To be honest, he was glad she'd escaped.

He wanted to kill her himself. He owed that to Mike.

He limped back around to the front of the jail. Teddy had moved the Explorer to the other side of the road, away from the furious heat. He was leaning against the front fender, face tinted red in the glow of the fire.

"I think she's out," Frank told him. "Through a vent in the foundation."

Teddy spat a stream of tobacco juice in the dirt.

"Why don't you go wake up old man Yates, if all this ruckus ain't woke him up already. Tell him to bring Coonie."

Frank didn't like being ordered around, least of all by Teddy. Growing up, Teddy had always been the butt of his and Mike's jokes, the tag-along and wannabe. Even after joining the sheriff's department he was still the same old dumpy loser, desperate for his daddy's approval and Frank and Mike's friendship.

But the events of the day seemed to have completely transformed Teddy from ass-sniffing runt to king of the jungle. Gone was his customary nervous laugh, ingratiating smile, halting manner. He was cool as a cucumber, as if they were doing nothing more than sitting around the trailer, drinking beers, watching a ballgame on their shitty TV.

Before tonight, Frank would never have credited Teddy with the guts to move his foot out of the way if someone was pissing on it. And now he'd gone and killed his own father, a man even Frank was secretly terrified of.

He hated to admit it, but for the first time in his life, Frank felt something besides a moderate disdain for Teddy. A touch of respect, yes, but more than that. A sliver of fear.

He hobbled down Main Street to Yates's place. The marshal's bullet had taken off the tip of his pinky toe. Teddy had bandaged it as best he could and given Frank four aspirin. And as Teddy was off getting a ladder and gasoline to burn the jail down, Frank had further medicated himself with a joint. But the foot still hurt like a sonofabitch.

When he pushed open the gate leading to Yates's front yard, Coonie leaped out of the shadows, jerking his chain, barking and snapping.

"Shut up, you fucking dumb dog," Frank snarled. Everyone in town was familiar with Coonie and his wild ways. Only Yates knew how to control him.

He stayed out of range of Coonie's teeth as he climbed the porch. He opened the front door, stepped inside.

"Yates!" he yelled. "It's Frank. Me and Teddy need your help!"

No response. Yates was old and deaf as a pile of dirt.

"Yates!" Frank yelled. "Wake up!"

Yates appeared at the top of the stairs. He was dressed in dirty underwear and tattered slippers.

"What's goin' on?"

"We need Coonie. Got some tracking to do."

"Tracking what?"

"That pretty little US Marshal."

"Huh?"

"Just get dressed and bring Coonie."

They arrived at the burning jail ten minutes later, Yates fully dressed and carrying a shotgun, Coonie tugging at the leash in his hand.

"Frank tells me that marshal's gone crazy and shot Big Ed," Yates said.

Frank winked broadly at Teddy.

"Yeah, that's right," Teddy said. "She, uh . . . She shot my dad, then killed Mike and locked herself in the jail."

"Goddarn," Yates said. "I knew she was trouble. She's after what's in the mine."

Teddy and Frank exchanged a look. Yates saw their confusion.

"The gold," Yates explained.

"Ah, yeah, the gold," Frank said.

"First she'll confiscate our weapons," Yates said. "Then the government will move in with their excavators, loaders, and whatnot."

"That's why we got to stop her," Frank said.

"We tried to burn her out, but she slipped

through a vent and is probably in the woods somewhere," Teddy said. "Think Coonie can catch a scent and track her down?"

Coonie whined. He was an ugly blend of Weimaraner and coon hound.

" 'Course he can. Best nose in the county. What you got that Coonie can smell?"

"Her car's right there," Teddy said. "He can smell the seat, and I don't know what else she's got in there."

"Maybe she's got some panties lying around," Frank said. "Give Coonie a snoutful of that!"

"Shut up, Frank," Teddy said.

Frank opened his mouth to retort but closed it without saying a word.

They walked to Helen's car, shielding their faces from the heat with their hands. Yates opened the passenger door.

"In," he said. The dog complied. Yates pushed Coonie's face into the driver's seat, around the steering wheel. The dog growled, wagged his tail happily.

"You smell her, boy?"

Coonie barked.

"All right, show me where she come out of the jail," Yates said to Teddy.

They all went around to the back yard, skirting the jail walls by a good measure. Coonie sniffed around the grass for a bit, then barked and pulled on the leash.

"He's got the scent!" Yates said.

"Frank, you go with Yates," Teddy said.

"What about you?"

"I'll stay with the Explorer. Make sure she don't double back and take the road out of town."

"My foot's shot up. Why don't you go with Yates and I'll stay here?"

"I'm sticking with the vehicle."

Frank put his hands on his hips.

"Seems like I got to do all the work around here."

"We'll talk about this later," Teddy said. He turned and walked away.

Frank figured Teddy wanted to stay close to the money, which was currently in the back seat of the Explorer. But what if Teddy just took off with the cash as soon as Frank entered the woods? Nah . . . Where would Teddy go? He'd only ever known Kill Devil Falls. Besides, if Teddy split, he knew Frank would come looking for his share.

"We goin' or not?" Yates asked.

"Yeah. Let's do it."

The old man gave Coonie some slack and the dog took off running, snapping the leash to its full extension. Yates hurried to keep up. Frank shuffled along behind.

■ ■ ■ ■

Teddy watched them disappear into the woods, Frank limping, Yates tottering along like the old man he was, both armed with shotguns. He figured it was fifty-fifty the two of them managed to kill the marshal and Lawrence. Better than fifty-fifty that one of them died in the process.

That suited Teddy just fine. It meant more money in his pocket.

He climbed into the Explorer and drove down to the red farmhouse. He considered bringing the duffel bag inside, but it was heavy, so he settled for locking the car doors. Using his flashlight, he entered the house, ascended the creaking stairs to the second floor, went into his bedroom.

He lit a few candles given to him by Mrs. P as Christmas gifts — they were homemade and smelled pleasantly of pine needles and cinnamon. He removed a backpack from the top of the closet and packed some clothes. Underwear, socks, pants, some T-shirts and sweaters. He added a few hundred bucks from his nightstand, a box of .357 rounds, another of .38s, and the snub-nosed police special he carried when he was off duty.

He looked around the room to make sure there was nothing else, nothing that couldn't just be bought and replaced elsewhere.

His dresser and shelves were empty of baseball trophies and track medals, his walls were bare of certificates of achievement. He had no collection of love letters or photos of old girlfriends. The emptiness of his room was depressing. He resolved to change things moving forward. The money was his golden ticket. A fresh start.

Teddy stripped off his deputy sheriff's uniform. He carried one of the candles into the bathroom and shaved off his beard. He'd worn it pretty much since he could grow one, and the touch of cold air on his exposed skin felt strange and unpleasant. It made him feel vulnerable, naked. Then he imagined himself on a sunny beach, thirty pounds lighter, tan, a little brunette in a littler bikini lying beside him in the sand, drinking cold beer. Beards and beaches didn't mix. Besides, for the time being, it was smart to travel incognito.

Back in his bedroom, Teddy dressed in cargo pants, a dark sweater, combat boots. He buckled on his gun belt. He shrugged into the bulletproof vest he kept under his bed. He appraised himself in the mirror by candlelight. Fucking bad-ass.

Teddy retrieved his go-bag from the closet. Inside were items he'd put aside in the event of a major disaster. Freeze-dried food. A first aid kit. Water. A heat blanket. And other equipment, some he'd found at an army surplus store, some he'd "requisitioned" from the sheriff's department. He set the go-bag on the floor outside his bedroom door.

Next, Teddy rooted around on the floor of the closet, shoving aside old shoes, comic books, nunchucks, and boxes of ammo and video games in order to reach an ancient, crumbling cardboard carton. He placed the carton on his bed, removed the lid. He pulled out several pairs of old underwear, a couple of shirts, a bra, some cheap jewelry. Stuff he'd stolen from Rita when she was a teenager. He chose a pair of red lacy panties (why she'd had such slutty undergarments at that age was beyond him), the bra, a V-neck soccer jersey she'd looked particularly pretty in, and a tarnished silver heart pendant that had been a favorite of hers until she'd carelessly left it on the bathroom counter one morning. He still remembered quite distinctly the way the pendant glittered as it rested just below the notch of her throat. These things he zipped into the front pocket of his backpack.

He carried a candle down the hall and into Big Ed's bedroom. He looked at the enormous oak bed with its lumpy mattress, the walls devoid of photos or paintings, the squat nightstand and barrel-chested armoire. The room was a reflection of his dad's personality — solid, cheerless, hard.

In the corner was a metal gun cabinet. Teddy dialed the combination, opened the cabinet, ran his fingers along the stocks of a dozen rifles stored inside. He chose an AR-15 with a flashlight attachment beneath the barrel. The magazine held sixty rounds. He grabbed a box containing another fifty rounds for good measure.

He took the assault rifle, backpack, and go-bag down to the Explorer, put them in the back seat next to the duffel bag. He paused for a long look at the red farmhouse. The only home he'd ever known.

Soon to be ashes. Like the rest of Kill Devil Falls.

An unfamiliar thrill prickled Teddy's flesh. He couldn't place the feeling for a moment, then all at once it came to him:

He was happy.

Helen led them through the forest, using her flashlight to pick out a path. Lawrence wheezed and gasped, stopping frequently to rest his hands on his knees.

"Lawrence."

"My lungs."

"I know. But we have to keep moving."

"I'm f-freezing."

He looked so pitiful, in his flip-flops and sweatpants, covered in dirt and smoky residue.

"Another five minutes, Lawrence. Come on."

She took his hand. He stumbled along in her wake. She heard a dog barking in the distance. She'd only seen one dog in town — in Yates's yard.

They were not far from the Trading Post. Another hundred yards and she expected to see the lights coming from Frank and Mike's trailer. That's where she planned to cut across Main Street.

The barking grew louder.

She halted. "Listen."

"What?"

"Barking."

"Uh huh."

"Getting closer."

"Yates's dog. Hunter. Tracker. Possums. Raccoons."

Helen grew up with Labradors and German shepherds. She loved dogs for their romping playfulness, their simple desire to love and be loved, their unquestioning loyalty. But she'd also seen what one could do with its teeth. She didn't want to find herself fighting some savage backwoods cur with nothing but a brittle tree branch.

She tightened her grip on Lawrence's hand, redoubled her pace. The ground was uneven, tough going. After a few minutes, Lawrence collapsed to his knees.

"I . . . I can't . . ." he said.

"You can."

He shook his head. "Lungs . . ."

"That dog. He'll go straight for your throat. And he won't let go, not until he's ripped a hole big enough to put a size twelve shoe through. I'm not waiting around to get my ass bit off. Pull yourself together or I'll leave you behind."

Wow, she thought. *I sound just like Dad.*

She started walking. After five yards, she stopped, turned. Lawrence struggled to his feet. She went back, grasped his hand, pulled him along.

The barking grew louder still. Helen realized they'd never make it all the way to Lawrence's house before the dog caught up.

"We need cover," she said.

She led him out of the forest, across the yard to the Trading Post's back door. She opened it and helped Lawrence inside, closed the door and locked it. She put her ear against the door, listened. Hopefully the dog would lose their scent, keep going.

"What's that smell?" Lawrence said.

"Rita's boyfriend. He's still lying on the stairs."

"Ugh!"

"Shh!"

She heard nothing from outside, and for a moment thought they were safe. Then Coonie barked furiously and Yates yelled hoarsely.

"Shit. He must have our scent. My scent, probably. My car's still right outside the jail."

"So he'll lead them right to this door."

"Let's head out the front."

She helped Lawrence through the restaurant and into the market. They stopped at the front door. Helen reached for the knob. Lights flashed through the window. She ducked, yanking Lawrence down beside her. The rumble of a car engine vibrated through the floor. She risked a quick peek.

"The Explorer."

"Teddy," Lawrence said. "Looking for us."

"We can't go out this way," she said. "Not while he's patrolling Main Street."

"Now what?"

"We need weapons." She bolted the door.

"Search the aisles for something we can use."

She scouted the leftmost aisle. She found a hammer, decided it was too unwieldy, returned it to the shelf. She was elated when she discovered a nail gun, but then she read the package: *Charge battery for two full hours before use.*

She combed through a shelf of Drano products. During her stint in the Navy, Helen had briefly dated an EOD Tech — the EOD stood for "Explosive Ordnance Disposal." It wasn't the rosiest of relationships, but it wasn't a complete waste of time. At least she'd picked up a few interesting tidbits of information, including that Drano had a million and one uses, and not just when it came to unclogging toilets. Add some Drano to a plastic bottle, slip in some wadded balls of aluminum — the foil reacts with the Drano to produce hydrogen gas — and in ten to fifteen minutes: BOOM! A low-grade bomb. Unfortunately, there was no way to time the explosion.

More useful was the knowledge that mixing ammonia and bleach created a toxic vapor similar to chlorine gas, and just a small amount of that was bad news. As World War I chemical warfare had proved, it had a devastating effect on the membranes of the eyes, nose, and throat.

Helen chose a bottle of bleach, unscrewed the cap, and poured half the contents onto the floor. She located a liquid glass cleaner, popped the lid, and tipped it into the spray bottle. She replaced the cap on the bleach bottle and shook it. She'd never tried this before, really had no idea what to expect. She was hoping for something really impressive.

Rowr-rowr-rowr! Coonie's rapid-fire barking startled her. It sounded like the dog was already at the back door. She snatched up two bottles of rubbing alcohol.

"Lawrence, come on!"

They raced through the restaurant and crouched by the entrance to the vestibule.

"Find anything good?" Helen whispered.

"Yes."

"What?"

Helen held up her flashlight to see. Lawrence showed her a pair of socks and rubber boots.

"Jesus, Lawrence, you can't stop a man from killing you with rubber boots."

"I have this, too." He showed her a six-inch knife.

"That's more like it, but still not much use against guns," Helen said.

"Maybe Mr. Patterson has a shotgun

337

upstairs. Around here, everyone has a shot-gun."

"Go look. I'll see if I can hold them off down here."

"Okay." He headed into the vestibule.

"Hey," she said.

"What?"

"Don't trip over the dead guy."

Rowr-rowr! Coonie scratched on the back door.

"Coonie, down!" Yates yelled.

The doorknob jiggled.

"Go!" Helen said. Lawrence hurried up the stairs.

Boots kicked against the door. Frank cursed.

Helen twisted the caps off the bottles of rubbing alcohol, tossed them away, splashed the liquid along the floor of the vestibule. She hurried back to the kitchen counter, rifled frantically through drawers until she found a book of matches.

Wood splintered and cracked. Frank and Yates were giving the door everything they had.

Helen put her flashlight into her pocket, ripped a match from the book, held it ready.

The assault on the door suddenly ceased. Helen's hand shook as she touched the tip of the match to the striking surface. She held her breath.

A shotgun roared. The doorknob and fragments of the brass doorplate skittered across the floor of the vestibule. Coonie barked and growled. The door banged open.

Helen lit the match. It fizzled. She heard Coonie's paws scrabbling on the slick floor. She desperately ripped out another match and struck it. It caught fire. She tossed it into the hallway. The rubbing alcohol ignited. Coonie yelped.

She heard a thud as Coonie, going out, collided with Yates, coming in. Yates hollered. Helen risked a quick look.

Coonie was already through the door and into the back yard. Yates stood in the open doorway, a shotgun in his arms. Flames sizzled along the floor, too low to do much more than cause an annoyance. Helen didn't see Frank but assumed he was right behind Yates.

She opened the bleach bottle, tossed it into the vestibule. A shotgun blast smashed a chunk out of the wall. She heard gagging, then the sound of Yates's boots as he clomped toward her.

So much for chemical warfare.

She scrambled to her feet, ran for the market. Yates came through the back doorway, fired. The shot buzzed over Helen's head. She cut left, slid across a table top, pulled it onto its side as cover.

Another shot shattered a section of the picture window in the side wall. Helen heard the click-click of a shell being ejected.

"I'm a federal agent!" she yelled.

"You're a goddamn murderer!"

"I don't know what they told you, but it's not true."

A roar from the shotgun, and a corner of the melamine table exploded. Plastic shards sliced her cheek.

"You killed Big Ed!" Yates yelled.

"Stop shooting! I'm unarmed. And I didn't kill Big Ed!"

"Bullshit!"

"It's true, Mr. Yates. You have to listen to me."

"You feds are all the same. Think you can just take whatever you want. If you can't do it legal, you do it by force."

"Mr. Yates, please. Let me explain, while there's still a chance. You're in as much danger as me. Frank and Teddy, they're after the money. They'll kill us both to get it."

"What money?"

"Lower your weapon and I'll tell you."

"You come outta there."

"Don't shoot!"

"Real slow. And keep your hands up!"

Helen raised her arms, slowly stepped out from behind the table.

"I am not armed," she repeated.

The feeble fire licking the floor of the vestibule lit Yates eerily from behind. He was dressed in baggy pants, boots, a thick coat, a flappy-eared tweed cap. Add the shotgun in his hands and he was an Elmer Fudd with very bad intentions.

"Closer," Yates said.

17

Helen stepped around the side of the table, approached Yates.

"Stop right there," he said.

"I did NOT shoot the sheriff."

"Who did?"

"Teddy."

"I look stupid to you?"

Helen glanced at the vestibule. The fire was nearly out. Where was Frank? And where the hell was Lawrence?

"No, you don't, Mr. Yates. Let me explain." Her hands were shaking. She had to make this old moron understand quickly. Before Frank burst in. "Rita Scroggins came up here to hide all that money she'd stolen. In the mine."

"Now why in the hell would she hide money in the mine?"

"Mr. Yates," Helen said. "Frank's going to come in that back door any second."

"He went around front," Yates said. "Don't

worry about him." He lifted the barrel of the shotgun. "Worry about me. Talk."

Helen spat the words out. "Rita planned to hide the money, turn herself in, do her time, and then come back to get it. She needed somewhere quiet, remote, safe. The mine was the best place she could think of. But she got caught before she could leave town. Teddy, Frank, Mike — one of them — figured this all out. They decided to kill her so they could keep the cash without anyone knowing it had ever been up here."

She heard a rattling noise coming from the market. Frank at the front door. She had only seconds left to convince Yates.

"The sheriff, he guessed about the money. Teddy and I found him down in the mine, looking for it. Teddy shot him, right there, in cold blood. Then he tried to kill me. I escaped. When I got back to the jail, Frank and Mike were waiting. They tried to kill me, too."

As the fire fizzled, the room slowly grew darker. She couldn't read Yates's face or see his features, only his outline and the shotgun pointed at her chest.

"I've known Teddy all his life," Yates said. "He wouldn't never hurt a fly. And Big Ed was his own dad, fer chrissakes."

"I know. It's shocking. But he wants that

money. He tried to kill me. And now that you know the truth, he'll kill you, too."

In the backyard, Coonie howled.

"We don't have much time," Helen said. "Help me, please, or we're both dead."

She reached out to him. He retreated into the vestibule doorway.

"Stay right there," he said.

"Why would I lie about this, Mr. Yates? Why would I come up here, a place I've never been before, and kill a sheriff I've never met?"

Yates didn't respond. The rattling noise from the market stopped. This worried Helen.

Yates cleared his throat. "How much money are we talking about?"

Ah-ha. A crack to work a finger into.

"I don't know. At least a few hundred thousand."

The barrel of Yates's shotgun suddenly jerked up toward Helen's face. She crouched instinctively, covered her head with her hands. But instead of shooting her, Yates dropped the gun and collapsed on the floor.

Helen saw a dark figure looming over his limp body. The figure didn't make a move toward her. Just stood there. She tugged out her flashlight, switched it on.

"Lawrence?"

"I . . . I . . ." He looked down at Yates.

Helen lowered the beam of the flashlight. The handle of a knife protruded from between Yates's shoulder blades.

"My God, Lawrence."

The sound of splintering wood and breaking glass signaled Frank's successful entry to the market. Helen stuffed the flashlight in her pocket, reached down, yanked Yates's shotgun out from under his body, grabbed Lawrence by the arm.

"Hurry!" she said.

"Yates?" Frank yelled, through the front door. "It's me, Frank. Don't shoot me, goddammit!"

Helen pulled Lawrence up the stairs, squeezed past Lee Larimer's body. Lawrence tripped on Larimer's leg and sprawled on the landing.

"Yates?" Frank called out, closer now.

Helen hauled Lawrence upright and around the bannister. She lay down at the top of the stairs. Lawrence thumped onto the floor beside her.

"Yates?" Frank said.

Helen aimed the shotgun at the doorway leading into the restaurant. She could just make out the spread-eagled shape of Yates's body lying across the threshold.

"Fuck!" Frank exclaimed. Now he'd seen the body, too.

She waited. She felt Lawrence tremble at her elbow.

Coonie barked and snarled.

"Shut up!" Frank said. "Fucking mutt!"

Helen remained perfectly still, apart from the violent pounding of her heart.

Finally: "You kill Yates, you heartless bitch?"

Helen concentrated on taking calm, even breaths.

"Your boyfriend with you? I'm gonna hurt you both, real bad."

Coonie whined.

"Fucking get in here and rip their hearts out, goddamn stupid dog!" Frank yelled.

A rivulet of sweat ran from Helen's hairline, across her temple and cheek, down her neck, into her collar. She kept her finger on the trigger of the shotgun.

Frank burst into the vestibule. Helen's shotgun roared, muzzle flash filling her eyes with hundreds of dancing white spots. Frank fired back. The top of the bannister exploded. Helen pumped the shotgun to chamber a fresh round, squeezed the trigger. The butt of the shotgun kicked against her shoulder.

She worked the pump again, pulled the

trigger, but it clicked on an empty chamber. Out of ammo.

She kept her head low, listened. Her ears throbbed. She blinked the spots away, waited for her vision to clear.

"I think you got him," Lawrence whispered. His voice sounded like it was coming from under water.

Helen raised her head for a look. There appeared to be two bodies now, lying in the gloom. She heard labored breathing.

"Wait here," she told Lawrence. She descended the stairs, took out her flashlight.

Frank lay half on top of Yates, curled into a ball, his sides heaving. He looked up at her in pain and fear, a sheen of sweat on his face. She saw his hands clutching his midsection, blood streaming between his fingers.

She dropped Yates's shotgun, reached down, picked up Frank's.

He tried to speak. Helen leaned closer. "What?"

"Help me," he whispered.

Helen stood up, retreated into the vestibule.

Rowr-rowr-rowr!

She nearly dropped the shotgun as Coonie lunged through the back doorway. She leaped for the stairs, turned halfway, extended the shotgun, and fired one-handed. The recoil jerked her wrist painfully. She raced up the stairs, treading across the top of Larimer's thighs. Coonie yelped and ran back into the yard.

Helen reached the second floor, fell to her knees.

"Helen!" Lawrence said. "Are you okay?"

Gasping for air, she nodded. Lawrence reached for her. She squeezed his hand. "I'm okay."

"Frank?"

"He's hit. Bad, I think. Dead soon."

"So . . . we're safe?"

"Teddy's still out there somewhere on Main Street, in the Explorer."

"Right. Shit."

Helen waited until she regained her breath, then pushed herself to her feet.

"Where's Mrs. Patterson?" she said.

"I don't know. I didn't see her."

"What? How is that possible?" Helen handed Lawrence Frank's shotgun. "Stay here. If Teddy makes an appearance, shoot him."

"I . . . uh . . ."

"Just do it, Lawrence."

"Okay."

Helen turned the knob for the bedroom door, opened it, poked her head inside.

"Mrs. Patterson? It's me. Deputy Marshal Morrissey."

She entered. The candles were still lit but the bed was empty, a wrinkled depression in the sheets indicating where Alice had been lying before.

"Mrs. Patterson?"

She checked the closet. Empty. She kneeled on the floor beside the bed. Lifted the coverlet, shined her flashlight into the darkness.

Alice lay squeezed into the narrow space between the floor and the bed frame, enormous breasts nearly touching the mattress slats, hands covering her eyes.

"Mrs. Patterson, it's me. Helen Morrissey. Come out of there."

After a bit of cajoling, Alice laboriously scooted out of her hiding spot. Helen sat her on the edge of the bed.

"Are you hurt?" she asked.

Alice sniffled, her mascara running down her cheeks in black streaks. "I'm so scared, Marshal. First Jesse, and then all the yelling and shooting —"

"I know," Helen said. "It's been a long, horrible night. And it's not over yet. But I won't let anything happen to you. Okay?"

Alice smiled, her lips quivering. "Okay."

"Good. Now, are you injured?"

"My ankle. I can't walk very well."

"But if you had to, you could? If I brought a car around front? Because we need to get out of here."

"Maybe with some help."

"Okay. For the moment, you just sit tight."

Alice reached out and gripped Helen's hand tightly.

"What about everyone else? Jesse, Big Ed?"

Helen didn't have the heart to tell her.

"Don't worry, Mrs. Patterson. You just wait here and I'll be back soon."

"Don't leave me!"

Helen remembered Rita asking her the same thing, at the jail. Before she was dragged into the woods and murdered.

"Lawrence will stay with you. Try to remain calm."

She pulled her hand loose with some difficulty, then slipped out the bedroom door.

"Hear anything down there?" she asked Lawrence.

"Just Frank dying," Lawrence said.

Helen's stomach roiled. She leaned on the railing.

"You all right?" he asked.

She gave it a minute before answering. "I'm going to make my way to your house and pick up your car."

"But Teddy —"

"Street lamps are out. If I avoid getting caught in his headlights, he won't see me."

"Maybe," Lawrence said.

"Where are your keys?"

"They should be on the kitchen counter," Lawrence said. "What if Teddy hears you start the engine?"

"We'll have to move fast. Give it two minutes, then help Mrs. Patterson downstairs and over to the front door. I'll drive up, you guys hop in, and we'll make a run for it."

"Uh . . . okay."

"So it's not exactly iron-clad," Helen said. "If you have a better plan . . ."

"No," Lawrence said. "I don't."

"All right. Wish me luck."

"Good luck, Helen."

"Thanks. I'll need it."

18

When Helen stepped off the stairs into the vestibule, the back door was still open, but there was no sign of Coonie. She wondered if she'd hit him. Maybe he was out back, curled up on the lawn, dead or dying — like everyone else in town.

She cautiously approached Frank. He was no longer gasping for air. Didn't appear to be breathing at all. She stepped over his body, walked through the restaurant, into the market, crouched by the open front door. Broken glass and wood splinters crunched under her boots.

No sign of headlights on Main Street.

Helen poked her head through the doorway. Frigid air numbed her face. She heard the hum of Frank and Mike's generator, but otherwise all was quiet. She squeezed through the door, raced across the pavement, huddled in the shadows on the other side of Main Street. She paused to watch and listen. All clear. She started for Lawrence's house.

Helen wasn't a strong runner, but she jogged a couple times a week for exercise, ran the occasional half-marathon. Now, however, each step forward was like moving through quicksand. Her legs shook, her lungs burned.

When she reached the porch of Lawrence's house, she dragged herself up the steps, completely spent. She stumbled through the front door, into the kitchen. She switched on her flashlight, scanned the counter next to the sink. No keys. Heart beginning to race, she ran the flashlight across the remaining counter space, the dining table, the floor. No keys!

She pulled out a chair, sank into it, rested her head on the table. One break. Why couldn't she get one freaking break?

She sat there, brooding, for a long while. Then she had a thought: *maybe Lawrence left the keys in his car.* She got up, rinsed her face in the sink, and gulped down handfuls of clear, cold water.

She peeked out the front door. Still no trace of Teddy or the Explorer. Could he have just decided she wasn't worth the trouble and split with the cash? Unlikely. He wanted everyone dead. So he could make a clean getaway. He was out there, somewhere.

She crept over to Lawrence's car, checked inside. No keys here, either. She pulled the latch for the trunk, went around back and looked inside. The knife glinted dully in the beam of her flashlight. She was certain now that it was the murder weapon. Planted in Lawrence's car to implicate him.

By whom? She'd been with Teddy from her arrival until the discovery of Rita's body. There'd been a small window of time when she was in the red farmhouse with Big Ed, but she doubted that was enough time for Teddy to run to Lawrence's and plant the knife. More likely, Frank and Mike were the culprits.

Yet both of them were at the Trading Post when Rita was killed. So who actually cut her throat?

Helen was certain her theory about Rita fleeing with the money, and Lee Larimer coming after it, was correct. And she was equally certain Lee Larimer wasn't Rita's murderer. No, there was a fourth party involved. And, as unlikely as it seemed, there was only one person it could be.

But solving the murder wasn't a priority right now. Getting out of Kill Devil Falls alive was.

She closed the trunk. She figured the killer was smart enough to not leave fingerprints, but the knife was still evidence, so she wasn't going to touch it.

She considered her next move. Hole up in the Trading Post, wait for Teddy to bust in? What if he just set it on fire like the jail? Leave town on foot? With Mrs. Patterson on a bum leg?

One thing was for sure. She needed a weapon. Between the two of them, she and Lawrence only had Frank's half-loaded shotgun. That just wasn't going to cut it. Because they weren't getting out of Kill Devil Falls without a fight.

She assumed there were lots of guns and ammo at Big Ed and Teddy's house. But that was all the way on the other side of town. Meanwhile, Frank and Mike's trailer was just up the street and they seemed like the type of good old boys who kept AK-47s stashed under the bed.

Helen crossed Main Street, jogged down to the trailer. The generator was still purring along. She opened the trailer door, stepped inside, squinted against the sudden brightness of the lights.

She took in the lumpy couch, trash-strewn kitchen counter, taped-up porn spreads. Pretty much as expected. She quickly tossed the living area. Incredibly, there were no guns just lying around, waiting to be snatched up. But in the bedroom, in addition to four plastic-wrapped kilos of marijuana, was a metal gun safe. She jiggled the handle. Locked.

Helen was shocked. *What kind of redneck dicktard actually stores his guns in a safe?*

She gave the trailer another once-over, found a collection of knives, including one that was a twin to the hunting knife in Lawrence's trunk. But no guns.

She'd been away from the Trading Post for ten, fifteen minutes. Time to get back to Lawrence and Mrs. Patterson. Think of a Plan B for making an escape.

As she was heading out the door, she spied Mike's crossbow on the wall. She lifted it from its mount, weighed it in her hands. It was shaped roughly like a rifle, with a shoulder stock, pistol grip, a barrel with a flight groove down the middle, and a bow apparatus sitting perpendicular to the groove. A sliding mechanism cocked the string. A foot stirrup sat beneath the barrel, along with a quiver of five arrows.

Helen placed the crossbow nose on the floor, slipped her foot into the stirrup. She pulled on the cocking mechanism, drawing the bow string back into position. She righted the crossbow, slipped an arrow out of the quiver, placed it in the flight groove. The tip of the arrow was serrated metal. Nasty looking.

She pointed the crossbow at the fifty-five-inch high definition television, the only object that appeared to have any value in the trailer. She pulled the trigger. The crossbow kicked. The arrow streaked forward, penetrated the glass screen, continued right though into the back wall. *Chunk!* Nice!

Helen reloaded the crossbow, slipped through the door, headed down Main Street. She was halfway to the Trading Post when she felt a rumble through the pavement, heard the growl of an engine. She turned. Twin circles of yellow light flashed.

Helen sprinted, but she knew she wasn't going to outrun the Explorer. She leaped over a wooden fence into the front yard of the nearest house. The Explorer jumped the sidewalk, its right bumper smashing through fence posts, flinging them away one after the other like a row of bowling pins. Helen sprawled on the grass.

The Explorer arced back toward Main Street, pulled a sharp 180, tires squealing, lined up facing the yard. Helen got to one knee. The engine of the Explorer roared, rubber burned, and it sped straight toward her. She aimed, fired the crossbow. Glass tinkled and the Explorer's right headlight went dark. She drew another arrow, tried to fit it into the flight groove, dropped it, realized she had forgotten to cock the string. But there was no time. She turned and ran up the porch steps of the house, yanked open the door, ducked inside. She reached up, locked the door.

She peered through a narrow window to one side of the door. The Explorer rolled to a stop on the grass of the front yard, cracking fence slats beneath its all-terrain tires. The single headlight spotlit the porch, its glare preventing her from seeing beyond it into the Explorer's cab.

She heard the engine die. A metallic clang as the driver's side door slammed shut.

The crack of a gunshot.

The front door shuddered, and a bullet punched straight through it. Helen ducked. A second bullet shattered the window, spraying her with glass. She flattened herself to the floor. Another bullet and another slammed into the door. Helen frantically searched for cover. Straight ahead were stairs leading to the second floor. To the right of the stairs was a hallway.

She slithered down the hallway.

She hurried past a closed door set into the side of the staircase. She kept moving, hoping for a back exit. At the end of the hallway was another door. Helen reached up, twisted the knob, pulled. The door swung open. She thrust her hand inside, touched a mound of leather, laces — old shoes. She reached higher, felt cotton fabric, nylon. Coats. A closet. Dead end.

A bullet ripped through the coats. Helen scooted back to the door in the staircase. She prayed it didn't lead to another storage closet. She opened the door, wriggled inside.

She heard more shots, more impacts, striking the front of the house. She switched on her flashlight.

She was at the top of a flight of cement stairs. Below, she saw boxes, tools, a ladder against the wall, a portable generator.

Shit. She was back in Yates's basement!

A splintering crash came from the foyer.

Helen put the flashlight in her mouth, stuck her foot in the crossbow stirrup, cocked the string. She placed an arrow in the flight groove, leaving one final arrow in the quiver. She took the flashlight from her mouth, switched it off, tucked it into her pocket.

She guessed Teddy would hesitate coming through the front door, uncertain of what weapon she might be carrying. And once inside, he would have to decide which direction to go — up the stairs, into the kitchen, down the hallway. He might pause, for just a second. Enough time to get off a shot with the crossbow.

She grasped the knob of the basement door, waited. It was an old house. Old houses had loose floorboards.

Squeak. Squeak.

Helen pushed open the door, swiveled her torso into the hall.

She saw a backlit figure in the foyer. A wide, bulky torso, huge goggle eyes, a trunk extending from its mouth. An alien creature, holding an assault rifle complete with a long clip and flashlight attached beneath the barrel. She heard a whoosh of artificial breath.

The figure swiveled its head, massive saucer eyes focusing on her.

Helen fired the crossbow. The arrow went wide. She leaped back through the basement doorway as series of rounds from the assault rifle ripped down the hallway.

She heard the thumping of boots running toward her. She slammed the door. There was no way to lock it from the inside.

She switched on her flashlight, stumbled down the stairs. Below, the generator sat atop the trap door. Above, the basement door crashed open. Teddy's boots slapped on cement. Helen frantically disengaged the generator's wheel locks, rolled it away, flung open the trap door, jumped.

She hit the floor of the shaft and felt her ankle twist. She got to her knees, flashlight in one hand, snatched up the crossbow with the other, crawled into the tunnel, huddled against a wall, out of sight from above. She switched off her flashlight and put it in her pocket.

She heard Teddy's bootsteps, the artificial sound of his breath. A beam of light nosed around the walls and floor of the space, sweeping back and forth like a prison-yard searchlight.

Helen fumbled in the darkness of the tunnel to reload the crossbow. Last arrow, last chance.

The beam of Teddy's light winked out. There was a metallic *pop,* like the opening of a soda can. Something fell into the dirt at the bottom of the shaft. Immediately, Helen's eyes began to water. Acrid smoke choked her throat. Tear gas!

She turned, hurried down the tunnel. She realized the saucer eyes, the dangling trunk — Teddy was wearing a gas mask.

She careened painfully off a rocky wall. She switched on her flashlight. The tunnel curved here. Another twenty or thirty yards and she would emerge into the ventilated chamber. Then what?

Helen heard the cough of a motor. The string of bulbs dangling from the ceiling flickered, bathing the tunnel in an anemic glow. Teddy had started up the generator, powering Yates's lighting system.

Now he would be coming fast, carrying a semi-automatic assault rifle, looking to finish her, tear apart her body with high-velocity rounds, leave her corpse to molder in the earth like Yates's abandoned mining tools.

Helen dropped her flashlight, redoubled her pace, ignoring the shooting pains from her injured ankle. The sickly yellow light from the bulbs strung overhead revealed a long blue tube snaking along the ground. Detonation cord. Helen saw it but was too focused on escaping to give it a closer look.

A jingling and clomping echoed down the tunnel behind her. Teddy was gaining. Helen moaned. Now she spotted flashes of red tangled with the detonation cord.

Ahead was the opening to the ventilated chamber. A breath of cool air tousled her hair. She rushed through, gulped fresh oxygen.

She paused. Which way?

At her feet, the det cord skirted the perimeter of the chamber, extended down the tunnel that led toward the mine exit at the bottom of the ridge. Those flashes of red, they were attached to it here as well, in clumps of two or three.

Helen digested the empty crates, sawdust scattered on the ground.

Dynamite!

Teddy had rigged the mine to blow.

Jingling keys signaled his approach. Another canister of tear gas shot out of the tunnel, bounced across the chamber floor. Helen coughed, ducked low to get under the smoke layer. To no avail. She scrambled on all fours, her lungs burning, searching for the nearest exit.

She located an opening in the wall, squeezed through, entered a passageway, this one unlit, eyes stinging, tears coursing down her cheeks.

Light from the ventilated chamber dissolved into darkness, and she kicked herself for ditching the flashlight. After a few minutes of blind groping, she felt the narrow tunnel give way to open space. She ran her hand across roughly hewn walls, hoping for a way out. She stepped into a crack, tripped, dropped the crossbow. She sank to her knees, patted the ground, found the crossbow, checked to make sure the last arrow was still in the flight groove.

A beam of brilliant white light flashed over her left shoulder. Seconds later, the light zeroed in on her face. The sound of Teddy's breathing was like something from a child's nightmare — a harsh, inhuman rasp.

Helen aimed just above the white light, squeezed the crossbow trigger.

The arrow made a satisfying *vroom* and a *thunk*. She heard Teddy fall and a tinkle of glass as the flashlight attachment on his rifle shattered.

She felt a thrill of triumph. A direct hit!

Teddy groaned. There was a clatter of metal on rock.

Helen rolled. Teddy fired his rifle, the gunshot deafening in the enclosed space. Bullets zinged into rock, pelting Helen with sharp little fragments.

She came up against something lying on the ground. She touched fabric. Cold flesh. The sheriff. Helen realized she was back in the wedged-shaped room where Rita had stashed her money, where Teddy murdered his own father.

Another shot rang out, the muzzle of the rifle belching flame.

Helen reached for Big Ed's gun belt, struggled to free his .357 from its holster.

Teddy fired again. He was shooting in the dark, but methodically, in a counterclockwise direction. The next bullet might be on target.

She frantically worked the holster snap, yanked out the heavy revolver, aimed over the sheriff's corpse.

BOOM! Helen felt Big Ed's body jerk violently. Congealed blood splattered. Helen fired the .357. It bucked violently in her hand, a bright muzzle flash reflecting off Teddy's huge saucer eyes. She squeezed the trigger again, and again, kept shooting until the hammer of the revolver finally clicked on an empty chamber.

She flattened herself behind Big Ed's body, pressed her cheek to the cold stone floor, the echo of the gunshots drumming against her tortured eardrums.

Thirty seconds passed. Sixty. Helen looked up but could see nothing in the pitch dark. She dropped the revolver, crawled over Big Ed's body. She felt her way along the wall toward the exit.

But as she stepped into the passageway, fingers clutched at her leg. She screamed, ran in the dark, bouncing off rocky walls, tripping over the uneven ground. In time, she saw a blush of light ahead, finally emerging into the ventilated chamber.

Threads of tear gas floated in the air, causing her to gag and wheeze.

She couldn't bear the idea of a long, frantic trek to the exit at the bottom of the ridge, not with Teddy still alive and possibly in pursuit. She turned right, into the tunnel leading back to Yates's basement.

She stumbled along, pain in her ankle forgotten in a rush of adrenaline, until she reached the shaft. Then she stopped dead in her tracks.

In her desperation to escape, she'd neglected to consider how she was going to get out of the mine. What would have made sense was for Teddy to use the ladder leaning against the basement wall to climb down into the shaft. But the ladder was still up there. Out of reach. Might as well have been on the dark side of the moon.

So Teddy must have jumped down. *Christ on a crutch.*

Helen peered back down the tunnel, expecting to see Teddy lumbering toward her, a bogeyman in black boots and a gas mask. She listened for the telltale sound of jingling keys. But the generator powering the lights chattered like a troop of Howler monkeys. She wouldn't be able to hear Teddy until he was right up next to her.

She turned her attention to the generator.

A sturdy black power cord extended from its belly, drooped over the lip of the trap door opening, ran down the wall of the shaft, and looped back up to connect to an electrical socket in the ceiling of the tunnel. The cord looked too thin to serve as a rope. But it was worth a try. It was either that or the long way out. Straight through Teddy.

She wrapped her hands around the electrical cord, put a foot on the wall of the shaft, pulled herself upward. The cord slipped through her sweaty palms. She wiped her hands on her pants, tried again. Gripping the cord tightly with both hands, she began to haul herself up, both feet braced on the wall. Almost there.

There was a sharp tug on her coat from below. Helen tried to hang on. The tug became a hard yank. She fell.

Teddy stood over her, in his black boots, gas mask, gun belt. She saw how he'd managed to survive the arrow and bullets. He was wearing an armored vest.

He removed the gas mask, dropped it onto the ground. His face was deathly pale. He looked shockingly young minus his beard. A nasty bruise on his temple revealed where she'd struck him with the halogen lantern.

Helen knew she should either run or attack. Do something, anything. But her body wouldn't cooperate.

Teddy grimaced. "Caught me with one of those .357 rounds." He laboriously tugged at the vest's Velcro straps, shifted it off his body, let it fall in the dirt next to the gas mask. He took a breath, winced, probed his ribs with his fingers. "Cracked, for sure."

He drew his revolver.

"Wait," Helen said. "Just . . . hold on." She had to speak loudly to be heard over the generator.

"If you're hoping to buy time for a rescue, it ain't gonna happen."

"Think about what you're doing, Teddy."

"I have. Now it's time to just do it."

"But . . . Teddy . . . Teddy, please."

Teddy rubbed his chin. She noticed he'd made a mess of it while shaving, leaving half a dozen tiny cuts and nicks. "I'm sorry, Helen. It ain't nothing personal. This is just how it has to be."

Stall. Distract him. Look for an opening.

"You're going to dynamite the mine?" she said. "Blow Kill Devil Falls off the side of the mountain? Then make a run for it? That your plan?"

"More or less." Teddy thumbed back the hammer on his .357. Helen saw his finger tighten on the trigger.

"When the cops don't find your body

among all the others, they'll know it was you," she said.

"Search and rescue might dig for months and never be sure they found all the dead."

"What about Frank? Isn't he your partner? What about Mrs. Patterson? You going to let her die, too? I thought she was the only person in town who was ever nice to you."

Teddy burst out laughing.

"Frank's a jackass. And Mrs. P ain't who you think she is."

Clearly, Teddy had become completely unmoored. Fallen too far down the rabbit hole to see the light of day again. He intended to destroy everything in his orbit and scuttle away from the rubble like a cockroach.

"You killed Jesse Patterson, didn't you?" Helen asked. "While I was with your father at the Trading Post."

"You heard him in the jail. Babbling. Who knows what he might have said to the doctors at the hospital once he was doped up on painkillers?"

"So . . . it was him. Who cut Rita's throat."

Teddy shrugged and nodded at the same time.

"What about his bad knee?" Helen said.

"His knee was just fine. For an old man. That was just to throw you off the scent."

"And after you killed Jesse, you decided splitting the money wasn't as good as keeping it all for yourself."

"You shot Mike, not me. And speaking of Frank, where are him and Yates?"

"Dead."

Teddy grinned crookedly, the spitting image of his father. "See? You did most of the dirty work for me."

"I was due back in Sac hours ago," Helen said. "My office probably has a whole convoy of agents cruising up Main Street as we speak."

"When I was supposed to be calling for backup, I told dispatch you had car trouble and to let your office know. I said me and my dad would help you secure the fugitive for the night and get you back on the road tomorrow. So no one's coming, Helen. Not for a long while, anyways."

Helen leaned back against the hard surface of the shaft wall. "I guess you outsmarted everyone," she said.

"You making fun now?"

"No. You have the money and the gun. I'm sitting on my ass in the bottom of a mine shaft. But . . . can you . . . I figured most of it out . . . can you tell me the rest?"

"Why? In a few seconds, it won't make a damn bit of difference as far as you're concerned," Teddy said.

"I want to know. That's not too much to ask, is it? Rita sneaks into town, stashes the money. But gets caught. Then what?"

Teddy rubbed his chin. Helen waited. It looked to her like he was trying to make a decision. Give her the story. Or just shoot her. Finally, he lowered the hammer of the revolver.

"Mike found her, in the middle of his pot patch."

Helen remembered the marijuana in the double-wide trailer. "Mike and Frank are pot farmers."

"They grow it, and Mr. P handles the distribution. Handled, I should say."

What a charming old man, Helen thought. *A murderer and drug dealer to boot.*

"Mr. P has . . . had . . . all these LA movie contacts from back in the day," Teddy continued. "That's who he sold it to."

"What was your end?"

"Me?" Teddy said. "Oh, I wasn't involved, not really. I just kept an eye on my dad, made sure he didn't get wise, checked for any info coming into the sheriff's department that might pertain to the operation. The inside man, you might say. Mr. P slipped me some cash every now and again, but that's about it. I don't think he made much money off it, either."

"Okay. So Mike finds Rita in his pot field."

"Yes. Hold that thought."

Helen watched, incredulously, as Teddy holstered his gun, removed a pouch of tobacco from his pants pocket, ran a thumb along the seal to open it. She considered bum-rushing him.

As if reading her thoughts, Teddy raised an eyebrow. "I'm a real quick draw," he said.

Helen let the moment pass.

Teddy stuffed a wad of tobacco into his cheek, slipped the pouch back in his pocket, drew his gun again. "Where was I?"

"Mike, Rita, pot field."

"Yeah. After Mike brought Rita over to the trailer, Frank went straight to Mrs. P to ask what they should do. These days, he don't wipe his butt unless Mrs. P says so. Mrs. P, she wasn't even *living* in Kill Devil Falls before Rita ran away, but she's heard all the town gossip and about the robberies and so forth."

"I thought you said Jesse was in charge of the weed business."

"I said Mr. P had the connections, but Mrs. P — she was the brain."

"What do you mean, the brain?"

"You want to hear this or not?" Teddy said.

"Yes."

"Then shut up."

"Okay."

"Next thing, I get a call," Teddy said.

"I thought there were no landlines up here."

"Well, Mrs. P's got a satellite phone. Should I continue or just shoot you now?"

"Um . . . Continue?"

Teddy massaged his rib. "Mrs. P calls me and says Rita's up here and Frank and Mike are sitting on her." He shook his head. "Helen, I about had a heart attack, let me tell you."

"Better luck next time," Helen said.

Teddy glowered.

"I'm sorry." She motioned for him to go on. "Please."

Teddy chomped tobacco for a moment, then resumed. "Rita told Frank she was just passing through. Mrs. P knew right away that was a lie. She figured Rita was in town to hide the money. I mean, why else would she be here?"

"So —" Helen started.

"Helen, I swear to God, if you don't quit interrupting me —"

"Okay. Not another word."

Teddy spat a stream of black tobacco juice against the wall of the shaft, wiped a dribble off his lower lip.

"We didn't have no way of knowing how much money there was, but given all those credit unions and banks Rita and Larimer ripped off, we guessed a fair amount," he said. "Split five ways, wasn't nobody getting rich, but it was enough to make it worth our while."

Helen raised her hand.

"Lord!" Teddy said. "What now?"

"How much do you consider a fair amount for killing your stepsister?"

"I didn't kill her. And don't you get all high and mighty on me, Helen."

"I'm not. I'm just . . . curious."

"Well . . . Frank and Mike was going to buy this satellite TV set-up so they could finally get some decent reception. I know Mr. P had been wanting to make a movie for a long while. Not a skin flick, a real one. He told me the plot once, but I didn't really get it, to tell you the truth. Mrs. P, she was just sick of living up here. She said she wanted to move someplace where you could get fresh sushi and a decent glass of Pino something or other."

"How about you?"

"Me? I was going to buy a new 4Runner."

"Jesus. You let Rita die in exchange for a new *truck*?"

Teddy's mouth twisted. "I said no at first.

I . . . I was fond of her. But there wasn't no other way. If we let her live, she'd find out we stole the money, sooner or later, and then who knows what kind of fuss she'd make? Maybe even tell the cops, just out of spite."

Helen couldn't believe her ears. A satellite TV. Sushi. And a truck. Talk about the banality of evil.

"Why even bother to tell your dad she was here?" she said. "Why let him call the marshal's service? Didn't that just complicate things?"

"That was the best part of the plan. Like you, we guessed Rita ditched Larimer and was going to keep the money for herself. But we couldn't be sure she wouldn't be tracked up here, one way or another, seeing as how she was one of California's Most Wanted. Maybe a hiker would find her car in the forest. Or an eyewitness might remember seeing her at a gas station along Route 49. Just in case, we needed to account for Rita being in Kill Devil Falls. But, of course, once she turned up dead, we'd all be suspects, a town as small as this."

"You needed an alibi."

He spat another stream of tobacco juice on the wall.

"That's where you come in."

"You did something to my car so it wouldn't start. Not Larimer."

"Not me personally," Teddy said. "I was in the jail with you, remember? But yeah. That was to get you over to the Trading Post. So you could see all of us there while Rita was . . . you know. Frank and Mike were going to fix the car right after. 'Course, my dad messed that up. Then you were supposed to head back to Sac to write up a nice little report putting us all in the clear."

Teddy, Frank, Mike, Jesse, and Alice. Collectively, they'd murdered Rita Crawford on little more than an impulse, as if it were no more trivial a matter than running down to the corner store for a gallon of milk.

"My legs are going numb, Teddy. I'm going to get to my feet, if that's okay. Don't shoot me."

"Can't make no promises."

Helen put a hand on the wall for support, slowly stood up. Her joints cracked.

"I feel like an old woman."

"You won't be getting much older."

Teddy's words were chillingly matter-of-fact.

"Alice Patterson," Helen said. "You said she was the brain. This was all *her* idea?"

"Well, none of us expected Lee Larimer to show up. He sure caught us with our pants down, shutting off the lights, beating the hell out of Jesse. If not for him, my dad woulda given Frank and Mike the go-ahead to take a look at your car and you'd be back home by now, snug as a bug in your little bed."

Helen's knees shook. Fear coursed like ice water through her guts. The situation really couldn't get any worse.

The real architect behind the whole sick affair was Alice Patterson. And while Helen was trapped in a dynamite-rigged mine shaft staring down the barrel of Teddy's gun, Alice Patterson was at the Trading Post with Lawrence. Just the two of them.

And Lawrence didn't have a fucking clue about the danger he was in.

19

Alice changed out of her nightgown and into a thick sweater and hiking pants. She pulled on a pair of tennis shoes, double-knotted them. She shrugged into a fleece pullover.

The time for playing possum was over.

She'd lied to Big Ed about having an injured ankle, thinking it was the best way to get him to leave her alone in the apartment, out from under his watchful eye. But that had proven to be a mistake. She'd remained trapped inside the Trading Post ever since, afraid of arousing Big Ed's suspicions, while outside gunfire crackled and buildings burned.

Twenty minutes ago, she'd watched from her bedroom window as Helen and Lawrence crossed the yard and entered through the back door. The two of them looked like they'd been swimming in a barrel of flaming cowshit. Alice had remained in her room, stayed quiet, waited to see who showed up next. It was Yates, Frank, and Coonie. So, Helen and Lawrence were on the run, with a dimwit, a geezer, and a mangy dog on their heels.

She wondered how Yates had gotten involved. Likely Frank or Teddy had fed him a lie about the marshal coming to take his guns and property, or some such nonsense. Yates was a real firebrand where the government was concerned. During the initial proceedings with the county, regarding the fate of Kill Devil Falls, he'd shown up at the Trading Post with a printed copy of the Constitution, suggested they form an armed militia and begin building defenses. When the case was resolved peaceably in court, he was sour about it for months.

Just before they'd started trying to kick in the back door, Alice heard footsteps coming up the stairs. She hid under the bed. The bedroom door opened and she spied a pair of dirty feet in flip flops. Lawrence.

Below, the back door crashed open and the shooting started. Lawrence stood frozen in place until it stopped, then quietly opened the door and left the bedroom. Alice stayed where she was, figuring under the bed was the safest place to be. Sure enough, there were more gunshots not long after.

When the shooting finally stopped, Alice gave it a moment, until her need to know what was happening outweighed her caution. She crawled out and put her ear to the door.

She heard Helen and Lawrence talking, learned that Frank was dead or close to it. Teddy was alive, and currently out in the Explorer. As for the others, the only one who mattered was Big Ed, and she assumed he was dead, too. Otherwise the sound of gunfire at the Trading Post would have brought him running.

With Big Ed gone, Alice was free to get back in the game. Good thing, because Teddy appeared to have forgotten all about her. Maybe he thought he was smart enough to go it alone. Perhaps he was even considering keeping the money for himself.

That wasn't going to happen. It was her plan. Everyone else — Teddy, Frank, Mike, Jesse — they were just the hired help.

She'd managed to slip back under the bed just before Helen entered the bedroom, the better to play the frightened, helpless old woman. It was obvious Helen had no clue as to her culpability. Good. That meant the situation was still salvageable.

First item on Alice's list, now that Helen was out scrounging up a car, was Lawrence.

He didn't look like much of a fighter. But still, he was a young man and she was a woman of, let's say, a certain age. A fact that might work to her advantage. Lawrence would never expect her to turn on him. But still . . . better to be armed.

Jesse didn't keep a gun in the house. Didn't believe in them. He was in many ways a cruel man, but never a violent one. He lacked the physicality for that. And the balls.

Which is why he was both the best and worst choice to kill Rita.

He'd nearly wet his pants when she'd told him what she had in mind.

"Is that really necessary, Alice?" he'd whined.

"You want to make that movie you've been going on about for the past twenty years? The one you don't have one red cent of financing for?"

"But I have to *kill* her?"

"Of course not, Jesse. Just ask her nicely where the money is. She'll be happy to draw you a map, complete with a little X marks the spot. And she'll never tell a soul that we took it. Do you have any other stupid questions?"

"Why can't Frank do it?"

"Because he looks like a murderer, you

old fool. You just look like an old fool."

The Pattersons possessed the one working phone in Kill Devil Falls, a GSP-1700, which operated via satellite link rather than cell tower and was used exclusively to contact their weed connection in Los Angeles. So she'd been able to reach Teddy in Donnersville, and as soon as he and Big Ed arrived to pick up Rita, she'd called the sheriff's department again to report a shooting in Sardine Valley. Teddy had said that according to protocol, Big Ed would have to respond immediately, leaving Rita with him. And that's exactly what happened.

Bolstered by three or four slugs of Scotch, Jesse was prevailed upon to wait in the woods outside the jailhouse. While the marshal was inside signing paperwork, he'd snuck out and disabled her car, according to instructions given to him by Frank.

The next part of the plan was dicey. When Helen learned her car wouldn't start, Teddy was to convince her to go with him to the Trading Post, leaving Rita alone in the jail. Given that Teddy was about as smooth as ground glass, Alice had her doubts he could pull it off. But pull it off he did.

As the two of them set off down Main Street, Jesse entered the jail, using the spare key from Big Ed's house. He'd hustled Rita into the woods, brandished one of Mike's nasty-looking hunting knives, demanded to know where she'd put the money. Her unexpected response had been to lower her head and rush him like a bull, despite the fact that her hands were cuffed behind her back. She'd knocked him down, gotten on top of him, bit him savagely in the neck. In a panic, he'd pushed her to one side and recklessly slit her throat.

Later, he showed Alice the bite wound. "What was I supposed to do, Alice? She latched on like a goddamn Rottweiler!"

Meanwhile, Helen was being served coffee at the Trading Post, providing everyone with their iron-clad alibi. Apart from Jesse. Diverting suspicion from him had been a matter of split-second timing. After an exhausting run through the woods, Jesse entered the back door of the Trading Post, climbed up to the second floor, quickly washed himself in the bathroom, combed his hair. He changed into the fresh clothes Alice had set out and checked the time. He went to the kitchen, gulped down two more glasses of Scotch, belched, his breath potent enough to light a fire.

Then he threw himself down the stairs.

Alice knew the plan wasn't perfect. It depended on a number of unpredictable variables. But it was feasible. It worked.

Until Lee Larimer pissed on her parade.

Alice assumed Larimer must have been hiding in the woods when Jesse dragged Rita out of the jail, probably looking to do the same thing — find out where she'd stashed the money and then kill her. Maybe Larimer thought Rita told Jesse where it was, so he'd followed Jesse back to the Trading Post, waited till everyone left, cut the electricity, and snuck in to beat the information out of him.

So much for a neat and tidy resolution. Now the dead were piling up like firewood.

But Alice was sure the money was still within grasp. From the start, Teddy had figured the most likely hiding place was the mine. If he was right, the fact that Rita refused to reveal its location to Jesse was immaterial. Maybe he or Big Ed had already been down there and found it. Maybe it was in the back of that Explorer he was driving around.

Anyway, first Lawrence. Then the marshal. Then Teddy.

Alice rooted around in Jesse's nightstand but found nothing useful. She went over to her vanity, combed through dozens of makeup brushes, styling utensils, eyebrow scissors. In the end, the only remotely deadly instrument she came up with was a nine-inch, sterling silver hair stick with a wickedly pointed end. It would have to do.

She slowly opened the bedroom door, poked her head out.

Lawrence was no longer guarding the stairs. She heard him humming from down the hall. She tiptoed to the second bedroom.

Lawrence sat cross-legged on the floor, his back to Alice, facing the goddess statue. He was drinking from the bottle of whiskey she'd placed at the altar as an offering. He'd opened the lids of the terrariums and removed some of her babies. The poor dears were coiled on the floor, too cold to move.

The sacrilegious little shit!

Lawrence sipped from the bottle, poked at a snake with his forefinger, completely oblivious. Alice gripped the hair stick like a dagger, crept toward him.

"Well, that's a hell of a story," Helen said.

"Yes, it is."

"As much as it pains me to say, Teddy — I'm impressed." The words were like putrid garbage in her mouth.

"Oh, bullcrap," he said.

"Seriously. It's like that thing Mike Tyson said: 'Everyone has a plan, until they get punched in the mouth.' You rolled with the punches. Stayed cool under pressure."

He shifted his stance, flinched in pain, touched his rib.

"Well . . ." he said.

"A lot of people underestimated you. Didn't they? Your dad, for one."

Teddy glowered. "He had it coming."

"You're probably right."

"Listen, Helen, I kinda need to get this show on the road."

Helen reached up, pulled the elastic band from her ponytail, shook her hair out. "What are you going to do with the money?"

Teddy snort-laughed. "Don't you worry about that."

"I am curious about one thing," Helen said.

"No. No more questions."

"Why did you give me Rita's old shirt?" She took a step forward. "You saved it all these years. It must be special to you."

"Stay right there, Helen."

Helen tugged at the shirt's hem, drawing the fabric taut against her chest. "Maybe I remind you of her in some way?"

"What? No!" But his eyes dropped down to her breasts.

"We could almost be sisters, Rita and me."

Teddy raised the .357, pointed it at her face. "Shut up."

"Same dark hair, right? Dark eyes. Is that what you like?"

She was filthy, bloody, bedraggled. A mess. But even so, she saw it in his eyes. The gnawing hunger. The desperate thirst.

"Teddy."

He shook his head, his finger tightening on the trigger of the revolver.

"Do you want to fuck me?"

"I . . . Lord." He blushed furiously, looked away.

Helen shot forward, slapped the gun aside, punched Teddy in his rib cage. He gasped, fell to his knees. She closed her hands around the .357, twisted. Teddy's grip loosened and the gun almost came free. But he managed to hold on.

Helen kneed him in the side. He cried out. She tore the gun away, turned it on him. Teddy shoved her and she fell onto her back. Teddy crawled on all fours, pulled himself atop her legs, straddled her hips. She aimed the revolver at his face. Teddy wrapped his right hand around the barrel, wrenched it up toward the ceiling.

His face was purple with rage and pain. Spit flecked his lips. An animalistic howl rose from his chest.

Helen struggled under Teddy's bulk. He controlled her wrist with one hand, began to slowly pry the gun loose with the other. Helen felt his strength, knew it was just a matter of time before he freed the revolver from her grasp. She let go of the gun with her right hand, thrust her fingertips into his ribs, felt something give.

Teddy doubled over, screamed. Helen put her feet flat on the ground, arched her hips, and turned onto her right side, rolling Teddy off.

She ended up on her knees, between Teddy's thighs. He was still holding the barrel of the .357 with his right hand while she maintained a grip on the handle with her left. He thrashed wildly, jerking the gun back and forth. Helen wrapped her right hand over her left, jammed her forefinger into the trigger guard.

She lurched to her feet, engaged in a desperate tug-of-war for control of the weapon. Then, using her superior leverage, she lowered the .357 inch by inch by inch down toward Teddy's face.

When it was lined up with the center of his forehead, she squeezed the trigger. But Teddy managed to slip a thumb under the hammer before it could strike the firing pin.

"Helen . . . wait!"

She pulled back, stripping the gun from his hands. He held out his palms, waved them frantically.

"Don't shoot! I surrender! I —"

Helen fired. The contents of Teddy's skull vomited onto the ground, a halo of blood and brain matter.

Helen stumbled back against the wall of the shaft, slid down to sitting position. She took a moment to catch her breath, allow the shaking of her hands to subside.

Teddy lay still, mouth open, frozen in the act of begging for mercy.

Helen slowly got to her feet, stuffed the revolver into the back of her pants, grasped Teddy's collar, lifted his head and shoulders. Bits of liquid matter dripped from the back of his head. She dragged his body to the shaft wall, push-pulled him into a sitting position. She put a hand on his shoulder, pressed down. Teddy tipped over onto his side. She hauled him back upright. His head lolled like a Mickey Mouse balloon on a broken stick.

She searched Teddy's gun belt, located his key ring, detached it. She picked through the keys until she found the one for the Explorer. She removed it, dropped the rest in the dirt.

Teddy's glassy eyes stared at her reproachfully, a crater between his eyebrows large enough to poke a thumb into.

"Suck it, you crazy sonofabitch," she said.

Helen placed her left foot onto Teddy's lap. A jolt of pain shot up her leg. She gritted her teeth, lifted her right foot onto Teddy's shoulder. His body crumpled an inch. She nearly fell, flapped her arms, regained her balance.

She took a breath and pushed off with her right leg, using Teddy's shoulder as a stepladder. She caught the edge of the trap door opening with both hands.

Her left hand slipped off and she dangled by her right arm, swinging side to side. She managed to get a foot on the crown of Teddy's head, base off it, slap her left hand back onto the lip of the opening. With a grunt and an upward pull, she hoisted a leg over the side. She hung like that for a moment, gathering her strength. Finally, she rolled herself out of the shaft and onto the floor of the basement.

The hard metal of Big Ed's .357 dug painfully into her back, but she was too exhausted to move. She lay there, feeling the vibration of the generator motor through the cement floor.

When she was able to muster the strength, she sat up, got to her feet, and limped toward the stairs.

20

Helen stepped out onto Yates's front porch. The Explorer sat in the front yard, its single headlight a bright yellow orb in the night. She slowly descended the porch steps, walked over, dug the key from her pocket, unlocked it. She climbed into the cab, pulled the door shut.

She placed the .357 on the passenger's seat and noticed an object already lying there: the transmitter Teddy had showed her in the mine, in that chamber with the dynamite and det cord. She switched on the overhead light, picked up the transmitter, turned it over in her hands. It was dented, scratched, covered with grit and grime. She noted the on/off switch, and a trigger under the main body of the device. She flicked the switch, saw a green light flash. She carefully turned the transmitter off, very gently laid it back down next to the revolver.

Helen craned her head around to look at

the back seat. She saw the dirty duffel bag, along with a backpack and half-empty gym bag. She started up the engine.

She backed onto Main Street, drove at a snail's pace to the Trading Post, watchful for sinkholes, and rolled to a stop. She switched off the engine, grabbed the revolver, climbed out.

She entered through the broken front door, listened. Silence. She wondered if Lawrence was dead. If Mrs. Patterson was huddled at the top of the stairs, Frank's shotgun in her hands.

Helen made her way through the market into the darkened restaurant. She put a hand on the wall for guidance, slowly, silently inched her way to the vestibule doorway. She knelt, searched with her hands. Her fingers touched fabric. She identified Yates by his hat, with its earflaps. But something was wrong.

Frank's body was missing.

Helen called out, softly, "Lawrence. It's me, Helen."

She extended the .357, pointed the barrel up toward the stairs. If someone was up there, it was too dark to see them. She slowly edged her way into the vestibule. Cold air wafting through the open back door ruffled her hair, whispered across her skin.

A low growl raised the hairs on the back of her neck. Coonie.

Helen sprang forward, slammed the back door shut just as Coonie attempted to race in from the yard. There was an enormous impact. Helen dropped the revolver, put her shoulder against the door.

Coonie barked, his nails scratching against the wood.

Helen knew the Kwikset lock was broken, useless, blown right out of the door by a shotgun blast. She ran her fingers along the door frame, struggling to keep Coonie from forcing his way in. A third of the way down from the top, she discovered a dangling chain and corresponding slide on the door. She tugged the chain, fumbled it into the slide.

Now the door would open only a couple of inches. Not enough for Coonie to squeeze through.

At least, that was the theory.

Helen leaned down and patted the floor, trying to locate the .357. Coonie suddenly rammed the door, knocking her on her butt. The door popped open. Helen's fingers touched metal. The revolver. She picked it up, spun around.

Coonie shoved his nose and muzzle inside. He snarled, but he was too big to get through the gap.

Helen prayed the chain held. Even after all the killing she'd done tonight, she didn't want to shoot a dog.

She backed away, to the foot of the stairs, looked up. She saw the dim glow of candlelight reflecting off of Lee's tarp-covered torso.

Helen crawled up the stairs, slipped by Lee Larimer's body, snaked around the bannister.

The door on her immediate right, the master bedroom, was closed. Further down, the wreckage of the bathroom door littered the hall floor. Directly across from the bathroom, Mrs. Patterson's room was open, candlelight flickering within.

A shadow played along the hallway wall. Someone was in there.

Helen crept to the open doorway. She adjusted her grip on the revolver, entered the room in a low crouch.

Lawrence sat with his back to Helen, wearing only his sweatpants, no shirt or jacket. He was fiddling with something, his shoulders and hands working, completely absorbed in what he was doing. As she watched, he reached out, took a bottle from the floor, drank.

"Lawrence," Helen hissed. He didn't hear her. "Lawrence!"

He slowly turned, smiled.

"Helen! Thank God. I was worried!"

He was covered in dried blood.

"Are you injured? Where's Mrs. Patterson?"

"I'm fine." He took another swig. Whiskey dripped down his chin.

"But you're drunk," Helen said.

Lawrence shrugged.

Helen stepped deeper into the room, glanced into the corners. She noticed Frank's shotgun propped against a wall.

"Where's Mrs. Patterson? And where's Frank?"

"In the bedroom."

"Whose blood is that? All over you?"

Lawrence lifted his hands, turned them over. "Whoa," he said, as if noticing the blood for the first time.

A collection of Alice's tools were on the floor beside his knee.

"What are you doing?" Helen asked.

"Making jewelry." He held up a partially constructed necklace. A string with pink blobs.

Helen shook her head in exasperation. Lawrence was three sheets to the wind.

Perhaps in shock. Most definitely out of it.

She left him there, moved silently down the hall to the master bedroom. She paused outside the closed door, unsure of what she would find. Had Mrs. Patterson laid low this entire time? Was she just biding her time, waiting to see who made it back, her or Teddy?

She threw open the bedroom door.

As before, the room was lit by a collection of candles. Tall white tapers, beeswax cones, thick squat ones that smelled of cinnamon and pine needles. Pools of warm yellow light contrasted with deeply shadowed nooks and crannies.

Frank lay on the four-poster brass bed, face up.

Mrs. Patterson sat in a winged chair placed in the left corner.

Only, that wasn't right. It took several moments for Helen to make sense of what she was seeing.

The body in the chair was dressed in Frank's clothes. Dark pants, boots, a Dickies jacket. But with Mrs. Patterson's face. Red hair piled into a messy bun, crimson lips, dark eye makeup.

The one on the bed was dressed in pants and a sweater, and featured Mrs. Patterson's exaggerated curves, rounded hips, large breasts. But Frank's head stared up at the ceiling from atop the neck. Well, it looked like Frank, but with some facial features excised. A jigsaw puzzle missing a piece or two.

Helen felt her gorge rise. She backed away. Bumped into Lawrence standing in the doorway.

"My latest project," he said.

"You?"

Lawrence nodded. "Didn't have much time. Or my equipment." He showed her the kitchen knife he'd used to kill Yates. "I improvised."

"Jesus Christ, Lawrence."

"You don't like it."

She raised the revolver. "Drop the knife."

"Okay." He opened his fingers. The knife fell to the floor.

"Back up."

"Helen?"

"Back up!"

Lawrence held up his hands, retreated into the hall. "Please don't shout."

Helen stepped out of the bedroom, closed the door behind her. She covered her mouth with her hand.

"Are you okay, Helen?"

"Not really, Lawrence. I don't think you're okay, either."

Lawrence laughed softly.

"No. Definitely not."

"I'm placing you under arrest. You're coming with me to Donnersville."

"I'd really rather not." He was carrying the bottle of whiskey. He sipped, wiped his mouth.

"I'm not giving you a choice," Helen said.

"Well, hear me out first."

Helen wondered where she might find a pair of handcuffs. Hers were in the charred ruins of the jail.

"Obviously, I have some serious psychological issues." He made a wry face. "Impulses. Compulsions. I'm not like other people, normal people. I never was."

"Stop talking," Helen said. "Put your hands on top of your head."

"It was little things at first. Bugs, insects, what have you. Those tiny lizards you find under rocks in the back yard. You know, just like any other kid. When I was nine or ten I had a succession of hamsters and mice. My parents couldn't figure out why they kept dying. Finally they stopped buying them for me. After that it was stray cats. A neighborhood dog. As I grew older, I craved bigger projects. I knew it was wrong. I just couldn't . . . stop."

Lawrence was wearing the necklace he'd

just made. He twirled it around his finger as he talked.

"Around the time I turned fifteen or sixteen, I discovered that drinking helped, a bit. Eased the itch. That's what I call it. The *itch*. And when drinking wasn't doing it any more, I turned to drugs. An attempt at self-medication. This went on for years and years. But the itch didn't go away."

"Lawrence —"

"Helen, *please*. Eventually, I got busted for possession and put in a program. I lied to you about that. I didn't go of my own free will. I fought it tooth and nail. But into rehab I went. They leeched the drugs from my system. And, of course, the itch came roaring back. Helen, you don't know how hard it was. To ignore the grating, fucking *relentless* little voice in my ear. The other patients had no idea how close they came to being mutilated with a plastic butter knife."

The .357 was heavy as hell, and Helen's hands began to shake, but she kept it pointed directly at Lawrence's heart.

"If there's one thing rehab accomplished, it was to make me realize that drugs aren't a permanent solution for . . . for my condition. I mean, I can't stay high 24/7." He smiled sheepishly. "So I decided to remove myself from society. A voluntary exile. Like a . . . a fox who padlocks the chicken coop. My plan was to live quietly, indulge my impulses in a minor way. Such as those projects in the cellar. Pickle myself in alcohol. Stay out of trouble."

He nodded at the bedroom door.

"You see how that turned out."

"There are people who can help you," Helen said.

"You think so? Because I don't. This is who I am. You can't change the color of your eyes, your craving for pistachio ice cream or whatever, and I can't change the part of me that wants to . . ."

His voice trailed off. He sipped from the bottle, wiped his mouth with the back of his hand.

"Helen, you can arrest me, lock me away for the rest of my life. Keep me in a cage, a padded cell. But I won't ever be *cured.* The need won't magically disappear. I'll be like a sailor adrift on a lifeboat. Water every-where. Not a drop to drink. Torture. I'd rather be dead. I really would."

"You can't be left free to run around . . . hurting people."

"Of course not. I completely, *totally* un-derstand that. But I have no intention of going anywhere. I'm good right where I am.

This place . . . it's not like anywhere else. Do you know what I mean?"

"Oh, yeah. Hell, yes."

"There's something in the soil. The forest. The rocks."

"Toxic levels of mercury."

Lawrence smiled. "More than that. Something deeper. Primordial. I can't put words to it. But it feels like home."

At this distance, Helen could see Lawrence's necklace more clearly. Those pink blobs — they were Frank's ears. And there appeared to be a bit of his nose, and some red stringy parts that may have been his lips.

"I belong here," Lawrence said. "And if your plan is to take me away, you might as well just kill me."

She considered shooting him. Just shooting him and getting far, far gone from here.

"Do you understand, Helen?" Lawrence asked.

Helen stared at the bare feet, baggy sweatpants, naked torso crusted with blood. The angelic features.

The revolting necklace.

She lowered the .357.

"Yes. I understand."

Lawrence set the bottle down on the floor. "Thank you, Helen. I knew you would."

He held out his arms. He wanted a hug.

Helen hesitated. Then she surprised herself by stepping forward and giving him a brief squeeze. She quickly disengaged and backed away.

"You take care," Lawrence said.

"Yeah. You too, Lawrence."

She kept her eyes on him as she rounded the bannister, slipped by Lee Larimer's body, descended the stairs.

Coonie barked as she passed through the vestibule. She ignored him, limped through the restaurant and into the market. When she reached the front door, she turned, half expecting to see Lawrence racing toward her, knife in hand, bloody foam dripping from his lips. But nothing moved in the gloom. Helen stepped out onto Main Street.

She shivered in the cold mountain air. The smell of the jail, still smoldering, reminded her of the few camping trips she'd taken as a kid. She hated sleeping bags, tents, swarming bugs, but loved sitting around the campfire, staring into its comforting warmth, smoke in her nostrils, listening to the pop and hiss of burning sap.

She climbed into the Explorer. She placed the .357 on the passenger's seat, started the engine, puttered down Main Street, skirting the wooden safety barriers. She paused outside the remains of the jail.

Her Charger was a hot mess, its paint job cracked and blackened. The jail itself was reduced to a heap of charred logs.

Helen accelerated down the access road. Fifty yards ahead, leaning crookedly over the shoulder of the pavement, was an old wooden sign with reflective letters that read *You are now departing Kill Devil Falls.*

Helen parked by the sign. She lifted the plastic transmitter from the passenger seat, got out of the Explorer, hit the on switch. A green light flashed. She counted backward from ten.

Pulled the trigger.

A series of violent explosions ripped through the earth. Orange flames erupted from the storefronts on Main Street. The ground heaved, cracked, buckled. The red farmhouse tilted crazily, collapsed into a hole. A swath of forest sank from sight into a sea of smoke and fire. Hot wind ruffled Helen's hair. She smelled a mixture of burning rubber, plastic, and pine.

She hurled the transmitter deep into the woods. She climbed back into the Explorer, closed the door, and rested her head on the steering wheel. The ground continued to tremble and shudder. Kill Devil Falls' last agonized death throes. As Rita had put it so adroitly earlier: *good riddance.*

Helen shifted into reverse, backed the Explorer up, gazed malevolently at the wooden sign. She gunned the engine and rammed it, snapping the post in half, flinging the board into a tall patch of weeds.

Better. Much better.

She eased slowly onto the access road. She couldn't wait to get home. Scrub herself thoroughly, head to toe, in a scalding hot shower. Have a drink or three. Sleep.

Knock out Chowder's front teeth.

She took a quick glance at the dirty duffel bag in the back seat.

As the only survivor to make it out of Kill Devil Falls, it fell to her to give an account of the night's events. She could make up any story she wanted. Three hundred thousand dollars, a hundred thousand. No one would ever know.

That wasn't her style, but it had been one holy hell of a night. She deserved a little more than a pat on the head and a commemorative plaque.

It was a three-hour drive to Sac. She had plenty of time to think about it.

A trace of a smile on her lips, a red glare reflected in the rearview mirror, and the road ahead lit by a single headlamp, Helen started down the mountain.

ABOUT THE AUTHOR

Brian Klingborg lives in New York City, where he works in educational publishing. He has written books on Kung Fu, and for television. *Kill Devil Falls* is his first novel.